I0654379

# SEVERANCE

## Wade Audrey

SWG Publishing

Massachusetts

SEVERANCE

ISBN: 978-0-9972782-1-7
First Edition 2016

Published in the United States of America
SWG Publishing
Ashland, Massachusetts 01721

# SEVERANCE

# CHAPTER ONE

Dark. No moon. She lay tight to the cold, damp ground. Waiting. Listening. She couldn't hear him, but she knew he'd be coming. She could smell the musty soil under the aspen and maple leaves that pressed to her cheek. She touched her lip with her tongue. A metallic taste. Blood. Her ribs hurt when she took a breath, but that wasn't the only reason she was breathing carefully.

She didn't want him to hear her. She didn't want him to find her.

Confused, her mind racing, she remembered flashes of the chaos. He'd been drinking. She stayed away as much as she could, stayed silent. She knew where it could go. She'd been there before.

She couldn't remember how it started, but she remembered how it felt when her back hit the living room floor.

She picked her head up off the ground a bit and listened. Nothing. She rested. Trying to think past the scenes from the previous fifteen minutes that were spinning through her head.

She remembered him lurching from the chair and knocking the lamp from the side table as he reached to try and steady himself. She remembered the sharp pain of the vodka bottle hitting her ribs. She remembered him tripping over the coffee table, falling on her, bringing them both hard to the floor. The sound of his fist hitting her face, his hard knuckles bouncing off the soft underside of her forearms as she held them in front of her trying desperately to stop the blows.

He punched. He screamed at her. He punched more. Her forearms took a beating, and a few blows glanced into her cheek. Then, as suddenly as it started, it stopped. He was out of breath. Spent. She didn't think. She thrust her thumbs into his eyes and pushed as hard as she could. He screamed and sat up straight, his hands to his face. Some of his weight came off and she squirmed out from under him. She didn't remember scrambling to her feet. She didn't remember running out through the sliding doors. Or running down the deck steps. Or running across the backyard into the woods. But now here she was, lying in the dark, damp woods. Waiting. Listening. Catching her breath. Listening.

Nothing. Maybe he wasn't coming. She winced as she slowly lifted herself to her feet. The bottle had really hurt her ribs, her forearms ached, and the side of her face was numb. She leaned against a tree and thought. She wasn't going back this time. Never again. He would never beat her again.

*Where to go?*

She looked for landmarks through the trees. She knew that she was between her house and the end of Kernwood Drive.

*Where to go?*

She touched the outside of her pants pocket and felt the bills and her debit card. She remembered going to the bank and the store earlier that day. She hadn't emptied her pockets. Maybe forty dollars. Maybe fifty. She didn't remember. But it was enough to start, and she had her debit card if she needed more. She started walking carefully through the woods trying not to make noise, but it was November and the leaves that covered the ground crunched beneath her feet. It only took her a few minutes to reach the clearing around the house at the end of Kernwood.

Feeling bolder, she started to run. She ran along the edge of the woods. She could see where she was going now. She stayed in the clearing as long as she could, skirted the woods. By the time she reached the condos on Bristol Drive she was too winded to run anymore. She leaned over, her hands on her knees, trying to catch her breath, but she had no time. She had to get away. She stood up and continued on, walking now. Around the condos, through a long open area, and up to the fence surrounding the self-storage buildings that sat near Highway 94. She stared at the fence for a few minutes, as if waiting for it to tell her something. She placed her hands on the chain links and leaned into it.

*Think. Think. What am I going to do?*

She heard a tractor-trailer whistle along the highway not more than four hundred feet away. She decided then and there to hitchhike somewhere far away. Anywhere. Away from Chelsea, Michigan. Away from the bastard she married.

She skirted to the right of the fence around the storage buildings, through a stand of trees, and across Brown Drive. She stood for a moment facing the highway. She was near the edge of the westbound lane. She thought. There was nothing for her to the west, but to the east her son Kyle was at college. In New York. She'd get closer to Kyle. She would go east.

The surface roads from where she stood led to the eastbound entrance ramp. She started walking in that direction, crossing the yard toward the highway and turning left behind the house under the cover of a few scattered trees. She stopped. She realized that the eastbound entrance ramp would be a long walk along the surface roads. He might be in the car now. Driving around looking for her. She looked at the highway through the trees. Traffic didn't look too bad, whatever rush there may have been earlier was long gone.

She decided to cross the highway. The eastbound ramp was just on the other side, near the intersection of McKernan Drive and Route 52. She knew it well. They used the ramp a lot when Kyle was young going to Tigers, Red Wings, Lions, and Pistons games. The boy loved sports. She walked past the trees and through the tall grasses that lined the highway. No guardrails. No cars. She ran across the westbound lanes to the median. Three cars were coming east. She stood on the edge of the median with her thumb out. The cars raced past, rushes of wind following each. Maybe too fast to see her, maybe too dark. She needed to get to the entrance ramp where the cars would be slowing. It was her only chance to get a ride.

She ran across the eastbound lanes. On the far side was a thick stand of trees that extended as far to her left as she could see but only a short ways to the right. She turned right and ran toward the open area. When she reached the opening, she jogged left away from the highway, ran along the edge of a stand of maples, and then sprinted across another opening.

"Crap!" she yelled aloud, startled by the radio tower looming directly above her. As surprised as she was, she also knew that the entrance ramp was very close to the tower. Just across a field to her left. She ran across an open field to McKernan Drive, turned right, and ran along the road until she was close to the intersection. At the terminus of the guardrail, she ran down the embankment to her right and collapsed between a tree and the base of a road sign to rest.

A few cars passed while she was resting. From her position below the road, she couldn't see the cars, but she could hear the tires humming. She stood, walked past the sign and up the embankment, and climbed over the guardrail. No cars in sight. She jogged across Route 52 and then sat on the guardrail to wait for a car. It didn't take long. Standing with her thumb out, exposed, it suddenly occurred to her that any car might be her husband. Her throat tightened. The car approached and slowed. Blinker on, it turned toward her and began to accelerate. She stepped back as it passed in front of her and sped away up the ramp. She sat back down on the guardrail. Sore. Tired. Cold for the first time since escaping the house.

Three cars passed without slowing down. She wondered if they even saw her. A long wait and finally another car. Standing, thumb out. The car slowed, stopped. She opened the door and climbed in.

Before she could close the door, the driver spoke, "Lady, are you alright?" His eyes were wide. She stared at him, not understanding. "You're covered with blood. You look like you've been in a fight. Are you alright?"

"I'm fine," she replied. "I tripped and fell. Where are you going?"

He stared in disbelief, silent.

"Are you going a long ways east? I need to get to New York."

It took him a few seconds to reply. "Uh, yeah, I'm driving back to Auburn. Straight through. I need to be home by tomorrow. You sure you're alright?"

She wiggled in the seat to get more comfortable. "Where's Auburn?"

"Just off the thruway about halfway through New York. Not quite to Syracuse. Eight hours drive from here."

She thought for a moment. Eight hours was a good start. She and her husband had driven their son to college through Syracuse. His school was only a few hours from there. She looked at him and asked, "Would you mind if I ride there with you?"

"Sure, as long as you're alright."

"I'm fine."

She shut the door. He put the car in gear and accelerated up the ramp and onto the highway. Margo Rank began to put Michigan behind her.

# CHAPTER TWO

The mug warmed Kris Jansen's hand, steam rising from the hot tea. Months of work preparing for the winter had left him sore. His hands felt swollen and stiff, but he was finally ready for it. As least as ready as he knew how to be. This would be his first winter in the cabin.

He gazed across the pond watching the mist rise, waking up slowly from what had been a fitful sleep. A lot of noise from Chance Pond Road overnight. Four wheelers. Seemed like armies of four wheelers driving back and forth. Kris hoped it wasn't going to become a regular occurrence.

The sun was almost ready to breach the spruce trees at the far east end of the pond. It was cold, probably even colder on the dock where he sat exposed to the pond. *November*, he thought, *but no snow. Wonder when.* A splash near the shore to his left caught his attention. A fish maybe? He looked but saw only a foam cup floating in the pickerelweed. He thought about fishing it out, but he was too tired. Too sore. And since almost everything that floated in the pond eventually washed into Kris's cove, a proper cleanup later in the day might gather more junk anyway. He sipped his tea and gazed across the pond.

The sun finally cleared the treetops, bright across the pond. Too bright, too much glare. Reluctantly, Kris stood up, gulped the last of the tea from the mug, and stretched. He loved sitting on the dock in the morning, even when it was as cold as today. He wasn't looking forward to the winter.

Kris walked back into the tiny cabin through the glassed-in porch. Inside, he took the fire screen off the wood stove. The logs that were burning nicely before he went out to the dock were nearly gone. He threw two more logs on the coals and replaced the screen. It only took a few seconds for the new logs to begin burning. He sat down in one of the rocking chairs in front of the wood stove and rocked. Today, for the first time in months, Kris had nothing urgent to do.

The cabin was small, no more than seven hundred square feet spread over two floors. On the first floor was a small kitchen with a metal table, the wood stove with a pair of mismatched wooden rockers in front, and a small area with a couch, a chair, his old television, and the VHS and DVD players. The second floor was an open room with five beds, two storage trunks, and two old dressers. All of the mattresses were old and lumpy. Kris didn't mind, though, this was home now. The cabin had a smell that wasn't like anything Kris had ever smelled before: wood smoke and pine boards mixed with a little bourbon. A good smell. Inviting.

The main part of the cabin had been built in the early 1920s. A single story addition had been added sometime within the past thirty years and held a small bathroom, a laundry area, and the pump system and water heater.

A large shed and an outbuilding were also on the one-acre lot. His little collection of buildings sat on a small pond just inside the northwestern boundary of New York's Adirondack Park, about eight miles from the nearest village. Built before the park regulations were in place, the cabin sat very close to the pond, only about twenty feet from the shore. He'd purchased the property from a local college professor about ten years earlier. A summer vacation spot.

Kris enjoyed a close relationship with his cousin, Erik, and the property was only about fifteen miles from Erik's house. Vacationing here meant that Kris got to spend more time with Erik and his family. They had all enjoyed it immensely, spending most of ten summers swimming, fishing, playing cards, and sitting around a campfire. Looking back, it seemed as if those days would never end, but changes came. Kris found himself unexpectedly out of work. He sold his house and moved north. He'd never planned on living at the cabin year-round; it had needed a lot of work to make it comfortable and safe for winter months.

Kris had worked on the cabin alone more often than not over the previous months. Erik helped when he could, but he didn't have much free time between his job at the Sefton police department and his family. Nevertheless, Kris had accomplished more than he expected since the spring.

First he'd tackled the outbuilding that Erik's two boys used as a bunkhouse during the summers. He needed a space for the consulting business he'd started and the outbuilding was his best choice, but it was too small and didn't have heat. He'd framed and finished a small addition, turning the square building into a rectangle with a small porch and a covered entrance. He'd finished the exterior walls with vertically grooved plywood siding and stained it white. Not fancy, but fast and easy. The roof was a simple peak with the gable facing the pond, and two large windows were added on to do the same. Since he would be spending so much time in this new office, he'd figured that he should at least have a good view of the pond. He'd insulated all the stud bays with fiberglass and paneled the walls with tongue and groove pine. A small wood stove in one corner provided heat, and satellite internet connected him to his clients and the outside world.

In the cabin, he'd replaced the old wiring with new and replaced the ancient fuse box with a new circuit breaker panel. He'd stripped the old paneling from the walls and insulated the stud bays there too. The cabin appeared to have been built without the aid of measuring devices; there wasn't a plumb or level board in it. Insulating had been easy, but putting up the interior paneling had taken more time than he'd hoped.

Much of the copper plumbing ran below the cabin, exposed to the air. Kris wrapped these pipes with electric heat tape, covered that with foam insulation, and secured it all with duct tape. His water supply was piped to the cabin from the pond, and he'd wrapped the water intake pipe with electric heating cable, insulated over that, and secured it with duct tape, just as he had with the copper pipes. To protect it from animals and ice movement at the pond surface, he'd fished it through corrugated black plastic pipe. He really would have rather buried it, but the ground was filled with roots from the spruce and hemlock trees, and he'd decided it would take too long to dig. He'd needed to finish all of the necessary projects before the snow fell. He'd bury it next year, but for now he hoped it was protected well enough for the winter.

Electrical service was tenuous at the cabin, outages frequent. In an extended outage, the heat tape on the copper plumbing and water intake pipes wouldn't heat and the pipes could freeze, a problem he needed to avoid. He'd constructed a small building to house a generator and a thirty-gallon gas caddy and installed a transfer switch to make it easy to switch between the generator and the grid when the time came. He'd built another small building beside his generator shed, this one to house the pump system and hot water heater. He'd insulated this little building as well and installed a small electric space heater to keep the equipment from freezing. Putting up the building itself had been easy compared to the disassembly and reassembly of the pump equipment and installation of the water pipes. He'd spent the time to install the pipes so they would drain easily and completely the next time he closed the cabin for a season. He wasn't planning to live here every winter.

With the pump equipment and water heater relocated to the outbuilding, he'd moved a wall in the bathroom to make enough room for a combination tub and shower. The old layout had only had room for a small square shower stall, and he needed a tub to use as a backup. If his water pipes froze, he'd be able to haul water in buckets from the pond, heat it on the stove, and fill the tub to bathe. It was a backup plan that he hoped he wouldn't need to use, but he really wasn't sure what to expect this first winter.

The cabin, like the outbuilding, was heated by a wood stove with a propane fired direct vent wall furnace as a supplement. As a vacation home, he'd mostly used the cabin during the spring, summer, and fall, so he had no idea how much wood he would need for the entire winter. He'd purchased ten cords of hardwood and stacked them in the woodshed that he'd built next to the shed. He'd also collected nearly three cords of spruce and hemlock from trees he had cut when he'd first started using the cabin. The spruce burned fast and gave less heat than the hardwood, so he planned to use that only if needed. He was prepared to conserve the wood as much as he could; he was worried about running short.

Work on the outbuildings and cabin had taken him into the autumn, in large part because he'd also needed to concentrate on his consulting business and his clients. Luckily, his clients hadn't demanded much travel this year. By early October he'd finished his work on the cabin and he'd began cutting and splitting wood on the ten-acre lot that he'd purchased in the spring. In fact, he'd spent the past week splitting wood on his lot, leaving the cabin every day before dawn and returning after dark. His firewood would come from his lot over the coming years, and it was on this lot that he planned to build a new, larger cabin where he could live permanently.

The fire was dying again. He got up and tossed on a couple more logs, then shuffled to the stove to heat water for another cup of tea. Thinking it might be a good day to stock up on supplies, he began writing a list, but he only managed to think of a few things, still too tired to function. The teapot whistled. He turned off the burner, poured the hot water into his cup, and shuffled back to the rocking chair. *Supplies can wait*, he thought, *I'll drink a little more tea.* He set the list and his tea down on the side table and watched the flames until he fell asleep.

# CHAPTER THREE

The rumbling of the four wheeler interrupted his dream, but it was the pounding on the door that woke him up.

"Kris! Kris! You in there, Kris?"

He jumped from the rocker, ran to the door, and yanked it open. Silas stood on the other side, stooped, flustered, and out of breath.

"Jesus Christ. Kris, it took you a long time to answer. You okay?"

Kris shook his head, his heart pounding from being startled. "Yeah, Silas, I fell asleep in my chair. Come on in. You want some tea?"

Silas shuffled into the cabin.

Silas and his wife, Violet, lived near the entrance to the camp road. They were the only people who lived on the pond year-round. Except for an oddball named Fisco, but Kris didn't pay much attention to Fisco. Silas liked to look after things on the pond. He patrolled the camp road on a rumbling, patched-together, powder blue four wheeler. Back and forth. Over and over. Every day. Almost as if he was running from something. He always dressed a little crazy, you might say flamboyant if he was city folk. In summer he liked to wear loose, white button-down shirts with baggy sleeves tied at the biceps by leather laces. In winter, a variety of knee-length coats with only the top few buttons fastened, so that, as he rode, the coat bottoms blew back like Guy Lafleur's hair during a Habs warm-up skate. The centerpiece was Silas's hat. It was a wide-brimmed, Rough Rider-style felt hat, the left brim curled up and fastened to the crown Teddy Roosevelt style. The front and sides of the crown were covered with pins and feathers, and a raccoon tail was fastened to the inner back sweatband. Silas could talk for hours about the hat; every appendage had a story. Over the years Kris had listened to many.

"Kris, I got a question to ask you." Silas almost hollered when he spoke. Kris figured it was because he couldn't hear very well.

"Silas, tell me if you want a goddamn cup of tea will you?" Kris hollered back at Silas, standing at the little stove grinning.

Silas paused, looked at him for a moment, and broke into a smile of his own. "Yes, for Christ-sake, Kris, make me a damn cup of tea." Silas shuffled to the rocker in front of the fire and sat down. "And put another log on this shitty little fire too." Silas smiled his droopy crooked smile, happy to be giving it back to Kris.

"Damn you, Silas. Never fucking happy, are you?" The teapot whistled. Kris turned the burner off, poured two cups, and took a seat next to Silas in front of the fire.

Silas leaned toward Kris, still smiling, and asked, "You been keeping track of your firewood, Kris?"

Kris stared at him for a second. "What do you mean?"

"Somebody's been stealing my firewood, Kris." The smile was gone from Silas's face. He stared at Kris and didn't speak another word.

"No shit, Silas. Who the hell would take your wood?"

"I don't know, but if I catch the bastard he'll get a load of birdshot in his ass, I'll tell you that, Kris." Silas sipped his tea and grinned, "Kris, I'm telling you because they're probably going after your wood too. You and me, we can't afford to lose any firewood."

"You're right about that, Silas."

They both sat silently, staring at the fire.

After a few minutes, Silas broke the silence, "Keep an eye on your wood, Kris, and put another log on that shitty little fire."

Kris removed the fire screen and placed it on the floor next to him. He reached to the wood rack behind the stove, grabbed a small chunk of birch wood from the top of the pile, and tossed it on top of the burning logs in the stove. It crackled and popped when it hit.

"Say, Silas, how's Violet doing?"

Silas stared into the fire for a few moments and shrugged. "She's the same as always, Kris. Reminds me that I gotta throw away today's lunch bag when I get back to the cabin." Silas got up from the chair and made his way to the sink with his mug. "I'll get going, Kris. What are you doing today?"

Kris looked at the list lying on the side table. "Groceries today, Silas, groceries. And maybe a couple bottles of whiskey. It's getting cold outside, and I might need a little hooch to keep me warm."

Silas smiled.

"You need anything while I'm in town, Silas?"

"No, nothing I can think off the top of my head. I might be back to drink some of that whiskey, though. And come to think of it, we need to play some cards so I can win back the money you stole from me last time."

Silas turned and shuffled out the door and down the steps to his four wheeler. He tossed the bottom of his coat over to one side as he climbed on and pushed the starter button on the handlebars to bring it rumbling to life. He waved as he started back toward his cabin. Kris shut the cabin door and went back to his seat by the fire. He picked up the list and pencil and tried to think.

Distracted again by a familiar rattle coming over the camp road and a couple of low shouts, Kris glanced out the window. A beat-up white van crested the hill and careened down the road past Silas. It was Tim Fisco starting his daily routine: speeding up and down the camp road. Back and forth, kind of like Silas, except Fisco wasn't ever paying attention to anything.

"Stoned motherfucker," Kris muttered aloud to himself. He had no idea what Fisco did for a living; all he knew for sure was that Fisco was a pain in the ass. He was always whining about something. And there were rumors that he was a hopeless pothead, living what life he had in a constant state of ignorant bliss.

As the van raced south on the camp road and disappeared over the rise, Kris tried once again to focus on his list. He couldn't. He wondered if his wood was being stolen. He got up from the rocker, grabbed his coat, and walked out to the woodshed. He couldn't tell if any wood was gone. He wondered how anyone could tell when wood was missing; there were so damn many logs, and they all looked the same. He walked back to the cabin to take one more crack at the list. This time he only sat for a couple of minutes.

*Fuck the list.*

He got up, grabbed his coat again, and stomped out the door to his truck. The driver's side door was unlocked. He never locked it. He never locked any doors here. It was one of the ways that he showed himself that his old life in the city wasn't nearly as good as this new life. Kris still needed convincing, though. He climbed into the truck and slammed the door shut.

*I'd better calm down before I drive this thing*, he thought. And for the next forty-five minutes, anyone who drove down the camp road past Jansen's place might have seen Kris, motionless in his truck, sore and tired, and wondering if the work would ever stop, even just for a day or two.

# CHAPTER FOUR

The slowing of the car startled her, and she opened her eyes. He was pulling into a rest area. She could see a large building, a parking lot with only a few cars, and a line of gas pumps beyond. Her sleep had been restless. She had never been able to sleep while riding in a car, and on this night her mind was reeling as well. Her neck was stiff, her head ached, and she was dirty and sticky. He pulled the car into an open space, stopped, and turned off the ignition.

"You're awake?" he asked apologetically.

"Yeah," she said as she straightened up and stretched.

"This is the last rest area before I get off the highway. You think it'll be okay if I leave you here?"

Her mind went blank. She was silent. She hadn't thought ahead at all when she fled Michigan. She hadn't thought about anything but the moment. "Shit," she muttered.

"I'm really sorry, but I don't know what else to do. I can't take you to my house. My wife, she wouldn't—"

She interrupted him, "No, don't worry, it's okay. I understand."

His relief was apparent to her, even though she was groggy.

He continued, "I've been in this rest area a few times. There's a couple places to buy coffee and food and plenty of tables you can sit at. And I've seen people washing up in the restrooms. Do you need money?"

"No, I'm set," she replied.

They sat in silence, both staring straight ahead. She turned and looked at him. "You want me to get out now?"

"Yeah." He didn't look at her.

"Okay, thank you very much for letting me ride with you." She opened the car door and swung her foot onto the asphalt. Her ribs hurt when she lifted herself out of the car. Tentative, she stood at the open door for a few seconds, then turned and shut the door. He waved an awkward wave. She returned it as he drove away. She had never felt as alone as she did at that moment.

A few dim parking lot lights struggled against the pre-dawn sky but threw enough light to help her avoid tripping on the curb as she made her way into the building. Inside, the lights were bright, maybe a little too bright. It was a large open space with a red and white tile floor set in a pattern that reminded her of geese flying south for the winter. Above, old painted canoes hung from the ceiling. *Not a bad place to land*, she thought to herself. Many of the vendors were closed at 6:30 in the morning. Only McDonald's was open, but she wasn't looking for food yet. She looked for the restrooms. She didn't want to see how damaged she was, but she had to clean up.

As she walked past the McDonald's counter, she heard gasps and whispers, suggesting that her condition might be worse than she'd thought, and as she turned the corner into the restroom and approached the sinks and mirrors, her fears were confirmed. She looked as if she'd been hit by a truck. Her left eye was swollen shut, her left cheek was badly bruised, and her lower left lip was swollen and split open. Blood had dried on her face below her lips and over her chin, spilling down her neck and onto the collar and front of her blouse. Her arms were both badly bruised between the elbow and wrist. She unbuttoned her blouse to reveal more bruises on her sore ribs that covered her from her left breast to her waist.

It hurt just to move her arms, but she removed her blouse, tossed it in the sink to her right, and began washing her face gently using the soap from the wall mounted dispenser. It stung as it hit the cuts. She ignored the pain, gently but persistently working away the dried blood, exposing the damage to the air. "I will heal," she whispered repeatedly, a mantra more for her fractured soul than her battered face.

Satisfied that she was as clean as she could get, she turned her attention to the blouse. She used wet paper towels to plug the drain, temporarily holding water in the sink. With repeated fillings, she managed to scrub the blouse with soap and rinse it pretty well. When finished, she took it to one of the hand dryers on the wall and soon had it dry enough to put back on. The blood had stained it a little bit, but looking in the mirror, she was satisfied that this was the best she could do under the circumstances.

"I will heal. I will heal. I will heal."

After a few deep breaths, she walked out of the sanctuary of the restroom and into the glare of the open space. She didn't think she'd been in the restroom for very long, but the building was more alive now than when she went in. A young girl was preparing to open the gift shop, a black man was mopping the floor, and there were two short lines at the McDonald's counter. She took her place at the back of a line and tried to ignore the stares and whispers. In early November in New York she would have stood out simply because she wasn't wearing a coat, but with her battered face and wrinkled blouse, she was causing a stir. With coffee in hand, she made her way to the furthest booth in the open seating area. Tucked in a corner with her back to the wall, it felt safe. Nobody behind her, nobody to her left, and a clear view of everyone who approached. She sat and thought.

*How am I going to get out of here? How am I going to get to Kyle?*

Margo sipped coffee and dozed, her head on her arms on the table. She got up to use the bathroom now and then and suffered through the McDonald's line for occasional refills and a burger when she was hungry enough. The day went by quickly. Most of the time she slept.

"Hi, hon. Are you alright?" The voice was gentle, as if from a dream. Margo picked her head up just enough to peer over her folded arms. A middle-aged woman was sitting across the table from her.

"Are you alright?"

"Yeah," Margo replied, her head still resting on her arms and still dazed with sleep.

"My husband and I have been worried about you, dear. You haven't moved a bit, and we've been watching you for at least forty-five minutes." The woman had a pleasant, round face, shoulder-length gray hair, and a canvas cap.

"What time is it?" Margo asked.

The woman looked at her watch. "3:45 dear. 3:45 in the afternoon."

Margo sat up, startled. She'd been asleep on and off in a busy rest area all day. How many people must have walked past her? Looked at her? And this woman was the first to check to see if she was okay.

The smile fell from the woman's face. "You're not alright, oh dear. You're badly hurt. Your face—" She turned to the table behind her. "Walter, this girl needs help!"

"I'm okay. I know I look pretty bad, but I'm okay. Really."

The woman slid to the side as Walter sat down beside her. "We want to help," he whispered.

Margo stared at him for a few moments. "I want to see my son. I came from Michigan last night."

"Where's your son, dear?" the woman asked.

"Paul Smith's College." Margo laid her head back on her arms for a moment.

The woman's smile returned. "We know where that is; we've been past it many times. We're driving to our cabin today, and it's near Paul Smith's. We'll be staying there for the week and then closing it for the season. Why don't you stay with us there and rest a little? We can take you to Paul Smith's when you're feeling a little better."

She couldn't believe what she was hearing. "Really? I could stay with you?"

"Of course, dear, it would be our pleasure." Nancy looked at her husband, her eyes asking for his reassurance.

Walter nodded and rose from his seat. "We should go now, though, if it's okay with you. We still have a few hours of driving, and we're not spring chickens anymore." He smiled and held out a hand.

"Where's your bag, hon?" the woman asked as Walter helped Margo up from the table.

"I don't have a bag; I left in a hurry."

"Not even a coat?"

"Nothing."

The woman looked stunned. They were silent for a moment while the woman looked Margo over. "I'm a little bigger than you, but I have an extra coat you can wear, and we can find some clothes from my bag for you when we get to the cabin. Walter, the coat's in the back of the car. It's the tan one. We'll wait here."

Walter nodded and hurried to get it.

"Hon, if you want to talk about anything I'll listen, and I promise it'll stay between us. Walter can be trusted too."

"Thanks, I might need a shoulder to lean on," replied Margo quietly. She still hadn't come to grips herself with what had happened. They stood in silence for a few minutes longer, neither knowing what to say.

"I never told you my name, hon. I'm Nancy."

"Margo," she replied.

More silence. Walter returned with the coat. It fit Margo fine, maybe a little big, but it was warm and dry.

"Let's get moving," said Walter.

# CHAPTER FIVE

Grocery shopping wasn't Kris's favorite chore, but he liked the drive between his cabin and the grocery store. The winding backwoods roads cut through walls of spruce and fir trees that crowded the roadside, broken only by an occasional marsh and a few ramshackle hunting cabins. With hunting season in full swing, most of the cabins were alive after being abandoned at the end of the previous season. Wood smoke spilled from metal chimneys, giving the crisp air an all-too-familiar, and welcome, fragrance.

The drive to Sefton took about a half hour in good weather. Kris didn't know how it might be once the snow and ice came. Grocery shopping was routine and mind-numbing. Kris could never remember what groceries were in what aisle, so he spent a lot of time crisscrossing the store before he finally checked out. At the deli case, he spotted the hot dogs that Silas always talked about and bought a few to bring back for him. After the grocery store, he made a quick stop at the liquor store to buy two handles of Wild Turkey 101 and then the hardware store for some light bulbs and batteries. He stopped next at the Village Diner where he took his time and read the paper over a turkey club sandwich, and he made one last stop at the gas station in

Cotswald to gas up the truck and fill a few five-gallon cans. All in all, it was about four hours before he was driving back through the woods toward the cabin.

Darkness had overcome daylight during the drive back from Sefton, and the thick walls of conifers lining the narrow road blocked what little light the moon might have shed if it had risen. As Kris neared Chance Pond Road, the walls of trees to his right gave way to a dirt parking lot lit by a single sodium lamp on a tall pole. A building that spanned the back of the lot revealed itself as the truck moved closer. Long and low and nearly windowless, Natty's Tavern, with dark brown siding and a plain, single-door entrance, wasn't particularly welcoming, but Kris knew the place well. This night, the lot was nearly full. Natty's was busy. A sudden desire for a glass of whiskey and a chat with Cindy, the owner, had Kris turn into the dirt parking lot.

Natty's occupied a lot at the corner of Chance Pond Road, about a mile from Kris's cabin. Inside, a single pool table filled the floor to the right of the entrance, a few tables covered with red checkered plastic tablecloths sat to the left, and the bar lay straight ahead. The door to the kitchen stood just to the left end of the bar, a door that Cindy spent much of her time walking through as she switched between cooking and schmoozing.

Natty's was full of hunters, the dinner crowd, and there was nowhere to sit at the bar. Kris found standing room at the far left end near the door to the kitchen and leaned on the bar's edge. Cindy was at the other end pouring beers, busy. It took her a few minutes to spot Kris, and when their eyes met, he grinned and lifted his chin. "Hey!" She held up one finger as if to say "just a minute" and finished filling a glass with Bud Light from the tap.

"Kris! Haven't seen you for a while!" Cindy's eyes shone as she set a rocks glass full of Wild Turkey on the counter in front of him. Cindy knew what Kris drank.

"I think I finally finished getting the cabin ready for winter."

Cindy winked, "You can always stay with me if it gets real bad, you know."

Kris raised his glass to her as if to toast, "And you know I'll be here if I need warming up!" He took a long drink of the whiskey while Cindy chuckled.

"Jesus Fucking Christ, how long do I have to wait for a beer down here?"

Cindy's smile evaporated into a frown. "The asshole's here again," she whispered. She turned and walked to the far end of the bar where a man with long gray hair in a ponytail and a flannel shirt was standing.

"It's about time, sexy."

Cindy looked him in the eye without smiling. "What'll you have?"

"Christ, honey, don't you know by now? Sam Adams. And I don't want a glass, just the bottle."

Cindy turned and took a bottle from the undercounter refrigerator, popped the cap with a bottle opener, and set it on the bar in front of him. "Tab?"

"You bet your sweet ass, honey. I'm in for a few of these tonight. Maybe you'll let me take you home when I'm drunk enough." He took a drink from the bottle.

Cindy turned back to the register and opened a tab. Her obvious lack of attention irritated him.

Back at the end of the bar, Kris watched nervously. Kris hated confrontation, but he was conflicted. He knew that somebody needed to set the guy straight. When Cindy returned, they just looked at each other silently for a few seconds.

"There's always one," Cindy whispered, "but this one's a real bastard. He's kind of new, been in a couple nights since the last time you were here, Kris. A professor at Sefton State if you can believe it. That scumbag teaching somebody's kids."

"Why do you serve him?" Kris asked.

"What am I s'posed to do?" Cindy straightened up and shrugged. "I can't refuse to serve him, can I?" Cindy looked down at the bar. "What a pain in the ass."

It didn't take long.

"Another fucking beer here!"

Cindy rolled her eyes, turned, and walked back to the professor.

"What the hell, sexy? Why don't you just stay the fuck here and talk with me when you're not pouring my beers?"

Kris couldn't take it. He walked around to the far end of the bar and wedged himself between the professor and the guy next to him. Kris's face and the professor's were almost touching.

"What the fuck do you want?" The professor was nearly shouting, and his spit flecked Kris's face.

"I want you to start treating Cindy with a little respect." Kris kept his eyes locked with the professor's.

The professor sneered, "And what are you gonna do about it, asshole?"

Kris didn't give him time to think. He grabbed the professor hard by the front of his shirt and slammed him against the wall. The room went silent. Some of the men at the bar started to back away.

"I'm gonna beat you so bad you'll never talk again."

They stared at each other for what seemed like minutes.

"Okay, Okay." The professor backed down, his hands in the air indicating that Kris had won this round. Kris eased him back from the wall but kept his grip tight on the professor's shirt.

"Now here's what's going to happen. When I let you go, you're gonna walk right out of this bar and you're not going to come back in here tonight. In fact, you're not coming back in here for a couple weeks, and then only when you can be decent to Cindy and everyone else in here." Kris gave him a hard shove against the wall and released his shirt.

"What about my beer?"

"No more beer. You're leaving. I'll pay your tab."

The professor turned and shuffled toward the door, looking down at the floor to avoid eye contact with anyone and grumbling softly under his breath. Kris returned to the end of the bar. Cindy brought the bottle and topped off his glass. "It's all on me tonight, Kris."

The rest of the crowd returned to their conversations.

Kris was a little shaken up by the confrontation and feeling funny about it. All of his life Kris had rarely been bold enough to act when he felt he needed to. He wondered where this newfound courage came from. He wondered if it was really courage at all.

A flurry of bar orders followed the confrontation and kept Cindy busy. Then, when the inevitable lull came, she again rested near Kris. "I lost my help yesterday, Kris."

"Sorry to hear that, Cindy. Anything I can do?"

Cindy smiled and winked, "You can move in here with me and take care of me and this place."

Kris took a sip of whiskey, his eyes locked with Cindy's. He liked flirting with her; she was attractive. In her mid-forties, she was stocky but fit and strong. She had raven hair and dark eyes. Eyes full of mischief.

"What do you say, Kris? I'd make it worth your while, you know."

Kris took another sip. "You know that I'd jump at the chance if I wasn't so busy trying to catch up with my work, Cindy. All this work on the cabin in the last few months has made it hard to keep current with my clients. I've got some catching up to do." Kris felt awkward. It wasn't really true; Kris never let himself get behind.

Cindy straightened up and tipped her head just a little to the left. Her smile broadened and eyes sparkled. She poured a little more whiskey into his glass. "I'm going to keep after you, Kris. I always get what I want."

Kris looked at the glass and then back at Cindy. "That's what I'm afraid of, Cindy." He raised his glass to her and took a sip. A call for a refill came from down the bar. Cindy gave Kris one more smile and a wink.

After a few more glasses of whiskey and a few more punctuated conversations with Cindy, Kris decided to head back to the cabin. He thanked Cindy, got up from his stool, and walked to the door. The bar became silent once again. He felt everyone watching him as he walked past the pool table, swung the door open, and stepped into the cold night. Bright stars hung in a cloudless sky with a moon now visible and half full. Headlights were coming down the road from the North. A tiny, lone SUV, nearly soundless as it approached. The hum of the tires grew louder as it teetered past.

Kris opened the door to his truck and climbed in. As he drove out of the parking lot and up the hill, he remembered that he had hot dogs for Silas. He decided to take them over in the morning.

# CHAPTER SIX

Nancy and Walter had a little SUV, a Toyota, or maybe a Honda. Margo didn't know, or care, really. It was packed to the roof with supplies. Nancy stood with Margo while Walter moved stuff around to clear enough of the back seat for Margo to sit. The wind was blowing steadily across the parking lot. Margo was glad to have the coat.

The highway was monotonous, but Nancy kept the conversation going. She tried hard to avoid the tough questions and kept it light. Margo thought Nancy was really nice and was quickly growing more comfortable in her company. A few strip malls and stores broke the monotony when they changed from Route 90 East to Route 81 North, but that was short-lived. Soon, the new landscape streaming past became even more monotonous than the old. Still, Nancy kept talking, and before Margo realized it, they were off the highway and on secondary roads. Signs said *Watertown* and *Route 11*, but Margo didn't recognize the area. She couldn't remember the route that she and her husband had taken to visit their son at college.

Darkness came fast, and any hope of understanding where she was vanished. Margo was in Nancy and Walter's hands, and she was comfortable with it. This was the first time since she fled her husband that she felt like she was going to be alright. She dozed, awakened now and then by the undulations of the roads as they moved further north and east. Through Gouverneur, Canton, Sefton. The roads narrowed further. Houses became scarce as the road climbed, twisted, and sank and the woods took over. At one point, Margo noticed a brightly lit parking lot. Strange, she thought, this far out in the woods. Lots of pickup trucks parked in front of a long, low building without many windows. One man in the parking lot was opening the door to his truck as they passed.

"Natty's," said Nancy looking out her window, "that's Natty's Tavern. It's a wonderful place." She turned back to Margo. "We'll come down here for some dinner one night when you feel up to it. We're almost at our cabin, Margo. Almost there."

It was only a few minutes later when they turned left onto a dirt road and weaved their way through the deepest woods of the trip. The moon was half full, the sky was clear, and Margo began making out what looked like water here and there through the trees to their right. Soon enough, the trees opened up as they passed cabins, and Margo could clearly see the water just beyond. Walter pulled off the dirt road into a flat area surrounded by tall trees and stopped the SUV. A tiny cabin lay directly in front of them. Wood shingles with dark shutters next to the windows.

"Here we are!" Walter exclaimed.

"Oh how I love this place," whispered Nancy.

Walter left the SUV's headlights on, and they all got out of the little truck. He unlocked the cabin door and wrenched it open, wood creaking against wood as it sprung free of the doorframe.

Walter turned toward the women, grinned, and shrugged. "Everything's crooked up here, but I guess that's the way we like it." He turned back toward the door and walked through it into the darkness.

Nancy placed her hand on Margo's shoulder. "We'll wait out here for just a second while Walter finds the fuse box and turns on the electricity." Only moments passed before a light came on inside. "Okay, let's go in." Nancy smiled and motioned with her hand, "After you."

The front room was wood paneled from floor to ceiling. It smelled a little musty, but pleasant. Walter had already hurried to the wood stove that sat at the far end of the room and was busy putting sticks and newspaper into it. Nancy began bringing armloads of supplies in from the SUV, and Margo helped, carrying paper bags full of cracker boxes and canned food and plastic water jugs. Even though the little SUV was packed full, it only took a few trips before they had everything inside the cabin and the door closed and locked.

Walter's fire was well underway, but it would be a while before the cabin warmed up enough to take off coats. Walter trotted up the stairs to the second floor with Nancy hollering behind him. "Walter, why don't you take some things up with you?" No sound from Walter except the creaking of the floorboards. "He's opening the windows upstairs. Seems kind of backwards I guess, but with the windows open the air inside can move and the place will heat up faster." Nancy started to follow Walter upstairs with an armload of things, and Margo moved to help. "Don't, hon, please. I know where everything goes, and it'll only take a few minutes. Sit and rest some." Nancy motioned toward two rocking chairs that sat near the wood stove.

Margo stared at the young fire from the rocking chair while Nancy and Walter scurried around the cabin putting everything in its place. The warmth of the fire and the creaking of the chair as she rocked were pleasant. She was more comfortable and relaxed than she would have expected. This place already seemed like a good fit. Before long, Nancy announced success and flopped into the rocking chair beside her. "We've come here so many times since we bought the place. Getting set up is routine now. I wish we could live here year-round; I'd love to be here all the time."

"Why can't you?" Margo asked.

"No real reason I guess. It's just that we take our wash water from the pond and the place isn't very well insulated." Nancy paused for a few moments and gazed into the fire, thinking. "I guess it would be kind of a big project, and Walter and I are getting old. Anyway, it probably wouldn't seem so nice if we were here all the time." She forced a smile, still staring into the fire.

Margo didn't know what to say.

Nancy broke the silence, "Are you tired, hon?"

"I'm really enjoying the rocking chair, Nancy. It's so relaxing here."

Nancy smiled, a real smile this time. "Why don't I show you your bed, and then if Walter and I call it a night before you're ready, you can stay and tend the fire as long as you want."

She rose from the chair and held a hand out to Margo. "Here."

Margo took her hand and they walked up the narrow stairs. The upstairs appeared to have two rooms: one open to the stairs to the right and another behind a closed door to the left. Nancy led Margo to the right. A full sized bed was positioned near the far wall under a window that looked out over the pond. Soft light came from a small table lamp on a nightstand beside the bed, revealing dark wood paneling on the walls and a tall vaulted ceiling. A brightly colored quilt and flannel sheets covered the bed, the colors rich against the wood of the walls and ceiling. The moon shone through the window and reflected off the still water of the pond. Tall evergreen trees lined the far side. Margo thought it could have been a picture in a tourism brochure. Or a postcard. Idyllic.

The three of them returned to the fire. Walter pulled a chair over from the dining table, and they sat together for a couple of hours. Small talk mostly, the women rocking and Walter occasionally rearranging the logs or adding a new one. By the time they all retired for the night, they had established that Margo would stay with them for the entire two weeks and they would call her son in the morning. Anything else could wait until they all had some time to think.

# CHAPTER SEVEN

Awake but unable to see, he ran his hands across the bandages that covered his eyes. He felt hard discs under the bandages. Protection to help the healing, he figured. The bed sheets were thin and stiff. There was a draft; the door was open. He could hear the nurses chatting and moving around outside his room as they tended to other patients. Low murmurs came from a television somewhere in the distance.

He heard someone approaching his bed, the soft shuffle of rubber-soled shoes on linoleum.

"Mister Rank?" She spoke in a soft but assured tone and touched his arm lightly. He turned his head toward her. Mute.

"Mister Rank, your doctor will be here shortly to remove the bandages."

The moment of truth.

She shuffled away, out to the hall, and on to the next patient. Efficient and diligent, but curt. He didn't care. Women were all the same to him.

It wasn't long before the doctor came. And someone else with him. Probably the same nurse, maybe more than one. "Mister Rank, we're going to remove your bandages and assess your vision." While he spoke, someone ran the motor that raised the back of the bed.

They were wasting no time. Hands began working the bandages at the back of his head, the dull, cold edge of scissors sliding against his skull as they snipped. With the unwrapping, the weight began to shed and the disc over his right eye fell away. The disc over his left eye remained, having been taped separately.

He couldn't see well with the one eye, but he could see. Blurry, like looking through Vaseline. The doctor stood to his right, skinny with glasses, and the nurse to his left, heavy. A police officer also looked on behind the nurse. A woman police officer. He looked around the room, not paying attention to detail.

The doctor asked, "Can you see, Mister Rank?"

# CHAPTER EIGHT

Monday morning came hard and fast. Kris was up at 4:30. He hadn't slept well, and his head was fuzzy. Down the stairs in the dark, he missed the last step and stumbled into the wall. Finally in the kitchen, he picked up the teapot to make sure it had enough water, set it back down, and turned on the burner. He shuffled to the bathroom and had a piss, then back to the wood stove to get a fire going. It was cold inside the cabin.

Just as the kindling began to catch fire, the teapot began to whistle. He put the fire screen on the wood stove, grabbed the box of matches, and went to the stove. Turning the burner off and picking up the teapot, he poured the hot water over his tea bag in the cup. He set the teapot back on the burner and latched the spout cover up to prevent it from whistling while the burner cooled down. He returned the matchbox to the closet near the refrigerator, went back to the counter for his cup of tea, and returned to the wood stove. The fire was roaring. He sat down in his favorite rocking chair and set his cup on the side table.

Six cups of tea and three logs later, the horizon began to brighten through the windows behind him. Kris had been considering his reaction to the professor the night before. Running through it over and over. He still couldn't figure out what had caused him to take action. Not that he regretted it. He didn't. It seemed to fit him in a way that it never had before. He'd always bottled it up, held it in. Frustrating. But last night he'd let it go. He'd gone with it and come away feeling liberated. Alive.

Kris threw a couple more logs on the fire and made some breakfast. Three eggs, green peppers, onions, and cheese all scrambled together. Topped with hot sauce. When he finished, he cleaned up the dishes and closed the doors on the wood stove. The rest of the day would be spent in his office, and he didn't want to chance a spark getting around the fire screen and doing damage. He decided to take the hot dogs to Silas before he settled in to work. It was late enough now; Silas and Violet would be up and about.

The early sun did little to warm the air. Kris could see his breath as he walked across the yard and through the hemlock stand, up the ramp Silas built for Violet and to the front door. Kris's knocking set the dog off, and it ran to the door barking. Silas followed.

"Come on in, Kris." Silas wore a sleeveless white t-shirt and his work pants. He hadn't gussied up for the day yet.

"I brought you some of the hot dogs you like from town, Silas. Wasn't meaning to stay."

"Bullshit, Kris. Get your ass in here." Silas turned and yelled, "Violet, put the water on! Kris is here, and he wants a cup of tea!"

Kris didn't think that she heard Silas.

Silas shuffled down the hall and turned toward the kitchen. "Violet! Violet?" He looked around, then back at Kris. "She must be outside, out the back door. Come on in, Kris. I'll get your...shit!" His eyes grew large. Silas was clearly surprised and suddenly very anxious. He snatched a brown paper bag from the counter and pushed past Kris back into the front bedroom. After shuffling around for a minute, he came back out. Relieved.

Kris must have looked puzzled.

Silas drew closer and whispered, "Violet packs a lunch every day for our daughter. She started doing that about a week ago." Silas paused and looked at Kris.

"I never told you about Brenda?"

Kris shook his head.

"Well, no time like the present. I'll fill you in while Violet is outside. C'mon, let's get that tea."

With cups in hand, they moved from the kitchen to the living area and sat. Silas set his cup on a TV tray next to his easy chair. He sat up straight, away from the back of the chair, and put his hands on his knees.

"Me and Violet had a daughter. Was a long time ago; she was born in '58. We all moved here to the camp in '69, so she started catching the bus to school every morning, right where our road meets Sefton Pond Road." Silas pointed in the direction of the road. "Every day she caught that bus, grade school right up through high school. One day in the winter, when she was in high school, there was black ice on the road." Silas paused and leaned a little closer to Kris. "You know there's black ice in the winter, right, Kris?"

Kris nodded, even though he didn't know.

Silas straightened up and continued, "Well, this one day she was waiting at the stop, and we think she got distracted by something. She wasn't paying attention to the bus coming. The stop's on a bad part of the road, on that corner where the road tips hard to the shoulder." Silas tipped his head to the floor and his back bent, almost like he'd just given up on sitting straight. He slowly shook his head and lowered his voice, "The bus driver hit the black ice and lost control. Nothing he could do, Kris. Brenda must not have seen it coming."

They sat in silence. No more needed to be said; Kris understood completely.

After a little bit, Silas raised his head and looked at Kris, "It took Violet a long time to get over it. I guess maybe she never did. In the last few months, her mind's been going away, and she's started doing some strange things, Kris. For the past week or so she's been packing a school lunch for Brenda every day. Like Brenda's still with us."

Another pause, then Silas tipped his head toward the floor again. "The first couple days I wasn't really paying attention, and I left the bag right where it was. When Violet saw the bag sitting on the counter, she got riled up, thinking that Brenda forgot to take it to school. She ran with it right out to the bus stop, Kris. I was scared that she was gonna hurt herself."

Silas picked his head back up as if it was easier to talk about now. "Since then, I grab it when I see it and I get rid of it without Violet knowing. That way she thinks Brenda took it and she doesn't get anxious."

Kris didn't know what to say. He finished his tea and thought before speaking. "Silas, life doesn't get any easier. You tell me how I can help out and I'll do what I can, okay?"

Silas nodded. Kris rose from his chair and put his tea cup in the sink.

"I have to get started with work, Silas. Remember, I want to help."

Silas rose from his chair. "Thank you, Kris. And thanks for the hot dogs. I know what I'm having for lunch today."

Kris walked out the door and headed for his office.

# CHAPTER NINE

Margo's first days at the cabin had been relaxing and healing, maybe the most relaxing time she could remember since getting married. Margo tried to help Nancy and Walter when she could, but there really wasn't much to do. She spent most of her time in the rocking chair in front of the fire, reading through the old books they kept on a bookshelf in the same room as the wood stove. She'd spoken with her son Kyle once. They agreed that he would call her back after a few days to arrange a meeting.

*Riders of the Purple Sage* had been a fast read, and a good one. She never really got into the Hemingway short story collection, though she enjoyed one story called *The Short Happy Life of Francis Macomber*, and for a day or so she'd been reading Sherlock Holmes stories from a collection. She really liked the Sherlock Holmes stories.

Her wounds were healing. At first she avoided the mirror, but after a while she felt brave enough to take a look. She discovered that the worst was passing quickly. Her left eye that had been swollen shut was now open almost fully, and the bruising around it was beginning to fade. The bruise on her left cheek was getting smaller and changing color too, and the swelling and splitting of her lower lip had greatly improved. She still stayed at the cabin when Nancy and Walter went for a walk or a drive, though. She wasn't quite ready to face anyone yet.

"Soon," she repeated aloud as she looked in the mirror, "soon. I'm healing."

On this morning she had just begun to read *A Study In Scarlet* when Nancy appeared suddenly next to her.

"What would you say to a ride into town, Margo?"

The idea startled her. Margo only managed to mumble, "Not sure I'm ready—"

"Of course you're ready dear. More ready than you think. And besides, the week will be over before you know it, and we need to start figuring out what you'll do when we leave." Nancy smiled and sat down in the rocking chair next to Margo. "Walter and I are going into town. You've told me a few times that you need to take money from your bank account. There's no time like the present."

Margo was speechless. Soon was coming sooner than she expected, and she didn't know if she was ready.

Nancy sensed Margo's discomfort. "You can stay in the car while we do our errands. Except, of course, at the bank. You'll have to do that yourself."

Margo thought for a moment. It would be nice to see a little bit of the area, and there was no way her husband could know exactly where she was. She was the proverbial needle in a haystack. She'd be safe.

"Okay, Nancy. Let's do it."

"Hooray!" said Nancy as she stood quickly, arms over her head. "Walter!" she shouted, "Margo wants to come with us. Let's get going!"

Walter walked into the room, dishtowel in hand, drying a frying pan. "I'll get my jacket."

The ride to town took nearly a half hour. Margo was awestruck by the scenery. For the first few miles, the road wound through a boreal Adirondack forest, twisting and undulating in what seemed to be a random fashion. Deep stands of hemlock and spruce lined the road punctuated by open marshes and hunting shacks with smoke billowing from their chimneys. On one curve, Walter stopped the SUV to let a family of wild turkeys cross the road.

Eventually the forest began to thin and the road began to unwind. Year-round houses began to appear. Yards filled with cars, small farm equipment, plastic kids' toys, and an occasional chainsaw carving, usually a black bear or an owl. After a long, steep descent, they arrived in the village of Cotswald and the landscape had changed permanently.

"This is Cotswald. The whole thing. Blink and you'll miss it," announced Nancy like the guide on a city bus tour. "We're halfway there."

Cotswald straddled the intersection of the Adirondack boreal forest and the agricultural St. Lawrence Plain. The hills were gone, only undulations remained. The forest was gone as well. Much of the land abutting the road was cleared, and they passed acres of pasture lined with maple, elm, and birch. Small family farms with dilapidated buildings popped up here and there as if having been dropped from the sky without thought of location.

Nancy asked, "It's pretty in an unusual way, isn't it?"

"It's beautiful," said Margo. The landscape reminded her of Western Ontario where she'd grown up. It reminded her of home.

As suddenly as the forest gave way to pastures, the pastures gave way to a village. Houses streamed past and the space between them shrunk. As they drove deeper into the village, the houses became larger and more ornate. Many were built with tall, steep roof peaks and intricate woodwork along the roof edges.

*It's just like home*, Margo thought.

Walter spoke softly, "We're here, Margo. This is Sefton."

The village center came on quickly, square brick buildings two to three stories tall full of pizza shops, used clothing stores, and restaurants.

Nancy turned back to Margo, "Do you care what bank we go to?"

"Nah, they'll all charge me a fee, Nancy. Whatever's easiest for you guys."

Walter pulled into a parking lot. The sign read *Community Bank*. The little SUV was silent for a few awkward moments. Margo hesitated. Stepping out of the car into a public space was unforeseeably intimidating.

"C'mon, Margo. I'll go with you." Nancy opened her door and stepped out. She turned to look at Margo. Margo looked back at her. Blank. Frightened. "It'll be fine, Margo. I'm here with you."

Margo took a deep breath before opening her door and stepping out. She stood behind the open door for a moment. *Not so bad*, she thought to herself. Finally, she stepped aside and closed the SUV door, and the two women walked side by side to the door of the bank and then into the little glass room with the ATM.

First Margo checked the balance on the account. She shared the account with her husband and had no idea

47

how much money he'd spent in the days since she left. The balance was $426.37. Almost nothing. She took $400, accepted the $3 fee and left him $23.37. She knew that he'd see the transaction and its location, but she reminded herself that she was a needle in a haystack. He'd look up the location on the internet and see that it was close to their son's college. He'd know she was on her way there, and that would be the most likely place he'd look for her. If he was looking for her at all. As long as she was careful about going to visit her son, she could reduce his chances of finding her to nearly zero. It suddenly occurred to her that if she took money from any other ATM or used her card at all, she would be leaving him a much better trail. She turned to Nancy who was standing behind her.

"I think I need to find a job, Nancy. I want to stay here now."

Their next stop was the grocery store. Margo didn't stay in the car; she went in with Walter and Nancy. People stared. Her cuts and bruises were not yet healed after all, but it wasn't nearly as hard as she had imagined. In fact, it became a badge to her, as if she was daring people to judge her. The feeling was relieving and empowering at the same time. Margo could feel her confidence coming back, and she liked it.

They made another stop at Walmart where Margo bought a couple pairs of jeans, a few long-sleeved t-shirts, bras, panties, a winter coat, a pair of boots, a small duffle bag, and a prepaid cell phone. Just under two hundred dollars including tax. She didn't know what she was going to do, but she needed some clothes. She'd been wearing Nancy's. And with the prepaid cell phone she could talk with Kyle without being tracked.

The trip back to the cabin was pleasant. It was lunchtime, and Margo was hungry. The scenery passing the SUV was just as beautiful to her in this direction as it had been on the way in. They rode in silence until the little SUV began winding into the forest. Nancy turned in her seat. "Margo, I've been thinking about what you said. About getting a job, about staying here. Would you be willing to stop at Natty's for lunch? It's usually not very busy this time of day, and the owner, Cindy, seems to know everybody and their business. I'd bet that she could help you figure out something, and if she can't, she'll know someone who can."

The trip had helped Margo. Getting out of the car and into public spaces had built her confidence a little. She didn't hesitate in reply. "Sure, let's stop."

There were two men at the bar and a man and a woman at one of the tables. Natty's was empty otherwise. When the trio walked in, everyone turned to look at them, but nobody stared for even a moment. They returned quickly to their own little worlds. The woman standing behind the bar turned also. She raised her hand. "Nancy and Walter!" she exclaimed at high volume. "Find a table. I'll be right there."

They sat at a table near the wall on the left side of the entrance door. The table was rectangular with a red checked plastic tablecloth and heavy wooden chairs. The woman was there almost before they sat down laying out forks, knives, and paper napkins. She looked at Margo. "I've known Walter and Nancy for years, but I've never seen you before. I'm Cindy." She held out her hand, and Margo shook it.

"I'm Margo."

"It's a pleasure to meet you, Margo."

Nancy spoke, "We came in to have lunch, but we also want to talk with you a little, Cindy. Do you think you might be able to sit with us for a few minutes?"

After they ordered and Cindy brought the food out, she sat with them and Nancy told her Margo's story, Margo filling in when needed. Cindy listened intently. Nancy ended by asking Cindy if she knew of anyone who might be looking for help and anyone with an inexpensive apartment or room to rent.

Cindy looked at Margo. "Have you ever worked in the restaurant business?"

"I have, a little," Margo nodded, "When I was in high school I had a part-time job at a Carl's, and during my two years at college I tended bar at a local place."

"How about cooking? Did you ever cook in a restaurant?"

Margo paused and thought. "Never more than filling in when I needed to. Salads, a sandwich or two, some eggs now and then. I wouldn't call it cooking, though."

A man called from the bar. "Cindy, how about a couple more beers?" He wasn't angry or aggressive, just honest, like he'd been waiting a while and was reluctant to ask. Cindy excused herself and fetched drinks for the two men. When she returned to the table, she sat silently for a moment or two, staring at Margo.

"I might be able to help you, Margo," she started. "A few days ago, maybe a week, I lost my help. I've been working the place by myself since then. If you'd be willing, I'd be happy to put you to work here. Waitressing mostly to start, but we'd work you into bartending and cooking as well. And there's always dishwashing." Cindy smiled, paused for a moment, and continued, "I can't pay much, but I can pay regular, and I'm always on time. I also have an apartment attached to the bar that I usually rent out, but I haven't had a renter for a couple months. Under the circumstances, I'd be willing to let you have the place no charge for the first few months so you can get back on your feet money-wise. After that, we can work something out."

Margo looked at Nancy and then back at Cindy. "I'll take it."

# CHAPTER TEN

"Yeah, I can see."

The doctor asked a few more questions, and Rank answered with short, incomplete sentences and a grunt or two. He was staring at the cop, and the cop was staring back.

"What's the cop doing here?"

After a pause, the doctor replied, "After I give her the okay, she needs to ask you some questions."

Rank never took his eye off the cop. "What's that mean? What's 'the okay'?"

No pause from the doctor this time. "I'll give the okay for her to talk with you when I'm convinced that you no longer need our help to heal and that you're healthy enough for the conversation. After she talks to you and gives me the go-ahead, I'll release you from the hospital."

"What do you mean release me with her 'go-ahead'? Am I under arrest here?" Rank sat up in the bed.

"No, Mister Rank," replied the cop, "you're not under arrest. I need to ask you a few questions about how your eyes were damaged and where your wife is."

Rank slumped back into the bed.

The doctor turned to the police officer. "I guess the conversation started without my okay. He's fine now anyway. You go ahead and talk to him." He turned to Rank. "Your right eye wasn't damaged severely, and it will heal further as time goes on. I expect that the vision will return completely. Your left eye was damaged so severely that we had to remove it. I'm going to schedule a follow-up for a few weeks from now. We'll check your right eye, and we'll set you up with an ocularist to be fitted for an implant in the left."

Rank was silent.

The doctor continued, "I'll leave you written instructions, but the basics are that you'll need to keep the left eye socket clean, bandaged, and covered with the hard patch. The nurse will change your bandage before you leave today and show you how to do it. We'll give you some pads and tape so you won't need to go to the pharmacy right away." The doctor turned to the cop before leaving the room. "He's all yours." The nurse scurried around picking up the last remnants of Rank's bandages and hurried to catch up with the doctor. She closed the door behind her.

The cop pulled a chair from the corner closer to the bed, sat down, and opened a notebook. "Mr. Rank, can you tell me how your eyes were so badly damaged?"

Rank hesitated. He'd been in trouble with the cops a few times before, always after he and Margo had fought.

"I think I'm gonna plead the fifth, officer."

The cop sat silently for a moment.

"I was afraid you'd say that, Mr. Rank. I can't make you talk to me, but I can tell you that your injuries are suspicious. In addition, you've got a history of spousal abuse, and we haven't been able to locate your wife. Do you know where she is, Mr. Rank?"

Rank looked down at the bed sheets and shook his head.

"If we can't find your wife very quickly, Mr. Rank, I'm going to have to start an investigation. Are you sure that you don't know where she is?"

Rank shook his head again. Silent.

"It'll be much easier for both of us if you cooperate, Mr. Rank."

Silence.

"Fair enough." The cop stood and moved the chair back to its original position. "You need to know that a missing person is a very serious matter, and without your cooperation, I can only assume that your wife is missing. We'll continue to look for her. I'll be back in touch, possibly with a search warrant for your home. Are you sure that you don't want to cooperate?"

Rank stared at the bed sheets. Silent.

The cop waited a few moments, turned, and left the room.

Rank continued to stare silently at the bed. After a few minutes, the nurse returned.

# CHAPTER ELEVEN

Kris had been rattled by his conversation with Silas. He depended on Silas and Violet more than he'd realized. They'd become good friends soon after he first bought the cabin, and they'd supported him during his transition from city life when he moved in permanently. He hadn't considered the possibility of even more change. The thought of Violet losing her mind scared him, and he knew it scared Silas too.

Kris busied himself with work over the two days following that conversation. The work was good for his head, helped keep him from thinking about Silas and Violet too much. He didn't see either of them during this time, though he heard Silas motoring up and down the camp road as always. He eventually realized that he'd been avoiding Silas. He'd found himself waiting until he heard Silas pass to leave his office or the cabin, making excuses to stay in either place. When he did leave one or the other, he walked as fast as he could between the two. He felt like a fool, but he hadn't been ready to face the reality.

Late on the third day, Kris quit work just before dark and was checking his wood when he heard Silas rumble over the rise and start down the road toward the cabin. *Enough is enough*, he thought, and he walked toward the road to flag Silas down. Silas pulled the wheeler into Kris's yard and shut it off.

"Any more wood missing, Silas?"

"Funny you should ask that, Kris. I just checked it and, by Jesus, I'm missing more than usual." Silas grinned at Kris. "You're not the one taking it, are you?"

Kris smiled. "No, I've got plenty." He turned toward the woodshed and motioned his head in that direction. "I was just checking mine, and it doesn't look like I'm missing any. Strange that someone would only be taking yours, Silas."

"I'm a lot closer to the main road, Kris, easier to get in and out without being seen I suppose." Silas got off the wheeler and stretched. "What gets me, Kris, they always know when I'm gone. They must be watching our place, but I've never seen a car or a truck out on the main road. I can't figure it out."

Kris nodded.

Silas continued, "Plus, they're not taking that much at any time Kris. Today I was out at the store and I checked when I came back, and there's only about ten logs missing. That's a lot more than the other times, but not enough to last long." Silas paused, looked to the ground, and shook his head. "Maybe the bastards are pulling wood from a bunch of people hoping nobody will notice."

It seemed ridiculous to Kris, taking any wood at all that is. "Has Violet seen anything?"

Silas looked up at Kris. "Violet sleeps a lot now, Kris. I'll bet she was sleeping the whole time I was gone today. She was sleeping when I left and sleeping when I got back a few hours later."

Kris changed the subject. "What would you say to dinner and a drink, Silas? Me, you, and Violet. I haven't been over to Natty's in a few days, and I could use a steak and a whiskey."

Silas smiled. "Boy, I'd like that Kris. Lemme go see if I can get Violet interested. How long before you want to go?"

Kris thought for a few seconds. "Well, Silas, I don't have much left to do today. What do you say we go in a half hour? Think that'd give you enough time?"

"Yessir." Silas nodded. "You stop at our place when you're ready." He jumped on the wheeler, started it up, and drove away.

Kris went inside the cabin and took a leak. He checked the wood stove, even though he'd been in the office all day, and then turned on the light that he always left on while he was out. He always left the light on so he could see enough to get around when he got back later, especially if he might be drinking whiskey. When he was satisfied that both he and the cabin were ready for him to leave, he sat in the rocker and waited. It hadn't taken him more than ten minutes to get ready, but he wanted to give Silas some time.

Kris pulled the truck off the camp road into an empty area across from Silas' cabin. It was half dirt and half grass, not really a parking area, Kris thought, but Silas kept his tractor and a trailer parked there, so it would be good enough for a few minutes. At least the truck was off the road. He walked across the road, up the ramp to the front door, and knocked. The dog came to the door barking as usual, and after a bit he could see Silas walking toward the door to open it. Silas was only wearing his sleeveless t-shirt. Not a good sign.

"I'm sorry, Kris, we can't go with you. Violet isn't right."

Kris could see the worry in Silas's eyes.

"Anything I can do, Silas?"

"Nothing, Kris. Thanks, though. I'll talk to you tomorrow."

Kris sighed, "Sorry Silas."

They looked at each other for a second or two, and then Silas nodded silently and shut the door. Kris stood for a moment before returning to the truck. He was at a loss.

Back in the truck, Kris sat and thought before starting it up. It'd been a busy few days and a steak and whiskey still sounded good. He'd be alone, but he was used to that. And Cindy would be there. It promised to be a lot better than sitting in the cabin. He started the truck and headed toward Natty's.

# CHAPTER TWELVE

Moving into the apartment had been easy; all Margo had was the duffle and the few clothes she'd bought at Walmart. Cindy gave her the grand tour, Nancy and Walter following like proud parents dropping their daughter off at college.

"There ain't much to it," Cindy said, sweeping her hand in front of her. "This here's the main room. The only room really."

*It certainly is the only room*, thought Margo.

It was the living room, bedroom, and kitchen. All in one. Tiny. To the left was an old, white enamel metal sink cabinet with a couple of shelves above and a few dishes and glasses on the shelves. The cabinet was rusty where the sides met the floor, but it looked clean. A tiny four-burner stove sat to the right of the sink cabinet. A small, white microwave oven sat on a shelf above the stove. Beside the stove and microwave stood a small, white single-door refrigerator. The scene reminded Margo of when she and her husband had redone their first kitchen, picking out cabinets and counters, appliances and paint colors. She'd been full of hope then; life seemed good. That was before he'd started beating her.

To the left of the entry door was a futon on a dark wooden frame. The futon frame's back was up, making it a couch, and a trunk sat in front of it.

Cindy noticed Margo looking at the futon. "That does double duty as the couch and the bed. Real comfortable. I've slept on it a lot myself."

Margo nodded.

Cindy continued, "There's sheets and blankets in the trunk, and the trunk doubles as a coffee table."

A small TV sat on a wooden crate next to the futon with a floor lamp between the two. The lamp was directly in front of the only window in the place, which was covered by a bamboo shade, the kind you'd see at Walmart, with poorly fitting horizontal slats spaced unevenly.

"The TV's an old fashioned kind, not a flat screen like a lot of folks have today, but it's hooked to the same satellite dish that the TV in the bar is hooked to." Cindy's voice lowered to a half whisper, "You're not s'posed to hook up more than one to a dish, but I've got a friend who knows how to get around that." She nodded a little nod, winked at Margo, and smiled. "You've got thirty-three channels in here."

The bathroom was on the far side of the room, opposite the front door. They walked over to it, and Margo peered in. All white again with a tub shower combination across the back wall, a sink cabinet to the left, and the toilet in between. Cindy didn't have much to say about the bathroom, only, "I keep towels and washcloths in the cabinet under the sink."

Margo looked around silently. Cindy could tell that she wasn't impressed.

"I know it ain't much, Margo, but it's clean and safe."

Margo spoke in a low voice without looking at Cindy, "It's perfect." She turned to Cindy. "I can't begin to tell you how much I appreciate your help. You won't regret it, Cindy. I promise."

Cindy smiled. "Okay, I forgot to mention that we have a washer and dryer in the back of the bar, off the kitchen. That's where you can wash your clothes and the sheets and the towels. Probably not up to code seeing's how we make food right there next to it, but I'm good friends with the town inspector so it works out."

Nancy had been silent, taking it all in. "I think it's going to work very well, Margo. Cindy is one of the best people we know, and you'll be back on your feet before you know it." She looked toward Walter. "Walter, we'd best get back up to the cabin." After a short pause, she turned to Cindy and Margo. "We'd love to have both of you up to the cabin for dinner before we close up. Margo, we'll be here a few more days and we'll check in on you at least one more time before we leave." Nancy gave Margo a hug and turned to Walter and nodded. They left. It happened so quickly that it took Margo by surprise.

"Those are the nicest folks I know," said Cindy. "Why don't I leave you to get settled? Poke around and get used to the place, and when you're ready c'mon over to the bar and I'll show you around there too. Maybe you can start helping me tonight. Might be busy. I hope."

Cindy handed Margo the key to the front door.

"I have spares if you lose it, but please don't. You got a last name, Margo?"

Margo thought for a few seconds. "Norling."

It was her maiden name. She was going to make a fresh start.

"Margo Norling," Cindy said softly.

Margo liked the sound of it. Cindy turned and left. Margo was alone.

Margo spent some time sitting on the futon looking around the place. She'd never imagined this, being in this place so far away from Chelsea, Michigan. It was frightening but exciting at the same time.

She opened the trunk to check out the linens. A quilt was on top, some sheets and a blanket underneath. She moved the trunk out of the way and folded down the futon to make it into a bed. She put the bed linens on, figuring that if she worked the bar tonight it would be late when she got back. She didn't want to have to make the bed for the first time when she was tired. With the bed made, she went into the bathroom, washed her face, and brushed her teeth. She used the toothbrush and toothpaste that Nancy and Walter had given her the day after they'd all arrived to their cabin.

In the kitchen she found a knife in one of the sink cabinet drawers, cut the tags off her new jeans, and put them on. They fit her nicely. Then she picked out one of the t-shirts, pulled off the adhesive tags, and slid it over her head and arms. Sitting on the edge of the futon bed, she put her sneakers back on before straightening up to have one more look around the room. She took a deep breath, got up from the futon, and headed over to the bar.

The two men at the bar turned and looked as Margo walked through the door and quickly returned to their conversation. Cindy was behind the bar wiping a glass with a towel. She nodded to Margo, acknowledgment that she saw her, and bent down to put the glass away. The bar was on the back wall of the place, shoved against the wall to the right and open on the left. Margo walked to the open end and leaned on the bar.

"I'll tell you what," Cindy started, "lemme show you around. It'll only take a sec, then we can get to work."

Margo nodded.

"I'll treat tonight and the next few like I was working alone, and we'll get you ramped up slow and easy."

The rest of the afternoon went by quickly, Margo chasing Cindy around the place trying to figure out what was what and where everything was. Cindy was patient, but she moved fast. Before Margo knew it, a few customers began to come in for dinner, and she was a waitress again. According to Cindy, they were all regulars, not a surprise to Margo considering that the bar was in the middle of nowhere. One customer, a man sitting alone at a table in the corner, seemed to be Cindy's favorite.

# CHAPTER THIRTEEN

Rank was silent during the cab ride home. Deep in thought. He fumbled getting the key into the front door lock; it was difficult with only a single blurry eye. Inside, the house was quiet. He stood in the archway to the living room and stared at the aftermath of the fight. No one had straightened it up. How could they? No one had been there.

The coffee table was on its side, TV controls and magazines on the floor. He was grateful that his drinking buddy had been home when he'd called for help. If he had called an ambulance, the police would have already been in here. He grabbed a beer from the fridge and sat down on the couch to think.

*Where would she go?*

The sliding doors to the deck were open.

*She ran somewhere. How far could she have gone?*

He drank the beer and considered his options.

There were messages on the answering machine. He listened. It was her mother checking in, her supervisor at the warehouse in Ypsilanti calling because she hadn't shown up for her shift, and the police. He erased the messages.

*She went somewhere.*

He grabbed another beer and turned on the computer they shared. He searched through their cell phone calls first. The cell phone company made the records available on its website. No real details, just the numbers called to and from each phone and the dates and times of each call. She hadn't used her cell phone since before the fight. No help here. He chugged the rest of the beer.

He was stumped. Back to the fridge. No more beer. An unopened vodka bottle sat on top of the fridge, but he could only find tonic to mix with it.

*Don't want a vodka and tonic.*

Not much food either. A trip to the store might help clear his head, help him think better. He checked his pockets for cash. Nothing.

*ATM.*

Driving was hard; distances were impossible to figure out with only one eye. He turned too quickly coming off Kernwood and ran his front tire hard into the curb. He heard something break, but he kept going. At the ATM, he walked around the car and looked at the wheel. The wheel cover was broken, only a few shards still held on by the wheel bolts. He shook his head and entered the lobby where the ATM was housed. He figured a couple hundred would hold until he decided what to do.

Card in, PIN, wait, withdrawal, amount, wait.

Insufficient funds.

*You're fucking kidding me.*

He pressed more buttons. Balance inquiry. Printout or On Screen? On screen.

$23 and change.

*Holy shit!*

He angrily pressed the buttons for a mini statement, whatever that was. It took a few seconds for the machine to spit out the little sheet of paper that showed the details of the last few transactions. At the top of the list was a $403 withdrawal.

*What the fuck?*

He jumped back into the car and drove home to sort it out.

At the house he studied the statement for a few minutes. The withdrawal was earlier that same day. Back at the computer he started the browser, navigated to the bank's website, and logged into his account. He closed the ad that always popped up and clicked on his checking account number to get to the detailed list of transactions. There it was, right on top:

Cash Withdrawal Community F423 Sefton/NY US.

*Sefton, New York?*

He opened a new browser tab and typed "Sefton NY" into the search entry field. A Wikipedia entry topped the results list: "Sefton is a town located in St. Lawrence County, New York, United States." He typed the word "Maps" into the browser's address field and pressed the return key. He clicked the first entry on the list, and when the page refreshed, he typed "Sefton NY" into the map search field. There it was. He zoomed out far enough to see where in New York this Sefton place was.

*Way up there. Not far from Kyle's college. She's gone to be with Kyle.*

He didn't close the browser or turn the computer off when he jumped from the chair. He ran to the garage, grabbed the stepladder, climbed to the rafters, and took an old toolbox out from behind a box full of old car parts. He spun the dial on the lock a few times quickly. He stopped at 34, then turned it to the right past 34 and stopped on 8, then left to 21. He pulled the lock open, pulled it out of the hasp, and opened the box. Under the tray was his stash. Booze money he'd squirreled away so she wouldn't know. He counted the bills. $226. It was enough to start.

He didn't put away the box or the ladder. He ran back into the house and threw some clothes into a small black duffle bag. Before zipping it up, he pulled a shoebox from the closet shelf and found his pistol, its magazine, and a box of shells. The pistol was a twenty-two caliber Ruger with wood insets in the handle. He'd bought it on a drunken whim years before at the Bass Pro Shops in Auburn Hills, after he'd seen the Lions play the Packers at the Silverdome. He checked the magazine. It was full. He snapped it into the pistol handle and put the pistol and shells in the duffle bag. On top. He zipped the bag and hurried for the car. He was on his way to New York.

# CHAPTER FOURTEEN

The place got pretty busy, busy enough that Margo forgot all about her bruises. Waiting the tables was easy, Natty's didn't draw the same size crowd as the place she'd worked in high school. It couldn't; it was tiny. There just weren't that many tables. Bartending was easy too. Nobody ordered anything fancy, mostly beers. Once in a while a rum and coke or a shot of whiskey. A couple younger guys ordered Jägerbombs, and Margo had to ask Cindy how to make those. Margo kept the customers happy while Cindy cooked and schmoozed. She schmoozed a lot with the guy sitting alone at a table in the corner. He drank whiskey.

"Wow, Margo, you're picking this up real fast," Cindy said leaning on the edge of the bar.

"Who's the guy in the corner?" Margo motioned with her head.

"That's Kris Jansen. He lives in a cabin up on Chance Pond. About a mile from here, up that hill right across from our parking lot." Cindy pointed toward the front door.

Margo looked over at Kris.

Cindy lowered her voice and leaned a little closer. "Margo, he's not like anybody else around here. He's nice and he's smart. He's owned his place for years, used to only come up in the summers, but this past spring he moved up here permanently. He told me he lost his job and couldn't afford to keep his house down near Boston."

"How about another beer, hon?" A guy sitting at the bar right in front of Margo. She turned and smiled at the guy.

"Blue, right?"

He nodded. Margo reached into the refrigerator below the liquor bottles, grabbed a bottle of Labatt Blue, swung around, grabbed the opener, popped the top, and set the bottle down in front of the guy. She did it so fast that it all looked like one single motion. As she added the sale to the guy's tab she looked at Cindy and asked, "Cindy, we're almost out of Blue here in the fridge. Think you could grab a few for us?" Cindy didn't hesitate. She hustled back to the beer cooler thinking just how lucky she was landing this girl and wondering how long she'd be willing to stay.

People came and went. As it got later, the dinner crowd left and the drinking crowd came. Couples were replaced by groups of men, although one small group of women stayed at a table drinking. *Girls night out*, Margo thought. At nine, Cindy turned up the music. Not too loud, just enough. All country songs, some new, some old. The girls-night-out crew sang along once in a while. There wasn't any room to dance. The guy that Cindy liked had finished his dinner and moved to a stool at the kitchen end of the bar.

"Beer?"

Soft. Almost a whisper. Margo turned, looking for the asker.

"Right here?"

He raised his hand and nodded. He was standing at the far end of the bar stuffed against the wall as if he was trying to hide in it. He wore a dirty hat with a deer on the front. His hair was long and greasy, and his ears stuck out between strands.

"What kind?" asked Margo.

"Budweiser please."

Margo got the beer for him. When she set it down on the counter, she noticed his hands were dirty too, his fingernails black.

"You need a tab?" Margo asked.

"Please," he replied. He seemed polite even though he was kind of hard to look at.

"You have bruises," he said softly.

Margo was suddenly self-conscious. She'd forgotten about the bruises when she'd started working that afternoon. She lowered her head, turned to the cash register, and set up his tab.

"Margo, come over here when you get a chance." Cindy was standing at the end of the bar talking with her friend. Margo nodded and finished with her customers.

"Margo, this is Kris."

"Hey, Margo. Nice to meet you." He extended his hand.

Margo shook it and smiled. "Likewise."

"Cindy's told me a little about you. She says you're catching on real quick, and she's hoping you'll take over the place so she can retire."

Margo was self-conscious. She'd forgotten about her bruises, and now they were all she could think about. With her gaze to the floor, Margo answered, "Cindy's been real good to me. I like her. I like it here. I hope to stay on, but I can see that only Cindy can run this place."

"Margo." Kris leaned a little closer to her. "I live right up the road. I'm a phone call away, and Cindy has my number. I'll be happy to help out any friend of Cindy's anytime. Okay?"

Margo shifted her eyes to Kris without raising her head. She nodded and turned her gaze to Cindy. "I'd better get back to it." She looked back at Kris and tipped her head toward his glass. "Ready for another one?"

"Why not?" He slid the glass a couple inches toward her. "Wild Turkey."

"101," Cindy added, "and we pour it heavy for Kris. Always a double."

"You'll have me walking home tonight, Cindy." Kris grinned.

Cindy winked at him. "I can always give you a ride if need be, but you'll have to invite me to stay."

Margo was pouring Kris's whiskey when she heard the low voice from the end of the bar.

"Another beer?"

She turned. It was the strange guy at the end of the bar again. He nodded and waved his hand so she'd see him.

Margo turned to Cindy and whispered, "Jesus. I gave him one just before I came over here to meet Kris." She finished Kris's pour, put the Wild Turkey back on the shelf, and turned to the dirty guy. "Bud, right?"

He nodded.

As Margo put the bottle down in front of him, Cindy hollered to her from the end of the bar, and loudly enough for everyone to hear, "Margo. I need a little help in the kitchen as soon as you can."

Margo turned to the bar. "Is everyone set for a couple minutes?"

Cindy was waiting in the kitchen. "I just wanted to fill you in on that little guy who ordered the Bud."

Margo whispered, "He's an odd one, kind of creeps me out."

"That's Danny Zelenco. They call him Dazzle. Local guy. Grew up in Cotswold. I was in school with him."

"Where'd anyone come up with 'Dazzle'?" Margo was grinning.

Cindy shook her head. "I'm not sure. I think it started in High School. His initials are DZ, right? And see, he was on the basketball team, and he could move the ball like one of them Harlem Globetrotters. He didn't have any friends, so I think he spent all his time practicing basketball. Reflects his personality good too, don't cha think?"

"What personality?"

"Exactly!" Cindy leaned in toward Margo and lowered her voice. "I think it stuck because it fit him more ways than one. Serious and sarcastic at the same time. He seems to like it, though."

"He could stand to wash his clothes," Margo added.

"He ain't a bad guy. Worked for his dad all through high school and after. His dad owned the scrapyard on the other side of town. Died a while back. Now Danny owns the place."

"So you've known him a long time Cindy?"

"Wouldn't say that I know him too well anymore, but yeah, since we was little kids in school. There was a time when we chummed around. Like I said, he's okay. Just a little odd. Keeps to himself. He'll drink a few beers, pay his bill, and leave before the rest of them."

Margo relaxed a little. "I'd better get back out there. Thanks for the heads-up."

# CHAPTER FIFTEEN

Rank stopped at the drug store and filled the prescription the doc had given him for pain. Tylenol with codeine. The instructions said to take one, but he figured two would be better. It took a while for the shit to kick in, but by the time he got to Toledo, he had a good buzz on.

Toledo was busy. The end of rush hour. The highway twisted and turned through the city, traffic weaved in and out, every car trying to beat the next car to the exit ramp. Rank held on tight and made it through, and after he was clear, he just cruised and enjoyed the buzz. He wasn't thinking about the traffic. Or driving. Or anything.

Route 90 was desolate after Cleveland. A little more than three hours in and he was getting bored and anxious. He fiddled with the radio. The few stations with a decent signal were broadcasting religious talk shows. Nothing he wanted to hear. He glanced at the dashboard for the first time since he left Michigan. A light was on, a little picture of a gas pump. He wondered how long ago it'd come on and looked at the gas gauge. Empty. Really empty.

The first exit he came to was 212. The sign read Madison. It would have to do. He looked for a sign that would confirm there were gas stations, but all he got was a sign displaying attractions and one showing that there was a McDonald's. He figured if there was a McDonald's there was a gas station. The exit ramp ended at a T, no signs pointing to a gas station. He turned right and got lucky, a station was just a little ways down the road. Marathon.

*Cash - Please Pay First* was written by hand on a lined yellow sheet of paper folded in half and taped to the pump. The kid behind the counter looked up and grinned as Rank walked through the door.

"You just made it; I'm about to close up."

"Better set the pump for sixty," Rank told the kid as he reached into his pocket for the cash.

The kid leaned to look past him out to the pumps, "Sixty dollars on pump number one. Yessir."

He took the bills and opened the register. Rank stared at the register for a second. It was like a bell going off in his head. He turned and walked out to pump his gas.

The pump ran slow. While he pumped, Rank looked around to see if there was anyone else close by. Nobody. The nozzle handle clicked home; the tank was full. Rank put the nozzle back in the holder and turned the gas cap through a few clicks to make sure it closed tight. He had one more quick look around, opened the rear door of the car, unzipped his duffle bag, and pulled out the Ruger. He checked the magazine and snapped it tight into the handle, pulled the bolt back to throw a bullet into the chamber, and snapped the safety off. He put the pistol in the front of his jeans under the belt, adjusted his coat to hide it, and shut the car door.

The kid behind the counter was ready for him when he came through the door. Ready to give Rank his change and close the place.

"You took forty-two dollars and twenty-six cents. Your change is seventeen dollars and seventy-four cents." The kid stretched both hands across the counter, the bills and a receipt in his left hand and the coins in his right. Rank reached his left hand out and took the coins first, then the bills, and then brought the pistol up with his right hand.

"I'll take the rest of your money too."

The kids jaw dropped and he stared at Rank in disbelief.

"Open the register and give me the cash." Rank didn't blink. The kid did what he said. He opened the register, took out the cash tray, and dropped it on the counter in front of Rank. As Rank was grabbing bills from the tray, the kid bolted for the back door. Rank didn't think, he raised the pistol and fired. The kid dropped.

Rank turned and looked out the front windows as he stuffed all the bills into his left coat pocket. The parking lot was still empty. He walked slowly toward the kid. He was laying face down, blood pooling on the floor near his right side. He was squirming and moaning softly. Rank stared at him for a moment, then looked up at the glass-front coolers just to his right. Beer. Busch. Rank opened the door and pulled out a cold thirty pack, then turned back to the kid as the cooler door swung closed. He stared for a few more seconds, stooped to get a little closer, put the pistol muzzle on the back of the kid's head, and pulled the trigger.

# CHAPTER SIXTEEN

Cindy had been wrong about Dazzle. He stayed. He kept himself stuffed against the wall and ordered beer after beer. And watched Margo. Late into the evening, most of the customers were gone, just three guys at the bar and two sitting at a table. And Dazzle.

"Another beer?"

Margo was at the far end of the bar drying a glass. She turned and nodded at him. "Be right there." When she turned back toward the kitchen, Cindy was coming through the door wiping her hands with a bar towel.

"He's still here, Cindy."

Cindy looked down the bar. "Never seen him here this long. Funny."

"It isn't funny to me, Cindy. He's creeping me out. He keeps staring at me."

"It's slow now, Margo. Why don't cha talk with him a little bit? Get to know him. I told you he's okay. You'll see."

Margo stared at Cindy. Blank.

"You're just tired, Margo. Besides, chatting up the customers is part of the bartender job. You know that."

"I'm not feeling chatty."

"When we were busy it was one thing, Margo, but now it's wide open. Hell, you might get a big ol' tip from Danny."

Margo dropped her shoulders and tipped her head to one side. "You're right. Crap." She put the glass she was drying down and swung the towel playfully at Cindy. She turned and walked toward the end of the bar, grabbing a bottle of Budweiser from the fridge on her way past. She set the bottle on the bar in front of him.

"So Cindy says your name is Danny."

"Yeah. And my nickname's Dazzle." He pushed the empty bottle toward her.

"Where'd Dazzle come from?" Margo was beginning to relax a little. This might not be so bad after all.

"I dunno." He looked down at the bottle. Shy all of a sudden. "I guess it's 'cause my initials are DZ and somebody just invented it from that."

"What do you do that you can stay out so late on a weeknight Dazzle? Are you taking some time off to hunt?"

"Nah, I ain't much of a hunter." He stared at the bottle.

Margo leaned down, elbows on the bar so she could see under the brim of his hat a little better. "So what do you do for work?"

Dazzle looked up at her. "I have a used car parts place here in town. I love cars and trucks."

Margo stood. "I've heard that used car parts can be a real good business. My dad knew a guy that owned a place back in Michigan. He told me once that the guy made good money."

"Was my dad's place. He's gone now. You from Michigan?" He acted like he was interested.

"Yeah. Most of my life until just a few days ago." She wiped the bar with the towel.

"Why'd you come here then?" Dazzle asked.

Margo wasn't ready to answer that one. "Stuff happens, you know? I wasn't planning to be here, but here is where I landed."

"D'jou come here 'cause of the bruises?"

*Geez,* thought Margo, *this guy's either stupid or just really nosy.* She straightened up and glared at Dazzle.

"Sorry." Dazzle raised his hands. "I didn't mean to be pushy. Sorry."

Margo relaxed a little. He didn't seem to be giving her a hard time. "Don't worry about it. It's just something I'm not willing to talk about."

"How about one last round, hon?" She'd been saved by one of the men sitting at the table. "Two Blues coming at you." She looked back at Dazzle. "Excuse me."

He nodded.

Margo grabbed two bottles of Labatt from the fridge, opened them, and walked them out to the table. "You ready for a check too?"

One of the men nodded.

On her way back to the bar, she spotted Cindy in the kitchen, her back to the doorway. She got close and standing in the doorway whispered, "Not so bad after all."

Cindy jumped. "Holy Shit!"

"Sorry, sorry." Margo couldn't help but grin. "I didn't mean to scare you. I was just telling you that talking with Dazzle wasn't so bad after all."

"Don't sneak up on me like that." Cindy's shoulders dropped a little as she started to calm down. "See, Margo? You're gonna do fine. Now look what time it is. We gotta close up real soon. Why don't you ask them all if they want one more round?"

The three guys at the bar took their checks. They were finished. The two guys at the table already had theirs. Dazzle had one more Bud.

"You never told me your name."

"My name's Margo." She handed him his check.

"Margo." He let it sink in while he pulled a few bills from his pocket. "Margo's nice." He counted the bills and put a few on top of the check. He slid the little pile toward her. "No change. It's for you." He picked up the bottle and took a long swig.

"Thank you. Should I call you Danny or Dazzle?"

He burped with his mouth closed, then chugged the rest of the beer. "My friends call me Dazzle." He put the empty bottle on the counter. "If we're friends, call me Dazzle."

"Okay, Dazzle."

He smiled, tipped his hat, and walked out of the bar.

Margo and Cindy raced around the place straightening chairs and wiping tables. Cindy had already cleaned up in the kitchen, and Margo kept the bar straight while she worked so there wasn't much left to do there. After the door closed for the last time, Cindy raised her hand above her head and stared at Margo. Margo high-fived her.

"We did a hell of a night tonight, Margo. I can't tell you how much I like you already."

"I told you, you give me a chance you won't regret it. What time do we start tomorrow?"

"We open early for the hunters. Breakfast. But you don't need to worry about working early; my brother-in-law comes in and opens the place and cooks breakfast." Cindy paused. "Tell you what, you come in here around ten or ten-thirty. I'll be here by then and we'll have some breakfast together."

Margo noticed a pickup truck parked on the side of the road as she walked out across the parking lot to the apartment. She didn't pay any attention to it. She was too tired to care about anything but sleeping.

# CHAPTER SEVENTEEN

Rank straightened up, turned, and walked toward the door. He stopped at the map rack. *Rand McNally Easy To Fold United States.* That would do it. He took the map from the rack and walked outside toward his car, looking all around carefully. Nobody. Not a single car had passed. He started the engine and floored it back to Route 90 as fast as he dared. It had all happened quickly, and he hadn't thought about it, but now it started weighing heavily on him. He figured he might have a few hours at best. He needed a plan.

After about twenty minutes of driving, he noticed something called a "Flying J Travel Center." He pulled off the highway. At least he could stop and think a little bit. The place was huge. He drove past the gas pumps and around the left side of the main building, then all the way across the back to see what was what. A lot of eighteen-wheelers, a few RVs, a few cars, and a pickup or two. He had an idea. He parked the car at the far corner of the lot, between a couple of the big trucks. He put the map in his bag, hoisted it to his shoulder, grabbed the beer, and walked around the side of the main building toward the front. The Ruger was still tucked in his pants.

He had been planning to go inside the main building, but he never made it. As he walked around an eighteen-wheeler and turned to walk around the side of the building, he spotted a pickup truck tucked tightly into the corners created by the grass that lined the parking lot. Someone was bent over beside it. He couldn't tell what he or she was doing. He stopped for a few seconds and looked around. Not another car or truck near this one.

She stood up quickly as he approached.

"Sorry if I startled you." Rank was close enough to see her now. Blond hair, kind of blond anyway, but dark in places. Long on one side, shaved on the other. Black vest, camouflage pattern pants tucked into tall black boots, and a thick loop of wallet chain hanging down at her side. She was big.

"You did come up on me fast and quiet." An open blue cooler chest sat at her feet.

"Anything I can do to help?" Rank nodded at the cooler.

"Nah, I'm good." She bent down and closed the lid, picked up the cooler and slid it into the back of the truck. She leaned over and looked at Rank as she slammed the gate into place.

Rank cleared his throat. "My car broke down. I'm wondering..." He paused and thought for a few seconds. "I'm wondering if, if you're going my way, if I might catch a ride with you."

She looked at him and then looked around the lot. "Where's your broken-down car?"

"In the back of the lot."

"Don't you want to get it fixed?"

"Yeah, but I need to be in New York by tomorrow. I'll have to call a shop in the morning and have it towed. Pick it up on my way back."

The big woman was clearly agitated. She walked around and stood in front of Rank. A little closer than he expected. She looked him over.

"What happened to your eye?"

It was Rank who was startled now. Up close he could see a tattoo covering the shaved part of her head and running down her neck.

"Shooting accident at the range. Buddy's pistol. I wasn't used to it, wasn't ready for the kick back."

She squinted a little, silent for a second. "I like to shoot too. I can see that happenin'. Sucks. New York, you said?" She walked around to that back of the truck and checked the gate and cap hatch. She leaned back over to look at Rank. "You up for helpin' me out some?"

Rank nodded.

"Get in."

The truck smelled like motor oil and dirty ass. Cups and wrappers and all kinds of trash covered the floor. It took a few cranks to start, but as soon as it did, she jammed it into gear and gunned it for the highway.

"We're gonna drive for a couple hours, then we're stopping in New York for the night. There's a few hotels all right near the highway. I think it's Hamburg. Just this side of Buffalo. That work for you?"

"Work's fine."

As soon as they got on Route 90, she worked it over to the left lane. At eighty-five miles per hour the truck shook like crazy and she was working the wheel like a dirt track driver. *This thing is a rat*, Rank thought.

"How about we drink a few of your beers and smoke some weed?" She leaned over and reached for the glove box, her arm rubbing against his thighs. No accident, that was obvious to Rank. She opened the glove box door and pulled out a bag and a pipe and closed it. She took her time sitting back up straight, rubbing her arm across his thighs real slow. She wasn't subtle. He had a pretty good idea now of the kind of helping out she wanted.

"Sounds good," he replied as he opened the cardboard box between his feet. He pulled out a can, opened it, and handed it to her. Then he did the same for himself.

She managed to fill the bowl, light the pipe, take a few hard pulls, hold the beer between her thighs, and saw away at the wheel with her knees, all while careening down the highway on the edge of control. Rank pulled a long swig from his can. He needed something to calm him down. The pills had worn off. She handed him the pipe and rested her hand on his thigh. He took a few hard tokes, just like she had.

They smoked a few bowls, drank beers, and made small talk all the way to New York. She kept her hand on his thigh and gave it a rub now and then when she wanted him to know that she liked something he said. Rank didn't fight it. He was starting to come up with a plan.

Rank was good and stoned by the time she exited the highway. She pulled into a Quality Inn but drove around the side and out toward the back to the entrance of a Super 8 that seemed to be connected to it.

"I've stayed here a bunch. It's cheap. Ain't bad neither." She squeezed Rank's thigh and smiled. In the light of the parking lot, Rank saw how bad her teeth were.

"I need to tell you something." Rank cleared his throat. "I'm on probation and I ain't supposed to leave my town in Michigan. With this eye patch I'm easily identified. I shouldn't go to the desk with you." He'd thought of that one somewhere around Erie, Pennsylvania.

"What the fuck you mean probation?" She turned angry. She took her hand off his thigh.

"Wait, it ain't that bad. I got busted with weed. A lot of weed. I wasn't selling, though. They gave me probation instead of jail time. Like I said, I ain't supposed to leave my town in Michigan."

She relaxed. "Weed? That's all? Shit, ain't nothin'." She grabbed his thigh again and squeezed. Hard this time.

It worked, she bought it. Rank continued, "We never talked about how I could repay you for the ride."

"No, we didn't. But I have an idea. Maybe you figured it out by now." She grinned.

Rank smiled back and nodded. "Tell you what. I'll pay for the hotel tonight. And I'll fill the tank when we leave tomorrow."

"And what else?" She cocked her head to the side a little and moved her hand from his thigh to his crotch.

"I'll give you a nice little night tonight?"

She moaned a low moan and licked her lips. "That's what I'm talking about, honey."

Rank dug into his pocket and pulled out some bills. He peeled four twenties off the top and handed it to her. "You go get us the room, and I'll wait here in the truck."

She took the bills, opened the door, and stepped out. Before she closed it she turned, leaned back in, and took the keys.

"I wanna make sure I get that sugar tonight, hon." She slammed the door shut and walked into the lobby.

*Shit*, thought Rank. *Okay, plan B.*

He pulled the Ruger from his belt, reached behind the seat, and put it in his bag. He buried it into the clothes a little bit. He didn't want her seeing it accidentally.

It only took her a few minutes. Back in the truck, she said, "Perfect, we can get to our room from out the back. Nobody's gonna see you." She pulled the truck out around the back and parked it. "Let's go fuck."

The room smelled like disinfectant and stale cigarettes. In the light of the room, Rank finally realized just how big this girl was. And ugly. This wasn't going to be easy. She set her keys on the TV cabinet, threw her bag down in front of the couch in the far corner of the room, and bent down to unlace her boots. "Strip down baby, let's get to it."

Rank knew this was going to be unpleasant, but he had to stick with it long enough to get the truck. He dropped his bag where he stood and took off his clothes. By the time he was naked, she was on her back on the bed, the bed covers pulled down and her considerable self on top. Her legs were spread wide open. Rank could smell her. He climbed onto the bed beside her.

She put her arms over her head. Her armpits were unshaven, and the hair was matted, greasy, and clumped together in places. She smiled at him. "I'm not much for kissing; I just like to fuck."

*Good thing*, he thought. "Tell you what, sister. How about I get you off once first before we really get it going?"

"I like the sound of that. What you got in mind?"

"I'm talented with my tongue."

She smiled wider, her yellow teeth showing loud and clear. "I like to be licked."

Rank grabbed the pillow that she wasn't using and raised it up.

"This here pillow we'll put under your ass, raise you up so I can get to you better."

She moaned softly, closed her eyes, and lifted her ass off the bed.

Rank pushed the pillow down on her face and threw his weight onto her. She arched her back, kicked her legs, and hit him on the back with her fists. Her screams were muffled by the pillow. Rank held hard, forcing himself down with all the strength he could find. He was exhausted when she finally stopped moving, but he kept his hold on her. He needed to be sure she was dead.

When she'd been limp for a few minutes, he relaxed a little. He wasn't convinced that she was gone, but he had nothing left. He slowly took the pillow away, thinking he was ready to stuff it back down if he needed to. He didn't need to. She didn't move. He held his ear to her nose. She wasn't breathing. He felt her neck for a pulse, pushing into the thick, damp flesh to find it. Nothing. She was gone.

He got up and put his clothes back on. He found the keys to the truck on top of the TV cabinet, then went through her bag to see what she had. The clothes weren't folded. They smelled and felt a little greasy. Under the clothes she had two plastic grocery bags, one with a dildo, a purple vibrator, and a well-used tube of KY jelly and another with a pistol and shells. She didn't seem to carry a toothbrush, shampoo, or deodorant. He went to the couch where she'd thrown her clothes and found the wallet in her camo pants. There were quite a few twenties in it. He stuffed the wallet in his rear pocket. He'd count the money later.

Rank put her pistol and shells into his bag and grabbed his Ruger. He pulled the magazine from the handle, added a couple shells, snapped it back into place, put it on top inside the bag, and zipped it up.

He opened the room door enough to look one way down the hall. Empty. He moved far enough out to look the other way. Empty. He walked into the hall, moved the *Do Not Disturb* sign to the outer knob, and gently shut the door. Rank figured the sign might buy him an extra hour or two before the maids found her.

He walked to the door they'd come in earlier and over to the truck and opened the passenger door. He put his bag on the seat, closed the door, walked around the truck, and climbed in behind the wheel. It still stunk. He rolled the window down a crack. The truck started with a rumble. He put the column-mounted gear shift into reverse, backed out of the parking spot, jammed it into drive, and headed for the highway.

# CHAPTER EIGHTEEN

Didier Mysliwiec didn't much like being dragged out of bed in the middle of the night, but he accepted it as part of the job. He'd just been promoted to a BCI Agent, and he was determined to make hay. Even when he was dog-tired. Like tonight.

The call came around two-thirty in the morning. It didn't take him long to get out of bed and out the door. The Crime Scene Investigation Unit was hard at work in the mini market when he got there. Yellow crime scene tape was everywhere and the place was thick with investigators, state troopers, and a local cop or two.

*Hangers on*, Didier thought.

"Dido!" It was Miller, Mysliwiec's partner. "It's a nasty one, Dido. A kid, couldn't be twenty yet." Miller was jacked up. Miller was always jacked up.

"Not good, Miller. Is everything still in place?"

"Jus' like we found it, Dido. Yep, jus' like we found it."

Miller had always been a little annoying to Mysliwiec with all his overabundance of energy and his "Dido this" and "Dido that." Mysliwiec didn't like being called Dido; it made him feel like a little kid.

Miller motioned toward the mini market, and Mysliwiec led the way. A middle-aged man was standing behind the counter staring at the scene. He was clearly shaken up with beads of sweat hanging among the few greasy hairs combed long across his bald head and a vacant look in his eyes.

"That's the owner of the place," Miller whispered.

They walked past the counter toward the beer cooler.

The kid was laying face down in a pool of blood. He'd been left in place, untouched, preserving the scene. Myslewiec knelt down to get a closer look, then stood back up and walked carefully around the body to see it from all angles. Satisfied, he glanced up at the forensics guy who was standing just to the side.

"Have you recorded everything you need so we can turn him over and get to work?"

The forensics guy nodded. Mysliwiec's gaze went from the forensics guy to the shelf behind him. He took a long, quick step over the body toward the rack, and the forensics guy moved to the side, puzzled. Mysliwiec reached for a bag of Shearers Krazi Kurls. The forensics guy stared.

"I'll pay for it." Mysliwiec opened the bag and tossed a few Kurls into his mouth. "Okay, let's turn him over."

# CHAPTER NINETEEN

Dazzle watched her walk from the bar to the apartment and waited after she went in. She didn't come out. He'd never paid much attention to the door at the far side of the bar, but he realized now what it was. She slept there. Tonight anyway. He started the truck and drove toward his place. Margo was all he could think about.

He didn't sleep much. Too excited. Up at three-thirty. Coffee in a travel mug in one hand and a Coleman lantern in the other, he walked out the back door into the junkyard. A Doberman Pinscher greeted him at the door, its breath visible in the cold air.

"Cold out ain't it, Blitz?"

Blitz ran free in the yard at night, chained only during the day when she might tear up a customer. Blitz walked beside Dazzle as they crossed the yard and wound their way to the far rear corner.

Dazzle opened the side door of the old motorhome and raised the lantern to light the step. He climbed inside, Blitz fast on his heels. The old thing had been sitting in this spot for as long as Dazzle could remember. All six tires were flat, and rust holes littered the sheet metal along the bottom edge of the body. It was big, though, and it only leaked a little bit. Tears, burns, and stains covered the green patterned fabric on the eating booth and couch. The white laminate table and the yellow counter around the sink had stains and burn marks too. Cabinet doors were missing, and the floor covering was torn. In the summer it smelled pretty bad, but the cold air helped that some.

He sat in the eating booth and sipped his coffee. Thinking. She might not understand right off. Blitz lay on the floor beside him. He had work to do before he opened the yard for the day, and he was getting hungry. One last slug of coffee and then up from the booth. Blitz scrambled onto four feet, startled by Dazzle's sudden move. They walked back to the shop together.

# CHAPTER TWENTY

Mind numbing. The drone of the tires on asphalt. The rattle of whatever shit she had in the back. The smell. But he was drained, and the only thing keeping Rank awake after an hour and a half on the highway was the constant need to saw at the wheel to keep the fucking thing pointing in the right direction. He fought it. He needed to make some time now. Distance. Get as far away from the gas station and that hotel as he could.

The weed they'd smoked and the beers they'd drunk wore him down. He needed a break. He'd been on the road for nearly two hours when he saw the sign. *Port Byron Service Area.* It had a McDonald's. McDonald's had coffee. He could take a piss too. A mile later, he was parked, wondering if anyone inside would recognize him. It was the first time he'd thought much about it. He wondered if the cops had even found the boy yet. The boy would be the first they'd find. The fat chick, she'd be a while. Not until the maids finally decided to go in the room. Maids are lazy. He stepped out of the truck and walked into the building.

Bright lights, empty building. Except the McDonald's. People staffing the counter and the kitchen. Rank walked quickly to the restroom. That was empty too. He pissed at the first urinal he came to. A long piss. Finished and at the sink, he saw himself for the first time. The eye patch had to go. It made him way too easy to recognize. He took off his hat and removed the patch. Weird. The eye was closed. He put the patch back on and figured he'd get some sunglasses as soon as he could. To cover it up. He'd get a haircut too, maybe a buzz cut. Didn't need to be messing around with his hair with all that he wanted to do.

He washed his hands and rinsed his face with cold water before realizing that there weren't any paper towels. Only air dryers. He turned the nozzle up and let it rip. After a few seconds he'd had enough. He walked out to the lobby, stepped up to the McDonald's counter, got himself a coffee, and walked back out to the truck.

He figured this would be a good time to check the back of the truck and see what kind of crap she had in there. The lot was almost empty, and the lights were pretty bright, that'd help. The hatch on the cap opened and flipped up pretty easily, but the gate was a little tricky, binding on the left side and forcing Rank to give it a hard tug. It opened reluctantly with a rusty metal-on-metal scrape. The blue cooler she'd put in there back in Ohio was front and center. He opened the lid and took a quick look inside. Whatever ice she'd put in had melted long ago, and everything inside was floating in water. The cooler would go. He slid it to the side and peered into the depths of the pickup bed. A wooden handle, maybe a shovel, with a rumpled blue tarp on top of it. Not folded. Rank pushed it aside, revealing that the handle didn't belong to a shovel, but a rake. Digging further he found a tire on a rim, an empty bottle of windshield washer fluid, and a few rags. And leaves. Lots of dried leaves. She must have been raking leaves.

The only thing that looked at all useful was a toolbox in the far corner up against the cab. Rank stepped back and looked around the lot hoping to see a dumpster. None in sight. He closed the gate and cap hatch, climbed in the cab, and fired it up. He drove slowly around the parking lot. Behind the main building, he spotted two dumpsters side by side surrounded by a fence. The fence gate was open. He pulled up close and started clearing the back of the truck.

It only took a few minutes; he moved quickly. With the bed empty, he climbed in and opened the toolbox. Basic stuff: pliers, a few box-end wrenches, screwdrivers. This he'd keep. He closed the toolbox and climbed out. As he closed the hatch and gate, he glanced down and for the first time saw her license plates

SXY BTCH.

That wouldn't do. He glanced around the lot again. Almost empty. Right. He needed to swap the plates with another car but it'd have to wait. He climbed back in and realized that he hadn't cleaned out all the garbage in the cab.

*Fuck it, later.* He had to move. He gassed up at the service area pumps and got back on the highway, working the wheel to keep the thing pointed in the right direction and sipping on his coffee. The coffee was cold now.

He kept at it through Syracuse, where he changed over from the thruway to Route 81 North. Traffic was a little heavier through Syracuse, but before long it thinned out and it seemed to Rank that it was only him and a few tractor trailers. He had a hard time staying awake now, even caught himself dozing off a few times. He rolled the windows down to let the cold air in. To help keep him awake. It helped the smell too. He exited on Route 3 in Watertown and found his way to Route 11 North. Toward Sefton.

The sky was just starting to brighten as he drove through Canton, and ten minutes later he spotted a Walmart on the right. He'd had enough. He was close. He was tired. He pulled into the Walmart lot and parked a ways away from the store. He sat still for a few minutes, not really thinking because he was too tired for that, just sitting. After a while, the sky brightened enough that he could see the inside of the truck clearly, and he got out. All the trash bothered him. The store was open twenty-four hours, so he decided he'd go in. He walked up the incline of the parking lot toward the store, now starting to think about what he needed.

Inside, he grabbed a cart. First he went to the sporting goods section and found a heavy sleeping bag, a roll up sleeping pad, a camping pillow, and a flashlight. He'd heard somewhere that Walmart stores let people camp in their parking lots. The truck had a cap, so that'd work for the time it took to figure out where she was. He was sure he'd find her pretty quickly, but he didn't know why he was so sure.

Next he found some food, things that didn't need special equipment to fix up. A couple apples, a box of crackers, some nuts, and a six-pack of ginger ale. He wasn't gonna be fussy or get too much. On the way to the checkout, he passed the optical department and remembered he needed sunglasses. Aviator style was fine. He took a pair from the rack. Enough. He paid for the stuff, walked back to the truck, and put it all in the back. He drove around the backside of the store looking for a dumpster and found one in the far corner. He spent a few minutes clearing all the trash out of the cab.

With the last reminders of the fat chick gone, he drove back out to the parking lot and found a suitable spot near the furthest corner of the lot. He parked the truck and climbed into the back under the cap. He unpacked the pillow, pad, and sleeping bag and left the rest of the stuff in the bags. He unrolled the pad and climbed into the sleeping bag with his shoes on. It couldn't have been five minutes before he was asleep.

# CHAPTER TWENTY-ONE

The truck wouldn't start. Dead battery. Seemed a lot colder outside this morning, so Kris wasn't too surprised. The battery had been on its way out for a while now. He opened the shed and pulled the charger off the shelf. *Red to positive, black to negative*, he thought to himself as he hooked the cables to the battery. He plugged the charger into the outlet on the side of the shed, turned it on, and walked back into the cabin for another cup of tea. He wasn't hurrying this morning. He wasn't looking forward to another trip to town.

As he rocked in his chair in front of the woodstove, he thought about the new girl working at Natty's. He'd been thinking about her a lot since the night before. Last night had been the first time he'd spoken to her much. Something about her, despite all the bruising. He did wonder about that, but something about the way she carried herself. The fire needed another log, and Kris needed another cup of tea.

Kris did a little reading in front of the fire and drank a few more cups. He could have worked, but he needed a break from it. When he'd given it an hour or so, he reluctantly dragged himself out of the chair. Coat on, he walked out into the cold, climbed into the truck, and started it. He removed the charger cables, put the charger away, and went back inside to close up the wood stove. He grabbed a pencil and a scrap of paper and made a quick list; he didn't want to forget anything and have to make another trip.

List in hand, he climbed into the truck, but as he grabbed the handle to shut the door, he heard a sound from up the road that he didn't recognize. Piercing, like a cat howling, but unearthly. He jumped from the truck and stood quietly, listening. Moments of silence, then it came again. From behind the shed, up on the camp road. He couldn't be sure, but it sounded like someone saying "Brenda." He raced around the shed, and there she was, stumbling down the camp road in her dressing gown and slippers with a lunch bag in her hand. Violet.

"Brennn-da!"

Kris walked toward her. "Violet! Violet!" No response. Either she couldn't hear him or she was ignoring him. As he got closer, he could see the confusion in her eyes.

"Brennn-da!"

"Violet!" It came from the top of the hill on the camp road. Silas coming for Violet. Silas in his work pants, t-shirt, and slippers.

Kris reached her first. "Have you seen Brenda? She forgot her lunch." Violet held up the bag for Kris to see. He didn't know what to say; he just stared at her dumbfounded. "I said have you seen Brenda?" Her eyes showed a little frustration and anger now.

"Violet!" Silas couldn't move fast, but he was doing the best he could. "Violet!" He finally reached her, out of breath. "That's Kris. He hasn't seen Brenda."

Violet turned as Silas spoke, then back to Kris. "You're Kris? Have you seen Brenda? She forgot her lunch."

Silas put his hand on Violets shoulder. "It's alright, Violet, Brenda will buy lunch today."

Violet looked back at Silas. "Those cafeteria lunches aren't any good, Silas, you know that. She'll be hungry."

"It'll be alright Violet; she's a big girl."

Violet looked down at the bag in her hand for a moment, then back up to Kris. "You're Kris?"

Kris nodded.

"Would you like this lunch, Kris? I made it this morning for Brenda. It's a ham sandwich. There's a pickle in there too." She held the bag up in front of him.

Kris looked at Silas standing behind her. Silas gave him a quick nod. Kris took the bag from Violet. "I love ham sandwiches. Thank you, Violet."

"There's a pickle in there too. A dill pickle." Violet smiled and turned to Silas. "I'm cold, Silas."

"It's alright, Violet. Let's go back to the camp and get warm."

Silas turned to Kris. "Sorry about that, Kris."

"No problem, Silas. Say, I'm on my way to town, can I pick up anything for you?"

Silas thought for a moment. "I don't think so, Kris, but thanks."

Kris nodded, then turned and walked back to the truck. He got in, shut the door, and fastened his seatbelt. He waited. He wanted to give them time to get back to their camp. Sitting in the heat of the truck, he realized just how cold outside it really was.

After a few minutes, Kris drove out the camp road and onto Sefton Pond Road. The truck slid a little on the very first bend. Kris caught it and kept it off the shoulder, but it startled him. Black ice, just like Silas had said. Kris slowed and took his time up the long hill, through the narrow curve at the top, and back down to the intersection at Natty's.

Natty's lot was pretty full. Kris had forgotten they served breakfast during hunting season. He pulled in. He hadn't had breakfast, and he still didn't want to go to town. Plus, he might see the new girl again.

Cindy was working a table in the left corner when he walked through the door. Kris glanced around, and, not seeing an open table, pulled up a stool at the bar. It took Cindy a while to come around to him. When she did, he could tell she was harried.

"Jesus, Kris, I don't think I've ever seen you here for breakfast. D'jou come in hoping to see Margo too?"

Kris smiled. "No, Cindy, I came in to have breakfast. I've never had your breakfast. To be honest, I'm on my way into town and I'm putting it off."

"Weren't you just in town the other day?"

"I was. My goddamn toilet's been leaking around the seal. Bathroom floor's covered with water every time it flushes. Needs a new seal. I've been putting it off, but I have a lull in my work today so seems like the right time to do it. And I need a new battery for the truck I think."

"When it rains it pours, Kris. Any idea what you want to eat?"

"How about two eggs over medium and black tea?"

"You got it." Cindy turned and put the order in the register then hustled into the kitchen. Kris realized that she was working alone.

Eggs don't take long, so Cindy was back out with Kris's plate and his tea in no time. He asked, "When you asked me about coming in to see the new girl it sounded like there might be a few guys doing that?"

Cindy leaned close to Kris and whispered, "Dazzle." She tipped her head a bit toward the far end of the bar. "That guy at the end of the bar. He's never come in for breakfast before either, and he's got a long drive to get here, from out the other side of Cotswald." She straightened up. Kris leaned back a little and glanced down to the end of the bar. The guy looked familiar but not so much that Kris would have known who he was. Cindy leaned back close to Kris. "He even asked about her when he came in. It's a little strange if you ask me. He was here last night until we closed."

Kris shook some salt on his eggs and thought for a minute. "Shit, Cindy, you might not know what you got yourself into."

"Tell you what, Kris, she works her ass off and that's all I care about. If she's got something going on that brings in a few more customers, that's icing on the cake if you ask me. I ain't complaining!" She straightened up again and looked around the place, raising her chin a little, acknowledging a request from one of the tables. She looked back at Kris with a grin. "She'll be in a little later this morning, just in case you were wondering."

Kris could feel himself blushing.

# CHAPTER TWENTY-TWO

Her little clock read ten-twenty.

"Oh no!" She sat up on the edge of the futon, dazed and fuzzy. She'd promised Cindy she'd be there around ten. She needed a shower.

The water pressure left a lot to be desired, but the water was hot and that was enough. She took a fast one, just enough to clean up and wash her hair. Her blow dryer was a distant memory. Her hair would dry by itself, and it would look the way it would look.

It took her twenty minutes to get ready, not fast enough. She didn't want to piss Cindy off. She stepped out of the apartment and almost directly into the grill of a red GMC pickup parked directly in front of her door. The parking lot was full. She locked the door and hustled across the lot to Natty's entrance. Just as she reached for the door handle, the door swung open.

"I'm sorry!" It was Cindy's favorite, Kris.

"No worries." Margo was startled and a little sheepish.

He backed into Natty's and held the door open for her.

"Thanks." She squeezed past him without looking up.

"Have a good one!" He left the place.

Cindy was behind the bar. "There you are, Margo!" She was smiling, a good sign. "Get over here and have a coffee." Cindy spun to the back wall and grabbed a mug and the coffee pot.

"I can use one." Margo pulled up a stool at the bar. "I'm sorry I'm a little late. I'm not used to the hard work I guess."

"Don't you worry about it. You're not late. We had a real busy morning, kinda strange to be so busy, but no complaints here." Cindy filled Margo's mug. "Slowing down now, though. Breakfast is over. I'd expect it to pick up some around lunch and a little after, and then it could get pretty busy tonight. Once deer season's over it'll settle down a little and just be the locals."

The coffee was good and hot. Margo needed it.

Cindy continued, "Whaddaya say I cook us up something to eat and we can talk about what you think of the place?" She didn't wait for an answer; she spun into the kitchen and started gathering pans and bowls. "How do you like your eggs?" She hollered without even turning around.

"Scrambled, Cindy. Thank you." Margo sipped her coffee and watched Cindy through the kitchen door. Cindy was fast, not a wasted movement. It was only a few minutes before she came out of the kitchen with two plates, both piled high with eggs, potatoes, and bacon. She cocked her head toward the corner tables and walked right past Margo.

Margo jumped off the stool and followed her to the table. "Geez, Cindy, I'll get real fat eating like this."

"Nah, you're gonna work it off fast. I can tell. You keep hustlin' like you were last night and you'll need to eat like this just to stay all thin like you are." Cindy ran back to the bar and grabbed utensils and ketchup. And the coffee pot. They sat silently for a few minutes while they both dressed up their eggs with salt, pepper, and ketchup. Cindy leaned forward and whispered, "D'jou see Dazzle sitting over there in his corner?"

Margo didn't look. "He's back this morning? Is he always here?"

"Nope. Until now he's only been around maybe once a month and always at night drinking beers. He's never been here for breakfast. Weird, huh?"

Margo took a bite of the potatoes. "Good home fries, Cindy. Really good."

"Hey, Cindy, can I get another cup of coffee?" It was one in a group of four sitting at a table near the bar.

Margo stood quickly and nodded to Cindy. "I've got it." She hustled to the coffee pot and then to the table and filled all the mugs. Cindy watched Dazzle watch Margo. He never took his eyes off her. He had a thing for her, Cindy was sure of it. She didn't think Margo noticed, though.

"Maybe me too while you're up please?" It was Dazzle. Quiet and polite.

Margo turned and moved a stool out of the way so she could stand right up beside him and fill his mug. He never took his eyes off hers, but she didn't look back at him until he thanked her. Even then it was a quick, polite glance.

Margo put the coffee pot back and returned to the table. She started eating again without a word.

*This girl's cool as a cucumber*, Cindy thought as she took a bite of her toast. "I like you, Margo. I like you a lot. I hope you'll stay on for a while. Have you thought much more about it?"

"Well…" Margo sat up, put her fork down, and wiped her mouth with a napkin. "I can't say as I've thought about it at all since yesterday." She sipped her coffee. "I have a good feeling about being here, though. And a good feeling about you, Cindy." She sipped the coffee again, leaned toward Cindy, and whispered, "I even kind of like Dazzle. In a sympathetic sort of way." She sat back up and sipped on the coffee again. "And I do like this place."

Cindy ate her last bite of toast and wiped her hands with a napkin. "I like Dazzle too. Me and Dazzle go back a long ways, I'll tell you about it sometime." Cindy pushed her chair back, stood from the table, picked up her plate, and reached for Margo's. "I hope you decide to stay. I think we're gonna get along real good. What do you say we get to work? Lunch crowd will be coming hard and fast."

Cindy was right. Just about as soon as they'd cleaned up the dishes and begun prep for lunch, the hunters started streaming in.

"Seems early, Cindy."

"They've been up hunting since dawn. Ain't early to them. They'll want to get back out as soon as they can 'cause the afternoon's short and it gets dark."

The place filled fast. Before long, all the tables were full and so was the bar. Cindy was making sandwiches and burgers as fast as she could, and Margo was waiting tables and pouring beers. And the occasional whiskey.

The crowd thinned almost as fast as it came, at least it seemed that way to Margo. Wasn't long before there were only two hunters left. Playing pool and drinking beer. A lot of beer.

"Hey, sexy, how about one more round?" The guy was big and scruffy, his hair looked like it hadn't been washed in a while, and he had a three-day beard. Margo brought two more beers.

"Shit, baby, why don't you take a break from work and we'll take a break from pool and we'll rock your world."

Margo gave him her best "Are you serious, douchebag?" look, picked up the empties, and turned.

"What the fuck?" the other hollered at her back, "you don't think you can handle two of us, bitch?"

Margo never turned back; she went straight into the kitchen.

"These two assholes have had way too much to drink."

Cindy peeked through the kitchen door. "Them two ain't locals. I've never seen them till today. I'll take care of 'em." She wiped her hands on a bar towel. "We're almost out of beers in here, Margo. How about you grab us a bunch more cases and fill up the bar fridge so we have a decent start on tonight? You remember, I keep them in a couple chill chests out in the storage room behind your apartment. There's a dolly in there too."

Margo nodded.

The two women left the kitchen. Margo walked out the front door while Cindy made her way to the pool table.

# CHAPTER TWENTY-THREE

It took Margo a while to get four cases of beer on the dolly, wheel it out of the back room, close the door, and wheel it around the side of the building. And a little extra time to avoid the pile of two-by-fours and scrap wood that was scattered along the side of the building under her apartment window. The two hunters were just coming out of the front door of the bar as she turned the corner near her apartment door.

"We ain't coming back to this piece of shit bar!" the big one hollered back into the bar as he walked out the door. Margo stopped, set the dolly back, and waited.

The smaller one spotted her and grabbed the big one's arm. "Lookee here!" They both stopped and stared at Margo for a second or two.

"Well how about that!" The big one started toward her and the small one followed. "Here you are. I knew you wanted a little fun with us."

Margo just shook her head. Silent.

They kept walking toward her. "Where we gonna go, baby? Out back of the building?"

Margo was frozen, scared suddenly.

Now they were standing close. Really close. The big one pushed her hair back around her ear with his finger. "You're pretty. Got a nice mouth."

Margo swatted his hand away from her head. "Leave me alone, asshole."

"Now don't you start pushing back. I'll hurt you."

"Kiss my ass."

He grabbed Margo hard by the upper arm. She tried to pull away, but the small one stepped in behind her and grabbed her around the neck.

"Cindy!" Margo yelled. "Cin—" The small one clamped his hand hard across her mouth.

She bit him.

"Fuck!" He pulled his hand away, bloody.

"Let her go!"

The big one spun away from Margo toward the voice. It was Kris running from his truck. In the commotion, neither the hunters nor Margo had seen him pull into the lot.

"I said let her go. Now!"

The hunter turned and smiled at Margo, then looked up at his friend and motioned his head toward Kris. He let go of Margo and turned toward Kris. The small one moved around Margo and stood beside him.

"You ain't the law, son. You're asking for big trouble."

"You got no reason to be manhandling this girl."

"I'll do whatever the fuck I want, needledink."

Kris looked at Margo. "You'd better get inside."

Margo started around the men, but the big one reached out and grabbed her. "We're all gonna have us some fun and ain't nothing you're gonna do about it, slick. You'd better be getting on your way."

Kris moved close to the big one. "Let her go, you drunk son of a bitch."

The big one smiled again and released Margo. Before she could move away, he lunged forward and pushed Kris hard with both hands. Kris stumbled back a few steps but stayed on his feet.

"Now if you think you want to get into it with us, you'd better get it started, fucker." The big one pushed his sleeves up on his arms a little.

Kris took a few quick steps forward, and before the big one could react, he swung a roundhouse right, hard against his jaw. The big one went down fast, moaning. The small one ran toward Kris and kicked him in the crotch. Kris wasn't expecting that. He buckled with the blow, falling to his knees, head into the ground. The big one worked his way to his feet spitting blood, and the small one just looked at Kris dumbfounded, holding his bloody hand.

The big one kicked Kris in the side, and the small one laughed and kicked Kris in the back of the leg. They didn't notice Margo running back to the side of the building. They didn't see her return with a two-by-four either. Kris was lying on the ground in a fetal position, the hunters standing above him.

"I say we kick the shit out of the fucker, Mel," the small one said, "teach him a lesson."

Neither one noticed Margo raising the wood over her head or bringing it down hard across the big one's neck and shoulder. He collapsed where he stood without making a sound. The small one looked over at him, startled and dumbfounded.

"Wha—" He still didn't see Margo as she brought the wood back like she was swinging a baseball bat, and when he did notice and jerk around toward her, the wood was already in motion and gaining speed. It caught him clean on the side of the chin. His eyes rolled into his head, and he collapsed.

Cindy must have heard the commotion; she came running from the bar just as the wood hit the small one.

"Margo! Holy shit! Kris!"

"They attacked me, Cindy. Kris came by and tried to stop them."

Cindy could tell that Margo was okay. She knelt down beside Kris.

"You okay, Kris?"

Kris nodded and sat up. "Yup, let me sit here for a minute. Catch my breath."

Cindy turned to the big one, who was starting to come to. "You bastards best get out of here now, before I call the cops."

The big one pushed himself up and stood, holding his shoulder, blood running across his chin. He nudged the small one a few times with his toe, then leaned down and slapped his face.

The small one came to. "Wha'd ja do that for?" He pushed the big one away and stood, rubbing his face. They shuffled to their truck, got in, and left the lot.

Cindy and Margo helped Kris up and into the bar.

"Whiskey's on me, Kris." Cindy grinned a tiny grin and winked at Margo.

# CHAPTER TWENTY-FOUR

"Dido! Dido! We have the car!"

Myslewiec nearly jumped out of his chair. "You scared the hell out of me, Miller."

"Sorry, Dido." Miller was out of breath. "We just found a car at a truck stop off 90 a little east of Madison. Matches the car in the videos."

By the videos, Miller meant the surveillance videos from the mini market where the kid had been killed. Myslewiec had spent the early hours of the morning reviewing the videos instead of sleeping.

The videos captured everything, everything except the kid going down. Myslewiec was thankful for that. There was one camera on the pumps that had good footage of the car and the guy who was driving it and one camera on the register that had captured the guy taking his change, pulling his gun, the kid running, and the guy shooting. The videos showed the guy's face as clear as could be expected from the cheap, low-resolution setup that the storeowner had installed. The guy hadn't even bothered to disguise himself, unless the eye patch was the disguise. But that didn't make sense to Myslewiec.

"Any details yet? You got the registration?"

Miller handed Myslewiec his notebook opened to the page with the registration noted. "I ran it. Chelsea,

Michigan. A guy named Rank. I called Chelsea PD and, get this, Dido, the guy's a wifebeater from way back and his wife's missing."

Myslewiec thought for a moment. "He's heading east, at least that's the way he started out."

# CHAPTER TWENTY-FIVE

The sun streaming through the cap windows was too much for Rank, and his head was spinning with worry. He'd slept some, maybe an hour or two, but now he'd given up. He was awake. He rolled over in the sleeping bag, grabbed the plastic Walmart bag that still held his food, and took out an apple. He rubbed it a little on his shirt to clean it off, then took a big bite. It was cold and good. He ate it fast and took another from the bag, beginning to realize why the apples were cold. It was cold in the back of the truck. Really cold. He wolfed the second apple down, pulled a ginger ale out of the plastic ring that held the six pack together, and made his way out of the back of the truck and into the driver's seat. He started it up and let it idle.

Wasn't long before he had heat, and he turned the heater fan to high. He began thinking about his next move. How would he find her? He had to ditch the truck and find something different if he wanted to stay below the radar. That might take a while, and he was on borrowed time now. All a cop had to do was run the plates to find out whose truck it was. And the maids would find the fat chick soon, if they hadn't already. He didn't have much time. He couldn't steal one, and he couldn't kill anyone else, that would be a sure way to show the cops where he was. Had to find a new vehicle some other way. He couldn't buy one, even if he had the money. He took a sip of the ginger ale. It was slushy, it was damn cold in the back of the truck.

With nothing coming to him, he decided to look around town. He put the truck in gear and made his way out of the parking lot and to the main road. He'd come in from the left, so he turned to the right out of the lot. It took about five minutes to get to the center of town. At what he thought was the main intersection, he had to keep straight, even though the street to his left looked the most interesting. He passed a hotel and some small professional buildings that were originally single-family homes. He quickly came to a stop light where he turned left, and then left again at the next light, circling back to that interesting street. He turned right. Within a block he saw the sign: *Community Bank*. He turned into the lot and pulled into a space in front of the ATM booth. He turned off the engine and sat staring for a few minutes.

"She was here." He said it aloud to no one. He was tired and confused. He knew he needed to get his head straight and figure out what to do before the cops found his trail.

He started the truck again and pulled out of the lot. No traffic either way, so he turned left back toward the town center. There was a street to the right just at the first block of the bigger brick buildings. He turned there and immediately found a parking lot directly behind the building. A parking lot with plenty of cars. He pulled in and found a spot a little ways back where the truck would be hidden by the other cars in the lot. Hidden from the street at least. He got out of the truck, locked it, and walked around to the street side of the building.

Right on the corner was a bar. He looked up at the sign and muttered to himself, "Magee's Tavern. Whatever." He went inside. There were a couple guys playing pool, a few guys at the bar, and a cute looking barmaid at the far end. Rank sat a couple stools away from the other guys. The barmaid was there immediately.

"What'll you have?"

"How about a Bud?" He smiled.

"Bottles are what we've got for Bud. That work for you?"

He nodded. She pulled one from the fridge below the bar, opened it, and set it in front of him on a coaster advertising Blue Moon.

"Tab?"

He nodded again. She wasn't as young as he'd thought, or as cute when she got up close. She had a few wrinkles and she looked a little hard, but she carried herself nicely. Brown hair down past her shoulders and parted on the side, a flannel shirt under a suede vest, and jeans that might be on the edge of too tight hugging her big ass and thighs. Her red painted nails and the rose tattooed on her hand just above her thumb made her sexy in a raunchy kind of way. He drank from the bottle without tipping his head back so he could keep looking at her.

When she set down his third beer she leaned down in front of him with her elbows on the bar and her chin resting in her hands. "Ain't seen you before. You're not from around here are you?" Hard to tell with his sunglasses on, but now that she was close, her eyes looked light brown.

"Nope. I just got here this morning."

"On your way through, or you staying for a while?"

"On my way through. No plans really. Haven't thought about staying or not. I don't even know anybody here."

She straightened up and stuck her hand out. Like she wanted to shake hands. "I'm Sherry."

Rank shook her hand, smiled, and replied, "Todd."

"There. Now you know someone. Your beer's almost empty. You gonna stay a while? I'll get you another one."

Rank nodded.

"How about something to eat?"

Rank shrugged and muttered, "I guess." He wasn't going anywhere, he liked this chick and the beers were calming him down. He was starting to think that with a few more he might be able to come up with a plan.

She slapped a menu down in front of him. "There's lots of stuff on the menu, but the burgers are real good and so are the turkey clubs. The wings sound good but they suck, and all the appetizers are tiny portions, not worth the money. And, Todd, you might be able to read it better if you take off those sunglasses. But what the fuck do I know, right?" She grinned, turned, and walked to the far end of the bar to help another customer, her big ass gyrating like she was trying to turn him on.

Rank opened the menu and looked through it without putting much thought to what he'd have. He was thinking about this chick Sherry. He left the sunglasses on.

# CHAPTER TWENTY-SIX

Kris sat at the bar and drank a few whiskeys. The afternoon crowd had been thin, thinner than Cindy had anticipated. Good thing, because that gave Cindy and Margo time to tend to Kris now and then.

Cindy stood behind the bar, and Margo sat on the stool next to Kris. They'd both been running around prepping for dinner, but it hadn't taken them long to get it under control. "How are you feeling?" Cindy asked as she dried a beer glass.

Kris smiled and raised his glass. "My ribs are a little sore, but the whiskey's damn good."

Margo added, "It was really nice of you to step in like that. Thank you."

Kris gave a little nod and took a sip from his glass. "I didn't do much except get the shit kicked out of me."

"You broke it up," Cindy interjected, "there's no telling what those assholes would have done to Margo if you hadn't stepped in. You did a lot, Kris."

Kris finished the whiskey in his glass, set it down on the bar, and stood. "I'd better be getting back to the camp, Cindy," he said nodding at the empty whiskey glass, "too many more of those and I might be the one trying to take advantage of both of you." He smiled and looked at Margo. "If you think seeing me getting beat up was ugly, you should see me drunk."

"You sure you're okay, Kris?" Cindy asked one more time.

"Yup. Thank you for the drinks." Kris pushed his stool back in place, nodded at Cindy and then Margo, turned, and left. Both women watched him leave.

Margo turned to Cindy. "I can see why you like him. He's simple. Real. No bullshit. And he doesn't think he's any better than anyone else."

Cindy nodded and added, "He ain't too hard to look at either."

The door opened, and a group of four came through, two men and two women. "Here we go, Margo." The door hadn't quite closed when it swung open again. It was Dazzle. Cindy leaned toward Margo and whispered, "I'll be a son of a bitch."

The group of four sat at a table to the left of the door. Dazzle sat at his usual spot against the wall at the end of the bar.

"You take the table, I'll take Dazzle," Cindy whispered. Margo stood, grabbed menus from a shelf below the bar, and walked to the table of four.

It only got busier. No break for either woman all night. The drinking crowd started showing up well before the dinner crowd was gone. Dazzle stayed put, except to use the restroom once in a while. He was the last to leave at the end of the night. He stayed a little longer than Cindy was comfortable with, but she didn't say anything to him. He was a paying customer after all. As the door closed behind Dazzle, Cindy rushed to it and locked it. Turning her back to it and leaning hard against it, she let out a loud sigh.

"Holy crap, Margo, it hasn't been that busy for a long time!"

"Good, though, right?" Margo was wiping down the bar. "We sold a lot of booze tonight. A lot of booze! Job security for me, you know."

Cindy laughed. "Job security for both of us, hon. Both of us." She walked back toward the kitchen. "I'll straighten up in here."

It wasn't long before Margo had cleaned up the main room and the bar and Cindy had the kitchen in order.

"What time tomorrow, Cindy?"

"How about ten again? You can come in earlier if you want; we'll have another good breakfast crowd. I'll leave it up to you, though."

"I'll try to get here earlier tomorrow. You can use the help for breakfast. You wanna lock up after me?"

"Shit no. I'm leaving with you." Cindy folded a bar towel and hung it on the oven handle. The two women walked out of the bar and into the cold night together. The sky was cloudy, and Margo thought she felt a little moisture, almost a sprinkle. After Cindy locked the door, the women bid each other one last goodnight and walked in opposite directions. Cindy walked to her car. She always parked at the far end of the lot so customers could park closer to the entrance. Margo turned the other way and walked to the door of the apartment. A streetlight to her right lit both the parking lot and her apartment door. It took her no time to unlock the door and get inside out of the cold. That streetlight lit her room too, a little too much, through the single window near the futon bed. She'd already decided to get a curtain for that window as soon as she had a chance. The light wouldn't matter tonight, though, as tired as she was. Stripped to her underwear, clothes tossed on the trunk in front of the futon, she climbed into bed.

Sleep came fast but didn't last long. The sound of glass breaking and thumping woke her. Dazed with sleep and wondering if the sound had been a dream, she sat up and fumbled for the light. Something was moving next to her. Something big. Uneven, jerky movements right beside the light. It wasn't a dream. She turned the switch.

Dazzle acted as startled as she was.

"Shit!" Shielding his eyes with his left hand he turned toward her. He held a knife in his right hand. A very large knife.

"What the hell?" she blurted.

He moved quickly, pushed her back down on the bed, and held the knife in front of her face. "Shhh! You be quiet now. It's only me. I ain't here to hurt you. This here's my protection. Our protection." He wagged the knife. It was large with a serrated back edge. The blade was almost as big as his hand. She'd seen knives like it before on late night TV commercials. She stared at the knife silently. Scared. Confused. He held her down, knife in front of her face. He looked over his shoulder, slowly taking in the room.

"This place ain't no good for you. Ain't safe." He turned and looked straight into her eyes. "See how easy I got in here? Jus' think if I wanted to hurt you. I could have cut your throat by now, nothing you could do." He wagged the knife again, as if to emphasize his point. "I got a place where you're gonna be safe. Safe with me.

Like you should be. 'Cause we're friends, right? You told me so t'other day. Didn't you?" He moved the knife a tiny bit closer to her face.

Margo's mind was racing now, deciding if she should fight. He was strong, holding her against the bed. Stronger than she would have thought. He smelled too. Like oil. Motor oil.

"Didn't you?" He demanded an answer.

Margo nodded silently.

He eased off her and straightened up, keeping the knife raised. Ready.

"Get up and get your clothes on. We need to get away from here." He smiled and pointed at her with the knife. "Us friends need to stay together. Away from here. I have a good place for us."

She rose slowly, feet on the floor on the side of the bed away from Dazzle. Thinking. Searching for an idea. He shuffled along with her, around the bed to the end. The trunk at the bed's foot was the only thing between them. He was staying close but not getting closer; he was ready for her to run. She didn't. She decided to take her chances and do what he said. This wasn't the time or place to fight. She was at a disadvantage. She needed to wait for a better chance. A better chance would come soon enough, she thought.

She took the clothes she'd worn that day off the trunk piece by piece and put them back on as Dazzle watched. When she finished, she stood and stared at him without speaking.

"Yer ready then?" he asked. Quietly. Almost apologetically.

She nodded.

He pointed the knife toward her front door. "We'll go out this way. My truck's just in front. You lock yer door when we go out."

She nodded, bent down, and took her key from the trunk. Standing up, she looked at him again but didn't move. He nodded his head toward the door and wagged the knife at the same time. "You go slow now. Don't move fast." He followed her to the door.

"I need my coat." She spoke softly and nodded toward the hook beside the door where it hung. He nodded back, never looking at the coat, his eyes fixed on her. She took it from the hook and put it on, opened the door, and stepped out, looking around the lot hoping someone was there. Empty. Aside from the pickup truck that was right next to her door. He stepped out, carefully moving around her. Making an effort not to touch her. She turned and locked the door. The light inside was still on.

"This here's my truck." He'd parked it just to the side of the door with the passenger door only a step away. She was between him and the truck. It was obvious that he'd planned this well. He leaned around beside her and opened the passenger door. "There you go. Get in."

She climbed in. He shut the door and ran around the front of the truck. The driver's door was already open, left open so he could get in quickly. For a moment she thought about running before he got in the truck, but where would she go? He was in with his door closed, the engine started, and the truck moving before she'd finished the thought. She hoped that a better chance would come. A better chance to run.

# CHAPTER TWENTY-SEVEN

Rank spent the next hour digging into Sherry's life. He was good at it; he'd always had a way with the ladies. He'd found out quickly that she was divorced, her kids were grown and no longer lived with her, and she didn't have a boyfriend. Beyond that, he now knew that she worked two jobs and had a little house cleaning business on weekends. She was just barely able to pay her bills, and she was having a hard time maintaining the house that she'd kept in the divorce. Lots of repairs needed, no money to pay someone to do the work, and no time to do it herself. She could hardly even cut the grass in her yard. Rank had the beginnings of a plan.

He waited for the best moment. Sherry was cleaning up near the end of her shift, and the bar was empty. He got off his stool and walked to the end where she was working.

"I have a proposition for you."

She grinned, tipped her head to the side, and batted her eyes a few times.

Rank continued, "I've got no place to stay and, like I said, I don't have much of a plan right now. You need some help around your place, sounds like things I can do. What do you say I do the work you need done at your place for room and board while I figure out what's next for me? You must have a spare room at the house, now with your kids gone."

Sherry looked at him without reacting. Thinking for a few moments. "That might work. I don't know you, but you seem like a decent guy." She returned to washing the bar glasses in the sink, looking in the direction of the sink but not looking at it. Still thinking. Considering the idea. Rank waited silently, he knew that was his best play.

She straightened up from the sink and turned to him. "I'll be taking a real chance, not knowing you. My intuition says it's okay, but I gotta be honest, it makes me nervous." She paused and stared at him. He waited. After a few seconds, she continued, "How about this. I've got a little time between here and when I start my shift at the hospital. Might be just enough to take you out to my place and show you around for a minute. Show you a couple things I need done quick, and show you where the tools are. I'll do my shift, you get to work at my place, and we'll see what happens when I get home."

"Sounds perfect."

She put the last glass in the rack and put the bar towel away. "One thing, though, at least for tonight. I need to make sure you don't just run off with my stuff. Once we get there, I'll need your car keys. I'll hold on to 'em until I get back from work."

Rank hadn't expected that, but he didn't mind it. Without hesitation, he stuck his hand out just like she had earlier. "Deal. I'll work on your place, you take my keys, and if you come home and don't like what I've done, or if you change your mind for whatever, I'll be on my way. No hard feelings. But if you like what I've done and you start feeling more comfortable, maybe we can work something out. That'll be your call."

Rank was removing as much of the threat as he could.

Sherry shook his hand. "Deal. Gimme a minute to get my stuff. Where are you parked?"

"In the lot out back. Green pickup with a cap."

"Okay, I'm back there too. Go ahead out. I'll be out the back door in a minute." She turned and walked into the kitchen. Rank watched her ass-filled jeans wiggle as she walked.

She was standing beside her car when Rank came around the corner into the lot. A beat-up silver Pontiac from the late nineties. They nodded at each other as he walked past and climbed into his truck. They left the lot together, Rank following. A right turn onto the main street, then a left at the first light and a right at the next. Soon, they drove past the west side of Sefton State University. Pastures overtook houses as they turned left onto Route 72, and after fifteen or twenty minutes of straight, two-lane highway lined by tended fields and small family farms, they arrived at the edge of a town. Sherry turned right on George Street, directly across the main highway from a gas station mini-market, and then about four hundred yards later turned right again on Picketville Road. A minute or so on Picketville, and she turned left into the gravel driveway of a small, single-story house.

"C'mon in while I change my clothes and I'll show you your room." She was moving fast. She skipped up the steps on the side of the house and through the side door. Rank had to jog to catch up, careful not to grab the broken rail. She was pulling off her vest as she disappeared down the hall on the far side of the kitchen. Rank stood near the entrance door, unsure of what to do.

"C'mon down here." She was out of sight down the hallway. He followed. Just as he entered the hall, she leaned out of the open door of the furthest room and pointed. She had already taken off her blouse and wore only a bra.

"This room. The first on your left. That'll be yours."

She disappeared back into the room and swung the door shut.

Rank peered into the room that she'd pointed to. A single bed, a dark dresser with a fake wood finish, a Bob Marley poster, and a single window with a white slatted blind. This would do just fine. Rank walked back out to the kitchen and waited. After a few minutes, she flew down the hall into the kitchen, now wearing black pants, black sneakers, and buttoning a light blue, long-sleeve blouse.

She spoke as she hurried past him back toward the kitchen door. "Sorry, had to change into my uniform for the cafeteria. I don't have much time. Lemme show you a few things I need done. Bring your bags to your room whenever you want."

She tucked her shirt into the black pants and took a coat from one of the hooks beside the door. "Everything I thought of on the way here is outside. Sorry. It's cold. Best I can do right now, though." She motioned with her head for him to follow and went outside. She was already down the steps and walking toward the back when Rank walked through the door. He hustled down the steps.

"The storms on all three of these windows back here are gone, been that way for a year. I have some plastic in the shed. If you can cover these with plastic that'll be good enough for the winter."

She didn't stop moving. She walked around the side of the house and pointed at a hose laying on the ground wrapped around a green metal hose hanger. "The hose holder broke this summer. You can get the hose drained and put that hanger back up. The hose can go in the shed."

Still moving, she walked around past the front of the house and to the side steps where they'd come in a few minutes earlier. "This rail's been busted for a long time. Needs to be fixed before it gets icy. C'mon over here to the shed."

The shed sat a few yards from the house at the end of the driveway. Tan metal with two doors and a barn-style roof. The doors squealed as she swung them open. "Plastic's in here and a bunch of tools my husband left. Nails and screws are in jars on the bench, and there's some wood over there and some more under a tarp behind the shed. I gotta go. Can't be late." She turned and walked quickly back to her car. "My shift ends at seven-thirty. I'll be back by eight or so. Thanks!" She was in the car and gone before Rank could respond.

He turned back to the shed and surveyed the contents. A small workbench against one wall, a few hand tools on a pegboard above it, and probably more tools in a couple old toolboxes on the floor. Also visible were a circular saw, a small portable table saw, and a drill on a shelf below with a few other tools. The bench top was cluttered with odds and ends and the jars with old nails and screws she'd mentioned. A few boards, some plywood, and some two-by-fours were piled against the back wall, a couple folding metal sawhorses hanging on hooks above them. The roll of plastic she'd mentioned was there too. Shovels and rakes leaned against the side wall, and a lawn mower and a small generator sat in the middle of the floor.

Rank was pleased. *This'll do nicely*, he thought. As he turned toward his car to fetch his duffle bag, he stuck his hands in his pockets. His keys were in one pocket. She'd forgotten to take them.

# CHAPTER TWENTY-EIGHT

The ride had been quiet except for Dazzle's attempts to whistle. More air than sound. It annoyed Margo, but she was too scared to tell him to stop. They drove down into the little town and then out a two-lane paved road for a few miles where they came to a junkyard. Dazzle pulled up to the closed gate.

"You stay put now. I have a Doberman, and she don't like new people much."

Dazzle jumped out of the truck, jogged to the gate, opened it quickly, and jogged back to the truck, repeating the moves when they were inside to close and lock it. The dog heard the noise. It exploded toward the gate barking furiously and then quickly became silent and slowed to a trot when it recognized Dazzle. Back in the truck, he looked at Margo and grinned. "You're gonna love this place."

He drove past the main buildings and through the junkyard with the dog trotting beside the truck next to Margo's door. They wound slowly along narrow dirt paths between rows and rows of rusted hulks, some recognizable as cars and others stripped beyond recognition. Eventually, a tall fence came into view with what looked like a stand of evergreen trees behind it. Dazzle turned to the right and the headlights revealed a large, very old motorhome. They pulled up beside it, and Dazzle stopped the truck.

"Here we are!" He was excited. "You stay put now while I get the lights going. Don't want Blitz to get confused about you not being a friend."

Dazzle jumped out of the truck and opened the two front doors to what looked like a plastic storage shed. He fiddled with something inside for a minute and then started pulling, like he was starting a lawnmower. When the engine started, Margo realized that it was a generator. Dazzle jogged to the door of the motorhome, leaned in, and turned on one of the inside lights and an outside spotlight mounted above the door. He turned back, stood for a moment in the doorway with a triumphant grin, pumped his fist once, and let out a rebel yell. He looked at Margo through the truck window. "You're gonna love this place!"

He jumped down from the step, shuffled the dog out of the way with his foot, pulled the knife from his coat pocket, and opened her door. "C'mon now. I'll keep Blitz away from you."

"You want me to go inside that, Dazzle?" Margo was doing her best to be friendly, trying to act as if nothing was wrong, hoping that acting naturally would help her talk him out of whatever plans he had. She wasn't pulling it off.

"Yeah! You're gonna love this place!" He pointed the knife at her and then wagged it toward the motorhome. "G'wan. Git inside."

Margo stepped out of the truck. The dog lunged toward her, barking, teeth bared. Dazzle caught the dog by the collar before it reached Margo. "Hurry up before

I get tired and let go of Blitz." As Margo walked past, the dog lunged again, straining against Dazzle's hold.

Dazzle followed Margo into the motorhome and closed the door. He left the dog outside. "Sit here in the booth for a minute," he said pointing the knife toward the table. She looked closely to make sure she wouldn't be sitting on anything disgusting and slid down in.

"I'm gonna go turn on our heater. Don't you move. And remember, the dog's outside." He turned and walked down the narrow hall. She could hear him fiddle with what must have been the heater he was talking about. As she looked around, her stomach started turning. She had no idea how to get out of this. No idea what he had in mind.

Dazzle returned to the table with two cans of beer. "I got a cooler in the other room with some beers for us." He put one down in front of her, opened his, and took a drink. She didn't move. "Don't you like beer?"

"Yeah I do, Dazzle, but I don't know why you brought me here. I'm kinda scared. What are you gonna do to me?"

Dazzle kept his eyes fixed to hers while he took another drink. He put the can down and looked down at the table. "It makes me sad that my friend don't appreciate that I saved her from that dangerous place she lived in." He stared silently at the table. He took another drink, still not looking at Margo. He put the can back down. "I don't like to be sad. I get mad when I'm sad." He raised his eyes to look at Margo. "You don't want me to get mad, right?"

Margo shook her head. "No Dazzle, I don't want you to get mad, but—"

Before she could say anything else, he stood and threw his beer can against the dashboard of the motorhome. "Too late!" He was breathing hard, and his eyes were wide. He leaned forward, held the knife in her face, and grabbed her neck with his other hand. Between clenched teeth, he sneered, "My friends only make me mad once. Only once."

He squeezed her throat. Hard enough to begin choking her. She brought her hands up and grabbed his arm, trying to pull his hand off. He was too strong. He held her throat tightly for a moment and then let go.

"I thought we'd have a nice time tonight, but you're being a bitch. Time you learned how to stop being a bitch." He motioned around behind him with the knife. "Git in the bedroom."

She was scared before; now she was terrified. She didn't know if she should resist further. She was afraid he'd hurt her. Or worse. She rose from the table and walked around him and down the small hall, passing a tiny bathroom on her right and a closet on her left. The cooler chest was on the floor of the closet.

The back room had two small beds, one against each wall, with a nightstand against the back wall between them. A small, round space heater attached to a propane tank sat in front of the nightstand, glowing hot. A heavy chain piled on the floor in front of the heater. Something that looked like handcuffs sat on one of the beds.

"Git on the bed."

*Shit*, she thought, *he's gonna rape me.*

She looked at him, her head shaking and her eyes pleading, "Please don't—"

"Take off your coat, and get on the bed." He was unmoved.

She slipped her coat off, tossed it on the bed, and climbed on beside it. He turned and took the object from the other bed. It was a belt with handcuffs, like the belts prisoners wear into a courtroom.

"Sit up."

She did. He started whistling again. He opened the belt, looped it around her waist, pulled it snug, and clasped it. The buckle was on the back. "It pains me to do this, but you need to learn not to be a bitch. Put your hands in."

She couldn't fight; she didn't have it in her. She put her hands in the open cuffs on either side of the belt. Dazzle clasped them tightly. They pinched a little. She winced.

He grinned. "Stay sitting up." He bent and grabbed the chain from the floor. As he picked up the end, she could see that it was looped through two holes in the floor, the loop padlocked together. There was also an open padlock on the loose end that she hadn't seen before. The belt around her waist had a metal loop on the front center that he could have locked the chain to. Instead, he pulled the chain up her back, between her waist and the belt, and then locked the chain to itself. She was captive, her hands secured and the belt around her waist chained to the motorhome.

"There. You can go to sleep now if you want."

It didn't sound as if he was going to rape her after all. She slumped down on the bed, and the chain pushed into her back. It hurt. She wished he'd used the metal loop on the front of the belt.

Dazzle walked back to the front of the motorhome and turned off the lights. The propane heater threw an eerie orange glow into the room. He returned to the bedroom, turned his back to her, and began taking off his clothes. Shirt first, then shoes, pants, socks, and finally his jockey shorts. He stood naked for a moment in the glow of the heater, his back still to her. He pulled down the bed covers and climbed into the bed opposite hers.

The room was nearly silent for a few minutes, then a rustling began. His bed covers moved. Short, rhythmic movements of the linens. And then heavy breathing, low at first but getting louder. As the linens moved faster, the pace of the breathing increased. Then suddenly, a protracted grunt, as if he was trying to lift something very heavy, and then a long, low breath. The linens stopped moving.

# CHAPTER TWENTY-NINE

"Would you eat another sandwich, Kris?" Silas stood on the stoop of the outbuilding in his work pants and wifebeater holding a lunch bag out towards Kris.

"Sure I will, Silas. Violet makes a damn good sandwich. What is it today?"

"Peanut butter and mayo."

"You're joking."

"I watched her make it, Kris."

Kris looked from Silas to the bag and back. He'd had a good morning; the work had come easy, and he'd been at it since before dawn. He was ready for a break, and Silas's knocking on the door provided a good excuse for one. But he damn sure wasn't going to eat a peanut butter and mayonnaise sandwich.

"Jesus, Silas, you know I'd like to help you out. But peanut butter and mayonnaise?"

Silas lowered the bag to his side. His shoulders and chin dropped. "I can't blame you, Kris."

Kris reached for the bag. "I'll take care of it, though. Maybe I'll cut it up and leave it for the squirrels and raccoons."

Silas handed him the bag. "More wood's missing, Kris."

"How can you tell, Silas? Is there a lot missing? I looked at my wood pile, and I'd have a hard time seeing anything gone unless they took a lot."

Silas was silent for a few seconds. "I guess I've been watching my wood long enough now. I can tell when some's been taken." Before Silas could say anything else, Kris's phone rang.

"C'mon in, Silas, grab a seat." Kris turned, stepped back from the outbuilding's door, and pointed to a plain chair in the corner as he picked up the phone. "Jansen." Kris's standard phone greeting.

"Kris, it's Cindy. Something's wrong. Margo's gone." Cindy was out of breath.

"What do you mean she's gone?"

"She's gone, Kris. Her window's busted and I can't find her."

"Busted window?"

"Can you come down here? I'm busy as hell with customers. I need some help. You can see it for yourself."

"Be right there." Kris hung up and stared at the phone for a couple seconds.

"What's going on, Kris?" Silas could tell something was wrong from the one side of the conversation he'd heard.

"Cindy's new help disappeared. Cindy's worried. Wants me to come help."

"Violet's asleep, Kris. I'll go with you. We can take my wheeler."

"Let's take my truck, Silas. That way we won't wake Violet when you start the wheeler up."

Natty's parking lot was overflowing, trucks parked along the roadside in front of the place. Kris parked on the side of the road closest to Margo's apartment. He and Silas looked at the broken window from the outside on their way past.

"Not much to see is there, Silas?"

"I ain't much of a detective, Kris. The window's busted good, wasn't just some kid's baseball. The glass is almost all gone. Hole's big enough for someone to crawl through."

Kris nodded. "Let's go see Cindy."

Inside, it was clear that Cindy was worried, and she was alone and having a hard time keeping up with the crowd. She was waiting on a table in the far left corner. Kris and Silas stood by the kitchen door at the edge of the bar and waited.

"C'mon in here," she whispered breathlessly as she hustled past them into the kitchen. They followed.

"It's best in here where nobody can hear us and I can keep cooking. If I fall behind this crowd, I'm in trouble." She cracked two eggs onto the griddle.

"We saw the window on our way in. What do you think's going on?"

Cindy stopped and turned, her eyes a little watery, "Kris, you have to keep this between us. You too, Silas."

Kris and Silas both nodded.

"I think it's Dazzle. Dazzle took her. Probably to his place."

Kris and Silas were silent.

"Look. I've known Dazzle since we were kids. He's not right. He's never been quite right."

Kris and Silas remained silent.

Cindy looked back and forth between them expectantly, as if she hoped they'd know something that they didn't. She continued, "I don't want Dazzle to get in trouble if he's got her. He won't hurt her; that's not what he wants."

"What does he want?" Kris asked.

"He just wants her to be his friend. He's got a strange way to show it."

"Kidnapping's more than strange, Cindy."

"I know, Kris, I know." She looked at the floor.

"What makes you so sure about Dazzle?"

Cindy stared at the floor silently for a few moments, then raised her head and looked at Kris. She had tears streaming down her cheeks.

"He kidnapped me once."

Kris and Silas were stunned.

"Cindy, why the hell do you want to protect him?"

"Kris, I told you, I've known Dazzle for a long time. Since me and him were in grade school together. I knew his family too. When we were kids we played together all the time. Dazzle never had many friends. He got teased a lot because his dad owned a junkyard. It was awful to watch. His Dad and Mom were grateful that I stood by him. I was his friend."

Kris interjected, "But he kidnapped you?"

"We were in high school. He broke into my bedroom window one night and forced me to go with him. He had a knife. I was scared. He took me way out in back of the junkyard where he had a motorhome. He took me inside it. I thought he was gonna do something bad to me, but he had a cooler full of beers and a deck of cards. He just wanted someone to hang out with."

Kris shook his head. "He kidnapped you to play cards and drink beer?"

"Yup."

"I still can't see why you want to protect him."

"We played cards and drank beer until it was daylight, when the beer was gone. The more beers he had, the more he told me. About being lonely, being picked on all the time. A few times he even cried. And I listened. He took me home, and when my parents were out shopping later that morning he fixed the window. They never knew. We stayed friends through high school, hung out together now and then. After high school he was working at his dad's place and he was real busy all the time. We kinda lost touch. A bunch of years later, when I was working as a waitress in Sefton, his dad came in to eat and asked me to sit with him for a few minutes. Wasn't busy so I did."

Cindy flipped the eggs one at a time.

"He told me about how hard it had been for him and Dazzle's mom. Watching Dazzle struggle growing up, being picked on, called names. Not having any friends. Except me. He said I was Dazzle's only friend. Then he told me about this place," Cindy waved her hand toward the kitchen door, "about how I should buy it and be my own boss instead of always working for somebody else. And then he told me it was for sale and he wanted to buy it for me. To repay me for being Dazzle's friend."

They all stood silently for a few minutes.

"Bottom line is, he did buy this place for me, and then a few months later he passed away. Pancreas cancer. He knew, but nobody else did."

Kris shook his head. "Jesus, Cindy, it's complicated."

"Yes it is, Kris. If he's got her, he ain't going to hurt her, and I want to keep this on the lowdown. I don't want Dazzle to get in trouble."

Kris thought for a minute. "Alright, alright. No trouble if we can help it. What do you want me to do?"

Cindy turned to the griddle. "Shit, my eggs!"

She grabbed a plate from above the griddle and slipped the eggs to it with her spatula. She turned back toward Kris. "First thing is to check and see if the motorhome is still there and if it looks like she might be in it."

"How do we get to the motorhome?"

"It used to be at the back of the junkyard, right at the back edge. The entrance to the yard is on Route 47, but Newton Road runs right across the back of it. They've got fences, but there's plenty of gaps where you can see in."

Silas broke his silence. "I know Newton Road, Kris."

# CHAPTER THIRTY

Rank did the windows first while there was still a little light. He'd ripped some two-by-fours into narrow strips and nailed them around the edges over the plastic. Sort of like the way narrow wood strips had held screens on the old screen doors he and his dad had fixed at his house when he was growing up. Figured that might hold better than just nailing the plastic up. The work went slowly with one eye, and as the light grew dim, he moved the sunglasses to his head. When he finished the windows, he made short work of the hose reel with a couple long sheetrock screws he found in one of the jars on the bench, and then he moved on to the step railing.

The railing took the longest. It was dark by the time he started on it. There were no lights in the shed and no spots outside, only a small outside light beside the kitchen door with a dim bulb. And it was cold as hell. Luckily the broken railing was made of stock two-by-fours, so he didn't have to rip anything to size, just cut to length. And angles. But he made the angles by eye, and they turned out pretty good. There were just enough three-inch nails in one of the jars to secure it all pretty well, and he was putting the last few tools back in the shed when Sherry's headlights came down the road and her car spun into the driveway.

"Shit, I wish I didn't have to work so damn much." She slammed the car door and smiled at Rank. "How are you doing? Glad to see that you're still here. I forgot to take your keys."

Rank was closing the shed doors. "I'm a man of my word, Sherry, and I just finished up." He latched the doors and turned toward Sherry. His sunglasses were on his head. "Cold out here, and I'm not used to working outside in the cold. Hope I did okay."

Sherry had already walked to the steps and was looking over the railing. She gave it a few tugs. It didn't budge. "Damn. This is nice work, Todd. Real nice." She looked at Rank. Her brow furrowed for a moment when she saw his eye, but she said nothing. She walked around the side of the house. Rank followed.

"Oh my god, where'd you get the little strips of wood? That's really smart."

"I ripped them from some two-by-fours that were laying in the shed. Hope it was okay to cut them up."

She glanced at him and shrugged. "Sure it is. What the hell am I gonna do with them anyway? Best to use 'em whatever way we can."

She walked around to the hose reel, pausing to admire the other two windows as she passed each. She reached down and pulled on the hose reel.

"Well, I'm impressed, Todd. Thank you." She turned and looked at him. "Thank you so much. What say we go inside and have a few beers?" She didn't wait for a reply; she walked right around the front of the house and ran up the steps and into the kitchen. Rank struggled to keep up. The girl moved fast.

Just like earlier, she disappeared into the hall just as Rank came through the kitchen door. "Open us each a beer, would you?" she hollered from the bedroom.

Rank took two Buds from the fridge, opened them both, and set one on the counter. He set his on the table and waited. It wasn't long before she came back down the hall, now in pajamas and a robe. She picked up her bottle and clinked his.

"Here's to a mutually beneficial arrangement," she declared, pronouncing "mutually beneficial" slowly as if being a little sarcastic. She took a long drink. Rank drank too.

"I've been thinking about the next bunch of stuff I need done. Got a long list in my head. If you're willing, the work could last a week or two, and I'll probably think of more."

Rank sipped the beer. "I'm in. Lay it on me."

Sherry nodded her head toward the hallway. "You know plumbing?"

Rank shrugged. "What I don't know I can learn."

She led him to the bathroom. "The toilet's been leaking for a long time. Dunno what it needs, but something. I hope I don't need a new toilet. The sink and tub faucets both leak too."

Rank could see that the vinyl floor was stained around the base of the toilet and that there were rust stains under both faucets where water had been dripping.

"Unlikely. You probably just need some new parts to stop the leaking. The floor might need some work, though. Looks like the leaks might have done some damage."

Sherry stared at the floor for a few seconds then took another drink from the bottle. "That would suck." She looked at Rank. "I don't think there are any plumbing parts in the shed. We might need to buy that stuff. You can look in the morning." She raised her beer bottle toward the bathroom door, motioning them out. Rank backed out and stepped aside. Sherry led him back into the kitchen. She finished her beer and rinsed the bottle in the sink. She took another from the fridge, and before closing the door, turned and asked, "Ready for another one?"

Rank held his bottled to the light. "Not yet."

Sherry pulled a chair from the table and sat. Rank followed suit.

"In the morning I'll give you some cash for the hardware store. There's a good one right around the corner from the bar I work at. If you need to, you can get the parts. You think that'll work?"

Rank nodded and then sipped his beer. "I'll need directions too. Hard to remember exactly how to get back there after only one trip out."

"I can give you directions tomorrow too. I'm too tired to do anything right now." She took a long drink from the bottle. Then she stared at Rank for a moment. "I think this might just work out, Todd. Might just work." She took another drink. "You mind me asking about your eye?"

Rank had forgotten that the sunglasses were off.

"Accident at the range. Trying a buddy's pistol, wasn't ready for the kickback." The story had worked before.

Sherry winced. "Looks sore." She took another drink, her eyes still fixed on Rank. "You'll want some time to figure out what's next for you too, right?"

Rank nodded again and sipped the beer.

"That's okay. You should feel free to do what you need to do. I don't expect you to spend twenty-four hours a day fixing my house." She tipped the beer back and drained it, then rose from the table. "That's it for me." She rinsed the bottle and put it in the sink. "The sheets and blankets on your bed are clean, and the towels are under the bathroom sink. I'll see you in the morning." She walked down the hall and shut her bedroom door.

Rank finished the beer, rinsed his bottle, and took another from the fridge. He sat back down at the table.

*She's all business*, he thought, a little surprised. And mad at himself for revealing his eye without a solid plan for explaining it. He sipped the beer. He thought about his next steps. How he might figure out where Margo was. It was clearer now than ever that he hadn't been planning, that the whole thing had been seat of the pants and he'd been lucky. Tomorrow he'd put some serious thought to it. Tomorrow he'd have time to think.

# CHAPTER THIRTY-ONE

Margo didn't sleep. She was too scared. Too uncomfortable with her hands bound at her sides and the chain digging into her when she tried to turn. Dazzle snored and talked in his sleep. Gibberish. As the light began to stream in through the filthy windows, she looked around the room. Looking for a way out. Any way she could find.

Dazzle farted and rolled in the bed. He coughed. He was starting to wake up. Margo pretended to be asleep and closed her eyes to slits. She hoped they were closed enough to fool him, but she wanted to keep them open enough to watch what he was doing.

"You awake?" Dazzle whispered.

No response from Margo.

"Shit." He got out of bed and stretched. Facing Margo, his junk staring her in the face. She wanted to squeeze her eyes shut, but she didn't dare move. Even a tiny bit. Dazzle took his time putting his clothes back on.

He whispered again, "You awake?"

No response. He left the room. Margo could hear him open the cooler and close it, then open a can.

He walked to the table and sat. Still and quiet. Thinking and drinking the beer. After few minutes, he got up and left the motorhome. Margo heard him talking to the dog as he walked away.

All she could do was wait. And think. She'd tried to loosen the cuffs during the night. No luck. She rolled to her side, swung her feet to the floor, and stood. The chain pulled on the cuff belt. Heavy. She stood and shuffled past the bathroom toward the front of the motorhome. The chain was long and heavy. She got to the table before it began pulling against its mounting on the bedroom floor. She threw her body weight against it a few times. It held fast. She sat on the edge of the dining bench and thought.

Before too long, the door swung open and Margo saw a foot jam against it. Dazzle appeared in the doorway carrying a McDonald's bag and a cup tray with two coffee cups. He looked up at Margo sitting in the booth and smiled.

"Hey, you weren't awake before. I got us some food."

He set the bag and cups down on the table. The dog was starting into the motorhome. Dazzle turned and shooed it out, then closed the door.

"Dazzle, you've got to let me go. This isn't right."

Dazzle didn't look up; he was busy removing the cups from the cup tray. "We're friends. I'm protecting you." It sounded as if he was trying to convince himself.

He set a cup down in front of Margo, raised his eyes but not his head, and stared at her silently. Margo stared back. She didn't know what to say.

Dazzle sat back, reached into his pocket, and pulled out a key. It was a ridiculously simple key, like something Margo thought she'd seen in an old black and white cop movie. A small ring for a grip and a rod with a small rectangle at the end.

Dazzle stood. "Turn so's I can get at your hands."

She shifted on the bench and turned. Dazzle stepped to her, bent down, and unlocked the cuff that was attached to the belt. Margo could lift her cuffed hands away from her body.

Dazzle sat down. "There. You can drink your coffee now. And eat."

He reached into the bag and removed two egg sandwiches. He set one in front of Margo, then a napkin.

Margo shook her head. A silent no.

"You ain't hungry?"

Margo shook her head again.

"Jeee-zus. You gotta eat." Dazzle sat back and took a big bite of his sandwich.

Margo brought her hands to the table and picked up the cup. She raised it to her mouth, but instead of taking a drink, she pushed it into the air toward Dazzle. It was an awkward toss due to the restraints, but it caught Dazzle by surprise. He didn't move fast enough. The cup landed on its side on the table in front of him, the lid came off, and hot coffee splashed onto his chest and lap as the cup completed its journey and tumbled off the table. Dazzle scrambled off the seat, too late.

"Fuck!" He stood leaning against the back of the bench with his arms raised at his sides, his muffin sandwich in one hand, looking at his coffee-soaked clothes. A few moments of silence, then Dazzle slowly raised his head and stared at Margo. Silently. As he stared, his eyes softened and he started to grin. He stepped out of the booth.

"Thes okay; I understand. But you'll come around when you see thet I'm helpin' you."

Margo stared silently.

He pointed the sandwich toward her hands. "Put 'em back down."

She shook her head, another silent no.

He stared for a minute, his face reddening and his grin suddenly menacing. He put the sandwich on the table and walked around to her. With a sudden lurch, he grabbed her neck with one hand and squeezed. Margo couldn't breathe. She held her hands up toward his face. He took his hand from her neck as quickly as he had grabbed her and grasped her upraised wrist. He pulled her hands down quickly and snapped the cuff to the chain between her handcuffs, locking her hands back down at her waist.

He walked back around to his side of the table. "You'll see."

He put the key in his pocket, picked up his sandwich and coffee, and walked to the door. He turned to her and nodded toward the table. "You go ahead and eat." He winked and smiled, opened the door, and walked out of the motorhome.

# CHAPTER THIRTY-TWO

Myslewiec dug down into the bag for the last Krazi Kurl, then licked his fingers and tipped the bag back to empty the crumbs into his mouth. He'd been living on Krazy Kurls and coffee for a couple days now. Not good. He was tired. Miller's chair gave out a long, low squeal as he turned around behind Mysliwiec.

"Dido." Not as jacked up now, Miller was tired too.

"Dido, I've got another one. In Western New York. In a hotel right off Route 90. The maids found her. Suffocated."

Mysliwiec turned. "What makes you think it's our guy?"

"Hard to say, Dido. Nothing really I guess. Maybe I'm just chasing my tail. They can't find her vehicle. Maybe he killed her and stole it. I dunno."

Miller turned back to his desk.

Mysliwiec thought for a few seconds. "Western New York, huh?"

Miller grunted, "Yeah," without turning around.

"That's in the direction we think he went. Can you get a description of the vehicle from New York?"

"I'll get on it." Miller still didn't turn around.

# CHAPTER THIRTY-THREE

The truck bounced down the narrow road toward Cotswald, Kris driving and Silas in the passenger seat. Both silent. When they reached the intersection with the main road, Silas pointed to the right. Kris turned and accelerated over the bridge and up the short hill. Faster than the speed limit. Much faster.

"Next left, Kris." Silas was hanging on tight to the door handle.

Kris barely slowed before turning left. The tires squealed just a little on the asphalt.

"Christ, Kris, you're gonna get us killed!"

"Sorry, Silas, lost my head." Kris slowed to a reasonable speed.

"Newton Road is just up here on the right." Silas held fast to the door handle, not really trusting Kris to stay near the speed limit.

A fence appeared on their left a little ways down Newton Road. Stockade style. Old. Lots of rot and gaps. Even at the speed they were traveling, Kris could see glimpses of cars in the junkyard on the other side. The fence had probably been erected on orders from the town years ago. A way to hide the ugliness of the junkyard. It hadn't been maintained.

The fence was on a small rise above the road and about ten feet back. Spruce and cedar trees grew here and there along the fence, along with patches of scrubby brush. Blackberries, Kris thought. He pulled to the side close to the fence corner and turned the engine off.

"I'm gonna scope it out a little, Silas. Wait here."

Silas nodded.

Out of the truck, Kris crossed the road and picked his way through some brush toward a large gap in the fence near its furthest corner. Thorns on the blackberry bushes grabbed at his shirt and pants as he picked the branches away and moved them aside. After a few slow yards, the brush gave way to clear ground, and he took the last few steps to the fence. The stockade fence was indeed just window dressing; it covered a heavy gauge chain link fence that actually protected the yard. At the first large gap in the stockade, rusted hulks of abandoned cars sat very close to the opposite side, and the view beyond was obstructed. Kris walked to his right to find more gaps.

After about fifty yards, a small gap that extended about two feet off the ground offered a view of what Kris thought might be the end of the motorhome, and in another ten yards, a larger gap revealed the side of the motorhome with the entrance door as well as a decent view down the row between junk cars. Kris guessed that was in the direction of the yard office. He watched the motorhome for a few minutes. All was quiet except what sounded like a small engine running. Maybe a generator. No signs of life.

He turned and surveyed the immediate area. He knew he would have to stake this out for some time and needed cover so as not to raise suspicions of anyone passing by. It was fairly wide open, a little flatter and wider near the fence than at the far end and the drop to the road a little steeper. No brush here; it was clear except for a couple medium-sized hemlock trees. A small moss-covered log lay at the top of the steep bank about six feet away from the fence. This would help conceal him some if he was to lie on his stomach. Across the road, he spotted a fallen hemlock. Its branches might make a decent blind. He stumbled down the incline and jogged back up the road to the truck.

"Whad ya find, Kris?" Silas looked anxious.

"A spot where I can watch the motorhome for a while, Silas. Hope there isn't more than one motorhome. I need my bow saw to get some branches for a blind. I might be here for a while, and I don't want to raise any eyebrows."

Silas nodded.

"And best to drop you back anyway. Violet might be wondering where you went to by now."

Silas nodded again. Kris started the truck, made an awkward three-point turn, and drove back to Chance Pond.

Kris dropped Silas at his door and drove over the hill to his cabin. He unlocked the shed, found his bow saw, and locked the shed back up. Inside the cabin, he found a pair of binoculars and an old snowmobile suit that he'd bought when he first got the camp but never really wore. He put on the snowmobile suit and a wool watch cap, took his warmest winter gloves, and drove back toward Newton Road.

He found a safe spot to park the truck in a trailhead parking area on Route 47, about a half-mile from

Newton Road. A simple wood sign painted brown with yellow block lettering announced that the trail led to Makwa Ledge and that it was a 1.7-mile trip that ascended 800'. Kris backed the truck in at an angle so it was pointing toward the road. He looped his binoculars around his neck, grabbed his bow saw, and started walking toward Newton Road. He didn't lock the truck. There was nothing in it that anyone would want, and he figured he might need to jump in fast on his way out.

He found his spot pretty quickly, walked across the road, and began cutting limbs from the fallen hemlock. The first few he laid on the ground for insulation and then a few more he leaned against the moss-covered log and adjusted to create a blind about four feet tall. Satisfied that he would be concealed from the road, Kris got comfortable on the hemlock branches and began to watch. It was just about lunchtime.

# CHAPTER THIRTY-FOUR

Sherry tossed two twenties on the table, grabbed a notepad and pen from a kitchen drawer, and scribbled directions to the hardware store. She spoke the directions as she wrote. "Right out of the driveway, left at the T, left again at the next T. Then you're straight on Seventy-Two for a few miles, then right on Fifty-Six." She looked up at Rank. "That's a T intersection too. Easy."

Looking back at the notepad and still scribbling, she continued, "Take Fifty-Six into town, left at the first lights, and then straight through the next lights. Hardware store is on the right, park on the street in front or they have a lot out back." She straightened up, tore the sheet from the pad, and tossed the pen and pad back in the drawer. She put the sheet on top of the twenties. "That's for the plumbing parts if you need any. I don't work my night shift tonight. Maybe we can grab some dinner." She took her coat from the hook near the door and was gone before she'd finished putting it on.

Rank sat silently at the table sipping his coffee. He heard the car start, back out of the driveway, and pull away. He was impressed with the way she gave directions. *Not like a girl at all*, he thought. And she was a force, pure energy. And pretty sexy. He shrugged to himself and finished his cup, poured himself another, and took it out to the shed to survey the tool situation.

They were disorganized and not very well taken care of, but there were plenty of tools in the shed. Everything he'd need from what he could see. He pawed through the wood leaning against the wall and found a couple small pieces of quarter-inch plywood and one piece of half-inch. He figured between the two they'd cover any floor repairs needed from the toilet leaking.

It took Rank about an hour to disassemble the toilet and the faucets and to figure out what he needed to make the fixes. He grabbed the two twenties and the directions from the table, put on his coat, and headed for the truck. It started a little harder than he remembered, but it started.

The ride to town was quick. It wasn't a complicated route, and Sherry's directions were spot on. Good thing, because Rank's thoughts were elsewhere. He was becoming conflicted. He liked Sherry a lot, liked feeling as if he was appreciated. He felt comfortable at her place, comfortable with her. But then there was Margo. And the things he'd done on the way here.

It had all been a flurry of rage. Unthinking. Spontaneous. Bad. He looked around the truck, and fear gripped him. *The truck. Shit.* A sudden realization that he was driving a truck owned by a woman he'd killed. It had been long enough now that her body had been found, probably by a maid at the hotel. The truck could have been identified, and they could be looking for it. He'd never swapped out the license plates. His calm was gone. Paranoia set in.

He got to the intersection in town where Sherry had told him to turn left. The light was red. Cars going straight through began to line up next to him, and cars turning left began lining up behind. He was exposed and trapped. To his left and across the street he saw the fire station. The police station was probably nearby. The light was long. Rank looked straight at it, focused, convinced that every person in every car around him was staring at him. They knew. He was sure of it.

The light turned green. Rank eased into the turn, not too fast, not too slow, careful not to draw extra attention to the truck. Traffic waiting at the opposite light was heavy, a couple pickup trucks, a Jeep, a Buick, a Prius, a Ryder rental truck, and a police cruiser. Rank looked straight ahead as he passed, stiff, holding his breath and self-consciously keeping an even speed. He watched the cruiser in his rear view mirror. No unusual movement. Clear. This time.

Beekman's Hardware was on the right just like Sherry had told him. He wasn't going to park the truck on the street, too visible. He passed the store, took a right into the back lot and pulled in between two Dodge Ram pickups. They were tall and would provide a decent screen, as long as they didn't leave before him.

The hardware store was big with multiple levels that were only a few steps up or down. Rank followed the signs to the plumbing department, up three steps and all the way to the back of the store on the right. A few other customers were wandering around, and he saw one clerk, but nobody looked at him funny. He found what he needed plus a can of WD-40 to help loosen up some of

Sherry's rusted tools. He hurried through the checkout and back to the truck.

His trip back to Sherry's place was nerve wracking but uneventful. Somehow he managed to hit the lights in town on green and never had to stop. By the time he got to Route 72 he'd relaxed a bit. He'd seen no police cruisers and almost no other traffic once he got away from town. Might have been that the bucolic scenery passing on Route 72 had also played a part in relaxing him.

The bathroom work was easy and went without a hitch. He took his time and made sure everything went together as it should. He was just starting to clean up when Sherry got home from work.

"Hello?" she hollered from the front door.

"In the bathroom. Just finished," Rank answered.

She appeared in the doorway, coat still on. "How'd it go?"

"Easy," Rank answered, "toilet needed a new wax ring, and I put in a new tank seal too, just to be safe. The faucets both needed new ball valves. The hardware store you sent me to had everything. I cleaned up some of your tools too and started sorting them a little. You shouldn't leave them all scattered, makes it take longer to find something 'cause you have to search all over for what you need."

Sherry was a little embarrassed. "I don't know shit about tools, Todd."

Rank smiled at her. "We'll have them back in order soon enough."

"I can't tell you how much I appreciate what you're doing for me, Todd. You had a great day, and mine wasn't terrible either. How about I get cleaned up and I'll buy you some dinner and a few beers?"

"That'd be great."

Sherry turned out of the bathroom. "There's a nice little place out near Chance Pond." She spoke as she walked into the kitchen and took off her coat. "Natty's. A friend of mine runs it. Good prices and decent food. And real laid back. And you'll like Cindy; she's easy to talk to. I haven't seen her for a while." The closing of her bedroom door punctuated the end of her sentence.

# CHAPTER THIRTY-FIVE

Margo didn't know how long she'd been sitting at the table. Her thoughts had carried themselves along outside of time. She was deeply confused. Dazzle was more complicated than anyone she'd ever met. Insane, absolutely. Threatening, sometimes. Gentle, quiet, easy to like other times. But here she sat, handcuffed and captive, with no idea what he had planned for her.

The sun had been streaming through the window over the kitchen sink earlier, but it was higher in the sky now. She was hungry and a little cold. She hadn't touched the food he'd left. She hadn't even tried to free herself. Something about Dazzle's reaction to her throwing the coffee at him had softened her. She no longer felt the degree of danger that she had since he kidnapped her. Instead, she was just very confused.

The door startled her when it swung open. His foot jammed against it to hold it open. He was trying to enter, keep the dog outside, and his hands were full, just like earlier. He managed to stumble in.

"Hey. You're still sitting there." He grinned, happy to see her.

Margo nodded.

He had a bag in one hand and a tray with two large cups in the other. He set them down on the table. "You didn't eat the breakfast." He sat down. Hard. He sighed. "I guess I don't blame you." He leaned forward and opened the bag and took out two sandwiches, both wrapped in paper. He set one down in front of Margo and one in front of himself before leaning back in the seat.

"You got to eat, Margo. I know I've made a mess of this, and I'm sorry. But you got to eat." He paused and sighed again. "If I unhook the cuffs from the belt will you eat a little? Please?" He waited.

Margo was even more confused. She tipped her head to the side a little, unconsciously. She nodded.

Dazzle got up and dug the key from his pocket. Margo turned so he could unlatch the cuffs. He sat back down, not as hard this time. He seemed pleased. He unwrapped his sandwich.

"This one's ham and thet one's turkey," he said pushing his chin towards the sandwich in front of Margo as if to point at it. "I like 'em both, but I figure you might not, so you choose the one you want."

Margo looked at Dazzle. "Turkey's fine. I like 'em both too." She unwrapped the sandwich awkwardly, raised half the sandwich to her mouth, and took a bite. Dazzle smiled and did the same.

They ate in silence for a few minutes. When Dazzle had finished the first half of his sandwich, he leaned back in the seat again, his signal that he was going to talk. "I jes want us to be friends. I don't have no friends, and you been nice to me at the bar." He paused.

Margo nodded, her mouth full. When she finished chewing, she replied, "It's no way to make friends, Dazzle, handcuffs and kidnapping and all."

Dazzle looked down at the table. "I guess." He picked up the other half of his sandwich and took a bite, picking his head up and staring at Margo while he chewed.

She felt like she might be getting through to him. "Maybe if you let me go we can start over and be friends the way most people are?"

Dazzle took another bite, thinking while he chewed. "I dunno about thet, Margo. I think I made too many mistakes by now."

"Well, you haven't hurt me, right?"

"I guess. Not bad anyway. Not so bad as whoever hurt you before me."

Margo realized that she still had bad bruising on her face and arms. "Yes, he hurt me real bad, Dazzle. He hurt me real bad. More than once."

Dazzle sipped from the straw in one of the cups, never taking his eyes off Margo. "He can't hurt you here. Nobody can hurt you here. This old motorhome is the place where nobody can hurt nobody."

"What do you mean?" She picked up the other half of the sandwich and took a bite. It tasted good.

"I mean thet this motorhome's the safe place. Nobody ever hurt me when I was in here. Nobody can hurt you while you're in here neither. They can hurt you outside here but not in here."

"Dazzle, people get hurt all the time. That's part of living. We can't stay in this motorhome for the rest of our lives just 'cause we might get hurt if we leave it."

Dazzle took the last bite of his sandwich and wiped his mouth with the back of his sleeve. "Sure we can. Well, not me 'cause I got to work. But you can. You can stay in here and be safe. I can bring you everything you need. You won't get hurt no more."

"You've got me handcuffed Dazzle. That's no way to live."

Dazzle smiled and nodded. "Once you get comfortable here and you know how safe it is, you're gonna want to stay and thet's when I'll take off the handcuffs. When you know it's your safe place too."

"What if I don't get comfortable, Dazzle?" She regretted saying it as soon as it left her lips.

Dazzle looked down at the table, his brow furrowed. He thought for a few seconds. "I dunno. I always thought you'd like it soon enough. I never thought that you might not." He looked up at her. His smile was gone. "You want to be safe, right? No more beat-ups like he did to you?" He pushed his chin toward her again, this time acknowledging bruises.

Margo nodded.

"I knew you'd come around to my way of thinking." He smiled again. "Hey, I got to get back to work. I got a few new wrecks thet I'm taking parts from and I want to get it done before we have dinner. I'm gonna surprise you with some real good food tonight." He stood and cleared away everything but Margo's cup. "I'll be back 'fore long!" He tipped his head in a quick nod, pulled the door open, shooed the dog away, and stepped out of the motorhome. The door swung shut.

Margo sat silently. She could hear Dazzle talking to the dog just outside. It sounded like he was feeding the dog the leftover food. He sounded relaxed. Happy. She might have begun breaking through. Talking to him like a friend, that was the key. That was the way she might break through. She looked down at her cuffed hands, one holding the cup. Dazzle had forgotten to clasp the cuffs to the belt.

# CHAPTER THIRTY-SIX

Kris hadn't waited long. The motorhome had been still for the first half hour, no one coming or going. But then, suddenly it seemed, Dazzle came along, both hands full and a Doberman beside him. The dog was either anxious or excited, trying to stay too close and tripping Dazzle a little now and then. Dazzle was carrying a bag in one hand and a tray with two cups in the other. He struggled with the motorhome door, partly because the dog was jumping up to try and get whatever was in the bag. After a few unsuccessful tries, he finally swung the door open, kicked the dog back out of the way, and entered the motorhome.

Kris thought back to what Cindy had told him about being in the motorhome. If Cindy was right and Margo was in there, she'd need to eat. Dazzle probably didn't cook much, so he might live on takeout. That could be what was in the bag. That most likely was what was in the bag since he also had what looked like two cups of soda. And the dog was jumping at the bag like it had food inside. The dog wouldn't be acting like that if there wasn't food inside the bag.

Two sodas. Not one. Two. Dazzle might drink two sodas with lunch. People did stuff like that. Kris had seen people buy giant buckets of soda at mini markets, buckets that must hold at least two big cups worth of soda. But why would Dazzle come all the way out to the motorhome to eat by himself when he could just as well eat in his office? Assuming that he had an office. All businesses have some kind of office, so he must have an office. Of some kind.

Kris had to fight to keep himself from jumping to conclusions. This was too serious to make a mistake. He wanted to run right back to Natty's and tell Cindy that Margo was in the motorhome, but he couldn't be sure. He waited.

It didn't seem like long before Dazzle came out of the motorhome. Now with a crumpled bag. No, two bags. And the tray. The tray was empty. The dog jumped up, nearly knocking him over. Dazzle held the bags high, away from the dog. Dazzle shouted, "SIT!" and the dog sat. Dazzle set one bag and the tray on the ground and pulled something from the other bag. Looked like fast food wrapped in paper. A burger or a muffin sandwich, Kris couldn't tell. Dazzle unwrapped it and set it in front of the dog. He straightened up and looked at the dog. The dog looked back, holding fast but struggling to remain composed. It made short twitches toward the food but never took its eyes off Dazzle. After a few seconds, Dazzle said "okay" and the dog dove into it. The food was gone in a flash. Dazzle picked up the bags and tray and started walking away from the motorhome. The dog watched him for a second, then rooted around on the ground looking for any scraps that he'd missed. Satisfied that it was all gone, the dog trotted to catch up with Dazzle.

Kris was pretty sure that Cindy was right. Margo must be in there. He wondered how he kept her captive. She wouldn't be a willing party to this. She couldn't be. She didn't even know Dazzle. He trained the binoculars on the motorhome windows. Nothing. No movement. He set the binoculars on the ground in front of him. Sure, but not sure. He shook his head. He had to wait longer. He needed something more definite. He hoped that if Cindy was right, if Margo was in there, she was okay. He hoped that Dazzle hadn't hurt her. He hoped that he could get Margo out before Dazzle did hurt her.

He waited. His mind spun with the possibilities that his imagination brought forth. He realized that the sky had turned gray and he thought he felt a mist. A frozen mist, if there was such a thing.

# CHAPTER THIRTY-SEVEN

Rank cleaned up, put on a fresh pair of jeans and a clean t-shirt. There weren't many clothes in the bag he'd thrown together back in Michigan, but enough for now. He was sitting at the kitchen table sipping a beer when Sherry came out of her room.

She was wearing a white, long-sleeve, button-down shirt, unbuttoned enough to show a little bit of the lacy white bra underneath. The sleeves were rolled up, and she had a bunch of silver bracelets on one wrist and a silver watch on the other. A pair of faded, bootcut jeans were stretched tightly over her thighs and ass, and a pair of high-heeled, Western-style boots made her look a little taller and a little slimmer. *A damn nice package*, Rank thought.

"Ready, Todd? I'm starving!" Sherry was moving fast, as usual. Rank slugged the last of his beer, rinsed the bottle, and grabbed his coat. Sherry was already getting in her car as he stepped onto the porch and closed the kitchen door.

She drove as fast as she moved, confident and comfortable with the surroundings. Rank held tightly to the door handle as she sped out of the driveway and then made a rolling stop at the main road and turned right, away from town. Open pastures quickly turned into woods, and houses thinned as the road climbed a long, left-sweeping hill past a huge blue water tower. Soon, all traces of civilization had disappeared. The road twisted, turned, dipped, rose, and dove through darkness. Sherry concentrated, sawing at the wheel, braking hard into the turns, and accelerating hard out of them. Rank held tighter.

It wasn't long before small camps began to appear here and there and the road became level and straight. As suddenly as they had left her driveway, Sherry turned into a dirt parking lot in front of a low, dark building and ground to a halt. She shut off the engine, and they sat for a moment.

Sherry turned to Rank with a smile. "Fun, eh? Helps me relax. Driving fast through here I mean. Almost never a trooper, but you gotta watch close for deer and turkeys." She opened the door and paused before getting out. "Natty's, Todd. This is the place! Let's grab a beer and see what's on the menu."

She was across the lot and in the front door of the place before Rank had even closed his door. He was doing all he could just to keep up.

By the time Rank got through the bar's front door, Sherry was sitting at a table and was talking over the small crowd to a woman at the end of the bar. They obviously knew each other. The woman came to the table just as Rank sat down.

"Hey, Cindy, this is Todd." Sherry motioned with her head.

"Nice to meet you, Todd." Turning to Sherry, she said, "It's good to see you, baby. I need a friendly face right now. What can I get you guys?"

Sherry ordered two Buds, and Cindy went to fetch them.

"Cindy and I were in school together. We ran with the same pack. We weren't too close back then, competing for the same guys and all, but we got closer once we were out of school and I got married. I come in here once a week, or so I think."

Cindy returned with the beers. She looked at Todd. "Check the menu on the wall. Prime rib's the special tonight, but we always have burgers and sandwiches." She looked back at Sherry. "How you holding up, babe?"

Sherry sipped the beer. "Same, Cin. Nothing's changed. 'Cept Todd here. He's passing through town on his way to fuck-knows-where, and he agreed to take care of some work at my place in return for a place to stay for a few days. He's done real good so far, fixed a lot of broken shit."

Cindy smiled. "I figured Todd to be your new boyfriend."

Sherry laughed. "He IS kinda cute, ain't he?"

Cindy nodded. "I guess, but I can't see all of him. You mind me asking how come you wear your sunglasses inside at night, Todd?"

"I accidentally put my eye out, and it's pretty gross-looking. If I take 'em off, all your other customers will run for their cars."

"Well leave 'em on then! Sorry to hear that you hurt yourself."

"It ain't that gross," Sherry chimed in. "Cin, you're still working this place alone aren't you? Didn't find new help yet? Need me to come in on my nights off and help?"

"I did find a new girl, but she ain't working tonight. She'll be back, though. Tell me what you want to eat, and when I bring it out I'll sit for a few and tell you about her."

They both ordered burgers and more beers, and Cindy went into the kitchen. The place wasn't too busy. Rank counted a half dozen other customers. He was having a hard time with small talk. Sherry was looking good, and she intimidated him. He let her do most of the talking, telling him about her day at work. She spoke like she moved, fast and steady. Non-stop.

Cindy came back with two large plates. The burgers were huge, and the plates were overflowing with fries. She set them down and rushed back to the bar to grab two more beers, and when she returned, she sat next to Sherry, across the table from Todd.

"So I stumbled on this new girl, and I have to tell you, she's great. Works her ass off and doesn't seem like she's uppity at all, real down to earth. The customers love her."

Sherry asked, "What do you mean you stumbled on her?"

"Well, there's these two folks who come from Rochester, got a camp up on French's Pond. She came in with them a few days back. I guess they found her at a rest stop somewhere on the thruway. She was really beat up, black eye and bruised face and arms. Running from some asshole in Michigan."

Rank couldn't believe what he was hearing. He nearly choked on the bite of burger he was chewing.

"You okay, Todd?" Sherry asked as Rank coughed.

He took a drink from the beer and wiped a tear from his cheek. "Yeah. Shit. Swallowed wrong. Sorry about that."

Cindy continued, "Anyway, she stayed with them for a few days up at French's and then they brought her here. They didn't know I was looking for help. She didn't know where she was going anyway, and she liked it here, so she hired on. She's staying in the apartment I've got over on the far end of the bar." Cindy nodded her head in the direction of the apartment.

Rank swallowed another mouthful of burger and wiped his mouth. "Did you say she's from Michigan?"

Cindy nodded. "She's got a kid going to school up at Paul Smith's. She says the only thing she could think of when she took off was getting close to the kid."

Rank nodded and took another bite.

"So where is she tonight, Cin?" Sherry asked.

"Not really sure. I just know that she needed a night off. And like I said, she works hard and she's already earned it."

The front door swung open, and a guy in a snowmobile suit rushed in. He and Cindy made eye contact, and her face turned white. She tipped her head toward the kitchen, signaling him that they would go in there. "Excuse me, guys. I got to talk to this one alone. Nice to meet you, Todd. Be careful of Sherry here."

Cindy shook Rank's hand, got up from the table, motioned to the guy in the snowmobile suit again, and rushed into the kitchen. He followed.

Sherry looked at Todd. "She's real nice, ain't she?"

Rank nodded and replied, "Yeah, real nice. Let's get some more beers." He took another bite of his burger.

# CHAPTER THIRTY-EIGHT

Margo stood next to the table, her hands in cuffs but no longer bound to the belt. She pulled the belt around her waist until the buckle came to the front and then unbuckled it. The belt and chain fell to the floor. She moved to the motorhome door and opened it.

Dazzle was on the other side. "What the—"

Margo had already committed to stepping down and out of the motorhome and couldn't stop herself. She collided with Dazzle, and they both fell to the ground.

"Shit!" Dazzle reacted quickly, grabbing Margo by the arms as he rose. Margo tried to roll out of his grasp, but he managed to keep holding her arm with one hand while he shuffled behind her to gain a better position. He grabbed the one arm with both hands and pulled her arms to the side. The dog growled and nipped at her pant leg. Margo stopped fighting. A cold mist was falling.

"I thought I could trust you, girl." Dazzle was out of breath.

Kris was watching as Dazzle returned and was startled to see Margo tumble from the motorhome and the ensuing scuffle. He watched through the binoculars, hoping Dazzle wouldn't hurt her and unable to do anything to help.

"Stand up." Dazzle tugged Margo's arm lightly as she worked her way to her feet.

"I just needed some fresh air, Dazzle. I thought you left me unhooked on purpose."

Dazzle didn't reply, he just tugged her arm and motioned to the motorhome with his head. She nodded. Dazzle held the motorhome door with one hand and her arms with the other, and they climbed back in. She let him put the belt and chain back around her waist and connect her handcuffs to the belt. He fell into the bench at the table. Margo sat back down across from him.

"Dazzle, I think you might be right. I might be getting more comfortable here. I wasn't going anywhere, I swear."

Dazzle stared at her, expressionless.

"You did leave me unhooked on purpose, right?"

Silence.

Margo pleaded, "Talk to me, Dazzle."

No reply. Dazzle got up from the table, fetched a beer from the cooler, and sat back down. He drank slowly and deliberately, never taking his eyes off Margo, not speaking a word. He set the beer on the table, got up, and left the motorhome. Margo sat in silence. Wondering. Afraid.

Kris watched Dazzle leave the motorhome. He barked a couple of commands to the dog, and the dog lay down directly in front of the motorhome step. Dazzle walked back toward the yard office. Kris scanned the motorhome windows. No movement. The dog lay perfectly still too.

Inside the motorhome, Margo sat in silence. It couldn't have been more than a few minutes before

Dazzle came back, now with a roll of duct tape. He swung the motorhome door open, climbed the steps, and jumped back in. The dog never moved.

"No, Dazzle. Please."

"Jes yer legs."

He didn't ask her to swing them out from under the table. He wasn't in the mood for negotiations. He dropped to his knees, shuffled under the table, and quickly wrapped the tape around her ankles. It was tight. He rose, set the tape down beside his beer, slumped back into the seat, picked up the beer, and took a swig. He smiled, and shaking his head, he whispered, "No more games." He took another swig from the beer. "Like I told you before, I got some work to finish and then I'm coming back with some dinner for us." He tipped the can high and finished the beer. "I guess it won't be quite like I hoped, but we'll eat together anyway."

Kris watched Dazzle exit the motorhome once again and walk away, this time with the dog. Now he was sure that Margo was there, and he knew the situation was becoming urgent. Time to act. He got up from his blind and jogged to the truck.

# CHAPTER THIRTY-NINE

"Sure as shit, Cindy, she's in the motorhome." Kris stood just inside the kitchen door, far enough to be hidden from the bar customers. Cindy paced in front of the grill. "He has her in handcuffs."

"Holy crap. He never handcuffed me. We gotta get her out of there."

"Police, Cindy. We need to get the police involved."

"No, Kris, not yet. I still don't think he's gonna hurt her."

"She's in handcuffs, Cindy. He's already hurting her."

Cindy paced. "Can you get through the fence, Kris? Can you cut a hole in it?"

"I suppose. I have an old bolt cutter at the cabin. But shit, Cindy, this's already gone too far. We need to get the police involved."

"All we need to do is get Dazzle away from her for a while. Buy some time. How long would it take you to cut through the fence and get her out?"

"You're talking crazy, Cindy. This is something that the cops need to be doing. We start fucking with this and it can go bad fast."

"He's not going to hurt her, Kris. I know him." Cindy stopped pacing and looked up at Kris quickly. "I've got an idea. We can get her out and nobody gets hurt. Listen."

Kris leaned against the wall, arms across his chest, resigned to listen but in protest.

"He's not going to hurt her tonight, so we wait till morning when there's daylight. Too hard in the dark, and my story ain't so believable until the morning."

"Story? What story?"

"Listen. Somebody always gets here real early now to open the place. Lots of the hunters get here real early to eat before they go out. Hunting season, right? So tomorrow it'll be me. I'll open the place. I'll call Dazzle and tell him that we got a truck that's been left in the lot. Dunno who it belongs to. Abandoned sometime during the night. Crossways, right in front of the door. Blocking the door, and customers are gonna be coming. Like it was somebody drunk during the night."

"Jesus, Cindy—"

"No, no, listen to me, Kris. It's hunting season. Crazy shit like that happens during hunting season. Lots of these guys come up here to cut loose. They do stupid shit like that. Dazzle's towed trucks away for me before. So I get Dazzle to hustle over here and tow that truck for me. Needs to be in a hurry so the truck's gone before too many customers get here. It'll take him a half hour just to get up here."

"And then when he gets here there's no truck?"

"That's right," Cindy nodded, "that's right, because the guy came and took it."

"Jesus, Cindy, he isn't that stupid, is he?"

"No, Dazzle ain't stupid. But he's towed for me before and it's hunting season. He'll believe me, and even if he don't, he'll already be up here by then, and it's gonna take him another half hour to get back to the yard. It'll give you an hour to cut through the fence and get Margo out."

"I dunno, Cindy. How about you go talk to Dazzle? Tell him you know he's got Margo?"

"Shit, Kris, put his back up against the wall? I don't know what he'd do then. Trust me, once Margo's out of there and safe, we can deal with Dazzle."

"Police would be better, Cindy. We're no fucking swat team."

"Kris, we call the police now and we start a shitstorm and we fuck up Dazzle and maybe some of the rest of us too and who knows where it ends. I don't want to fuck up Dazzle."

"You hear what you're saying, Cindy? He kidnapped Margo. He already fucked up. What about Margo? How's protecting Dazzle gonna help anything? What if he hurts her? Or worse."

"He ain't gonna hurt her, Kris. Nobody up here's a saint, you know. Dazzle's the same as the rest of us. He's just weird. Does weird stuff. We get Margo out of there and then I set down with Dazzle. Talk with him. It'll be over, and it'll stay over. I know him, Kris. And Margo's tough; she'll be fine. We can do this and nobody'll get hurt and we don't need to get anybody all wrapped up in Dazzle's shit."

"Cindy, what do you know about Dazzle that you aren't telling me?"

Cindy tipped her head a little and stared back at Kris in silence. Tears began to well in her eyes. "I'm sorry, Kris. Please trust me just a little longer. This'll work,

Kris. This'll work." She shook her head as the tears began to trickle down her cheeks.

Kris thought for a minute. He was confused as hell. This felt like a bad idea to him, but Cindy was persuasive, and Kris always had a hard time saying no to a woman. Especially Cindy. Especially when she started crying.

"Please, Kris."

"Fuck me up the ass!" Kris muttered. It was his favorite curse when he was frustrated. He shuffled.

Cindy tipped her head, wondering where the hell that had come from.

"Okay, Cindy. Goddammit. We'll do it. But I sure hope this doesn't go wrong. I need a whiskey."

# CHAPTER FORTY

Kris knew he wouldn't be able to sleep, and he figured Margo might not be as safe as Cindy thought. He ran it over in his head as he headed back to the cabin to get his bolt cutters and a flashlight. They'd planned it out at the kitchen end of the bar over a glass of whiskey. Cindy drank one too. Unusual for her.

The plan had Cindy calling Dazzle a little before five the next morning to come tow the truck. She'd ask him to come quickly since it would be blocking the door and the hunters would be coming in for breakfast. After she talked to Dazzle, she'd call Kris to let him know. Kris would have already pulled his truck close to his stand, near where he was going to cut through the fence. After Cindy's call, he'd either wait for Dazzle to leave the motorhome or he'd wait fifteen minutes if Dazzle didn't come out of the motorhome. They guessed that they could be pretty sure where Dazzle was by watching for the dog; it would be dozing near Dazzle, wherever he was. Probably near the motorhome step if Dazzle was in there, just like it did when Kris had watched the motorhome earlier that day.

When the coast was clear, Kris would cut through the chain link fence, get Margo out of the motorhome and into the truck, and get her back to his cabin. Taking her to Natty's or her apartment there was too risky, Dazzle might go right back to Natty's, and Cindy wanted a chance to talk with him before he saw Margo again.

As he drove back to the trailhead parking lot, Kris ran it over and over in his mind. Still didn't make sense to him, far too dangerous, but he couldn't turn Cindy down. She knew Dazzle better than most anybody he supposed. Kris decided he'd take Margo back to the cabin the long way, up Route 56 and down Stark Road, because he figured Dazzle would head straight back down White Hill to Cotswald as soon as he found out there was no truck to tow. He didn't want to take a chance that Dazzle would see them if they passed each other.

Back at his blind, Kris settled in for a long, cold night. It was dark; he wasn't worried about being seen. The motorhome was lit outside by a small utility light on a pole, the generator was running, and lights were on inside and over the door of the thing. He scanned the windows with his binoculars. Margo's profile was clear in the largest window near the door of the motorhome. Not moving much at all, but she looked fine. Kris guessed by her position and the position and size of the window that she was sitting at the motorhome's table.

Inside the motorhome, Margo was wondering if she'd been wrong about breaking through to Dazzle and what was in store for her. Dazzle had been gone for a quite a while, longer it seemed than any other time since he'd kidnapped her. She didn't have to wait much longer.

Kris saw movement in the corner of his eye and lowered the binoculars. It was Dazzle, a pizza box in one hand and a duffle bag in the other, and the dog next to him jumping at the pizza box, both walking toward the motorhome. He watched Dazzle put the duffle bag on the ground in front of the motorhome step, open the door, hold it with one leg while he grabbed the bag, straighten up, and step into the motorhome while shooing the dog out with his foot. The dog stared at the door for a few seconds as if expecting it to open again, and then, realizing that it wouldn't, laid down in front of the motorhome step.

Inside, Dazzle set the duffle bag on the motorhome floor and the pizza box on the table.

"I got us a pizza from Sefton. Might be the best you ever ate. You want a beer?"

Margo thought for a second and nodded. Worst case it might help take the edge off, best case Dazzle might let his guard down if he thought she was relaxing. Dazzle grabbed two wet cans from the cooler, sat down across from her, and opened them both. He took a sip from his and stared at her, puzzled that she didn't pick the beer up and take a drink.

"My hands are cuffed to my waist, Dazzle."

"Oh shit." Dazzle jumped up and dug the key from his pocket. "Sorry 'bout thet. I forgot." He unlocked the cuffs from the belt, shoved the key back in his pocket, and sat down. He swung the pizza box open and turned it so they both could reach in for a slice. The open lid rested against the motorhome window.

"Dig in!" He smiled and then turned and rummaged through the duffle bag, pulling out a baggie full of marijuana, a big glass pipe, and a lighter. "Pizza's always better when you got a good buzz I think." He filled the bowl of the pipe, held the lighter to it, and took a long drag. He held the pipe toward Margo and motioned with his head, holding the smoke in as long as he could.

Kris could see Dazzle now through the motorhome window. He was sitting across from Margo. He watched Dazzle smoke from the pipe and then hold it over the table. The box lid covered part of the lower edge of the window, but Dazzle held the pipe high as if to avoid whatever was below it. When Margo reached for the pipe, he could see that her hands were still cuffed. Dazzle stood, leaned over the table, and held the lighter to the bowl as Margo toked.

Kris was stunned. Margo was getting high with the guy.

"The weed's my own," Dazzle bragged. "I grow a little for myself, and my friends." He took another long toke and spoke while holding it in. "It took me years to come up with this hybrid, and it's real powerful."

He handed the pipe back to Margo, no need to keep the lighter on it now. She pulled the smoke into her lungs and held it. It had been years since she'd smoked marijuana, since before she'd been pregnant with Kyle, and she was already feeling it. She started to wonder if this was going to be a good strategy.

They shared the pipe, sipped beers, and ate pizza without much talk. When the bowl was finished, Dazzle carefully emptied and cleaned it and returned it to the duffle bag. As he sat up, he thrust his hands below the tabletop and squirmed around a bit. Margo heard his belt unbuckle and his pants zipper pull down. He levered up with his back on the bench and pulled his pants down. When he sat back down his right hand stayed below the table.

He took a sip from his beer. "I need your help in a little while." He was playing with himself.

"Oh, Dazzle." Margo shook her head. She was scared. "Please don't make me have sex with you."

"Ain't like thet, Margo. We're friends, right? I never make my friends do anything they don't want to do."

"You got me tied up and handcuffed, Dazzle, and I don't want to be tied up and handcuffed."

"I know, but that's to protect you." Dazzle smiled, sipped the beer, and kept on playing with himself. "The help I need is you to be my buddy system. Keep me from going too far."

"I don't know what you mean."

"I like to get high and then get myself off. Best way to get off that I know is to run out of breath right when I finish. I read how to do it on the internet. Lots of guys use ropes and stuff, but that's too complicated for me. I use a plastic bag."

"Oh, Dazzle, no." Margo shook her head again, no longer quite as scared and now somehow sympathetic.

"I know it's weird, Margo, and mostly I do it when I'm alone. But it scares me 'cause if I go too far I might kill myself." He sipped the beer. "I read about a lot of guys that killed themselves accidental."

Margo looked at him silently, his hand working a little faster under the table.

Dazzle continued, "But because we're friends, I'm okay with you knowing about it, and you can help me by making sure the bag comes off my head and I don't kill myself. Would you do that for me? Please?"

Margo was overcome by pity. She knew he was dangerous, and she knew he might hurt her at any moment, or maybe worse, but he was pathetic, and she was starting to buy into his friend thing. She was actually starting to believe him. She was actually starting to think that his holding her here wasn't so weird after all.

"Dazzle, you promise you're not gonna hurt me? Promise that after you're done you'll let me go?"

"I ain't ever going to hurt you, Margo. I promise. But I can't let you go just yet. I promise, I really, really promise, that when you're ready I will let you go, but I don't know when you'll be ready jus' yet."

Margo thought. He was trusting her. Maybe she was breaking through. Could she stand another night here? "Dazzle, promise me that when you're finished you'll clean everything up yourself and you'll let me go to bed."

"I promise. I'll clean up and you can go to bed." Dazzle smiled.

Margo took a deep breath. "Okay. Tell me what I have to do."

Dazzle leaned over and pulled a plastic grocery bag from the duffle bag. He stood away from the table, his pants at his knees and his erect penis in plain sight as he stroked it. He shuffled next to Margo and got down on his knees.

"Take this bag off my head as soon as I come if I pass out and can't do it myself." He stopped masturbating long enough to fit the bag over his head and adjust it to his liking, then he wrapped his hand around his penis again. Margo watched as he got down to business.

# CHAPTER FORTY-ONE

Sherry had one more beer and Rank had two while they finished eating. Small talk, awkward when they had to raise their voices over the rising and falling din in the place. Rank tried his best to concentrate on Sherry, but his mind was spinning in disbelief. Margo was here somewhere. He'd found her.

Rank concentrated hard on the ride home. He needed to remember the way back to the bar. Not difficult as it turned out. As remote and undulating as the road was, it was a straight shot from Sherry's place to the bar. Just the right turn away from town where her street met this road.

By the time they pulled into Sherry's driveway, they were both tired.

"Hell, Todd, I was thinking we might spend a little time getting to know each other better tonight, but I'm dragging."

Rank grinned. "Well hold that thought. I'm gonna be around a little while."

Sherry put her hand on his thigh. "Thanks, Todd."

He followed her out of the car, up the steps, and into the house. She wasn't moving as fast as usual.

"Tell you what, Todd, lemme get into my bathrobe and I'll show you a few more things that need doing around the house." Sherry walked down the hall unbuttoning her blouse. Rank pulled a beer from the fridge and sat at the kitchen table. She was back quickly, tying the bathrobe sash around her waist. Rank couldn't help but look at her bare legs and feet, exposed from the knee down. She noticed him looking.

"You like 'em?" She swung one side of the robe off her leg and stuck her leg out in front of her in an exaggerated pose. Her leg was muscular and smooth. All she had on under the robe was a tiny pink pair of lace panties. A little pubic hair was peeking out from the edge of the panties.

"Yeah, I like 'em." Rank took a swig from the beer bottle.

Sherry laughed and, without missing a beat, tossed the robe back in place and walked past him into the front room. "Lemme show you the next couple things that need doing."

Rank set the bottle down and followed. *Shit*, he thought, the image of Sherry's leg temporarily diverting his thoughts from Margo.

Sherry stopped at the front entry. "This door leaks air like crazy. Think you could put in some new weatherstrip?"

Rank nodded. "Easy."

She turned and pointed to the floor at her feet. A large rectangular area of slate sat in front of the door, between the carpet in the living room and the hardwood floor in the dining room. "Slate entry floor. S'posed to be kinda fancy except the grout keeps chipping away."

Rank offered, "Might not have been installed right the first time. I could just patch the grout, but it might chip back out."

"What's the right way?" Sherry asked.

"Right way will be to take the slate up and do it like it should be. I did it at my house. They make a thing called an uncoupling membrane that you put between the subfloor and the tile. That should keep it from chipping out after."

"Expensive?"

"Not so much as doing it over every year."

Sherry stared at the floor for a few seconds. "Okay, do it then." She turned and walked through the living room, into the hall, and into her bedroom. From the bedroom, she shouted, "I'll give you money in the morning." She closed the door.

Rank fell back into the chair at the kitchen table, finished his beer, and took another from the fridge. His thoughts were bouncing around. He'd be going to the hardware store again in the morning and he was worried about being stopped by the police. Before the hardware store, he figured to go back up to the bar and scope it out in the daylight. Find a place where he could watch without being seen. He took a swig from the bottle.

Margo. Finding Margo and getting revenge was his priority. But this Sherry chick was nice. He liked her. And she kind of made him feel like he could start over. He looked around the kitchen. It was worn. Lived in. Not even very well built, the cabinets anyway. But it was neat and clean. Sherry made an effort. A new start would be really nice.

Except he'd killed two people. No taking it back now. His thoughts turned back to Margo, and he finished the beer.

# CHAPTER FORTY-TWO

Kris clicked the rubber button at the base of the flashlight and aimed it at his watch. Four twenty-two. There had been no visible movement in the motorhome since the lights went out around ten the night before, and Cindy would be calling Dazzle soon. Probably a good time to get the truck. Kris tossed aside the boughs that helped keep him warm, stood up, and stretched. A thin, cold mist was falling.

As he walked back to the trailhead lot, he recounted the previous night's events. Margo and Dazzle had sat across from each other, eaten, drunk beers, and shared a few pipes. Probably weed. At some point, Dazzle had seemed to get down on his knees beside the table and put what looked like a plastic grocery bag over his head. He'd been still for a few minutes, and then he'd disappeared, fallen backward as far as Kris could tell. At the same time, Margo had lunged forward toward the floor, and after a few more minutes, they'd both returned to the seats across from each other and shared the pipe again. Then they'd moved to the back of the motorhome, and the lights had gone out. It was confusing. Margo wasn't acting like she was a hostage, even though her hands were clearly bound. And Dazzle wasn't acting like a hostage taker. But then again, Kris didn't know how hostage or hostage takers were supposed to act.

By four forty-five, Kris had the truck where he wanted it and was kneeling at the fence with the bolt cutters ready and his cell phone in hand. The phone began to vibrate at four fifty-three.

A light came on at the back of the motorhome as Kris answered in a whisper, "Yeah."

It was Cindy as expected. "He's on his way, Kris. I just talked to him. Says he'll be up here in about twenty minutes."

"I'll get to work like we planned." Kris didn't want to talk much for fear of waking the dog. It was asleep in front of the motorhome steps.

"Good luck, Kris. Be careful."

"Okay." Kris hung up and waited. Within seconds, the light in the front of the motorhome came on and Kris saw Dazzle rush across toward the door. The light went out, the door opened, and Dazzle jumped down the step to the ground next to the dog, startling it. The dog growled as it rose and followed Dazzle toward the front of the yard. Kris was relieved that the dog went with Dazzle. One less complication.

As soon as Dazzle and the dog were out of sight, Kris tore a few rotted boards from the privacy fence to expose as much chain link as possible and began cutting. One link at a time. Slow but easy. Before too long, he had a hole that was big enough to walk through in a crouch. He moved a few stray branches aside to allow clear passage, and with flashlight in one hand and bolt cutters in the other, he stepped through the fence and into the yard.

He walked toward the motorhome slowly and carefully with the flashlight turned off. He wanted to stay as invisible as possible. The light in front of the motorhome only created indistinct shadows across the already dark ground at this distance, making it very hard to see objects in front of him. He did well, picking his way carefully. Silently. Near the motorhome, he began to rush and his concentration slipped. He stepped on something tubular-shaped that rolled under his foot. He lurched and instinctively put his hand out toward a pile of tires and hubcaps at his right front, dropping the bolt cutters and knocking a few hubcaps from the pile. The hubcaps made a racket as they hit the ground and rolled. The dog barked in the distance. It'd heard the noise. Kris hoped that the dog was alone, hoped he didn't have to deal with Dazzle. Too complicated. He grabbed the bolt cutters and crouched behind the tire pile, watching for movement in the direction that Dazzle and the dog had gone.

Almost immediately, the dog came running through the yard at full pace, barking and growling. Kris had no choice but to face it head on. He stood and walked around the pile directly toward the dog. He dropped the flashlight, took the bolt cutters in both hands, and readied them at his side, prepared to swing. The dog came to a sudden halt directly in front of Kris when it realized he wasn't moving. Kris hauled the bolt cutters back and swung them hard at the dog's head. It never reacted; its head snapped hard to the left as the bolt cutters struck it. It's legs buckled. It collapsed.

Kris' heart raced as he found his flashlight. He trained it on the dog, making sure he wasn't a threat, and then on the motorhome. He walked carefully. Listening. The yard was still as he crossed, only the generator growling. He stopped trying to be quiet when he reached the motorhome. Time was critical, and from this point on there was no need to be quiet. He threw the door open and stepped in.

"Margo! It's Kris. Cindy's friend."

"I'm in the back."

Kris was in the back room with Margo by the time she finished saying it. She was on the bed, partly upright. Startled. A heavy comforter covering her, a propane heater blasting beside the bed.

"I'm handcuffed. They're hooked to a belt at my waist."

Kris threw the comforter aside and trained the flashlight on the cuffs.

"Lemme stand up."

Kris stepped back to give her room.

"Unbuckle the belt and release the chain," Margo said as she stood and turned her back to Kris.

The chain fell to the floor and the belt swung to Margo's front when Kris unbuckled it.

"Okay," Kris motioned with the flashlight, "turn around and let me see the cuffs."

Margo turned and raised her hands, the belt hanging from the cuffs on her wrists. Kris cut the chain between the cuffs. The belt fell to the floor. The cuffs remained on her wrists, but Margo's hands and arms were free of the belt.

"My truck's on the other side of the fence. Let's go."

They left the motorhome door open as they stepped to the dirt.

"Walk slowly, right behind me. There's all sorts of stuff scattered on the ground."

They passed the dog, still not moving. Kris shone the flashlight on the ground at their feet, and they began picking their way toward the fence. At the fence, they both crouched to get through, Margo first then Kris. The ground was clear down the bank to the truck.

# CHAPTER FORTY-THREE

Cindy was waiting in the Natty's doorway when Dazzle pulled up in his flatbed truck. She walked out to meet him as he stepped out.

"I'm sorry, Dazzle, the guy came and got it just a few minutes ago. I figured you were almost here anyway so I didn't call you.

"It's okay, Cindy. Shit happens."

"I'll pay you for your trip, though, and I'll make you breakfast for your trouble. C'mon inside"

"Thanks, Cindy, but I'll come back later. I gotta get back to the yard." Dazzle's cell phone rang. He answered, "Zelenco," then paused and listened. "Yeah. Okay. On Fifty-Six near the Snow Bowl. Got it. It'll take me twenty. Right." He closed the phone and put it in his pocket. "Guess I ain't getting back to the yard yet. Accident on Fifty-Six, and I got one of the cars."

Cindy nodded. "Well, next time you get a chance, you get back up here and there's a meal with your name on it, okay?"

Dazzle nodded and climbed back in the truck.

# CHAPTER FORTY-FOUR

"We'll go the long way, Margo. Out Seventy-Two to Fifty-Six, up to Stark and in the back way. We'll go to my cabin. Cindy's gonna bring some of your stuff over. You can stay at my place for a day or two. Cindy needs to get your window replaced. She wants a chance to talk to Dazzle too before you settle back in over there." Kris looked at the road while he spoke. Margo said nothing.

Kris glanced at her and continued, "I thought we ought to get the police involved. This rescue shit is dangerous. Cindy insisted we do it this way."

Margo turned to Kris. "Cindy's right. This way's best."

"The guy kidnapped you. And put you in handcuffs."

"He's mixed up. Really mixed up. He didn't hurt me, and he never would have. I'm not saying that I'd rather have stayed, I'm grateful for the help. Just that Dazzle ain't so bad."

"Jesus." Kris shook his head.

As they turned onto Route 72, the back end of the truck broke loose. Kris fought with the wheel to keep it from spinning, and it straightened out.

"Black ice. We gotta take our time." He slowed.

They rode in silence up Route 72. It was slow going, a fine mist freezing to spots on the windshield. At the intersection with Route 56, they turned left to go south.

The sky was beginning to brighten. Margo watched as they passed houses, rolled over a bridge with a wide river on the left, and soon came to camp roads marked by white sign posts stacked with the names of the people who owned camps there.

The flashing lights surprised them both as they eased around a bend and came to a stop behind two other pickup trucks. An accident. Police directing traffic through the single open lane. Their turn to pass came quickly, and they were back in motion. Kris kept a slow pace to make a lot of room between him and the truck in front. The black ice made him anxious. He didn't need an accident now. They were still a long ways from the camp.

Dazzle left Natty's and headed for Stark Road, then north on Route 56. He too was being cautious, but Dazzle was never much for just watching the road. It was getting light enough to see inside passing cars and trucks. Dazzle was daydreaming, looking at the people inside other vehicles, imagining where they were going.

On a long, left-hand bend that passed beneath a power line, Kris slowed as he passed a truck off the road to the right. The black ice had caught someone else out. Kris normally would have stopped to help, but today there was no time to waste, and there was already another vehicle stopped and people were helping. Kris didn't notice the flatbed truck pass him in the opposite direction.

Margo noticed.

"Kris, I think that was Dazzle!"

"No it wasn't, I saw all three real good. None were Dazzle."

"Not the people helping that guy. Dazzle was in the truck that passed us just now going the other way. I swear it was Dazzle."

Dazzle noticed too. He got a good look since they were going slow. It took a few seconds to register. "Jesus Christ!" He swore out loud, very upset. It was nearly a mile before the next side road. When he reached it, he turned around.

Margo's insistence convinced Kris quickly.

"Think he'll turn around and come after us?" Kris asked as he alternated from watching the road ahead to watching the rear view mirror for signs of Dazzle.

"I don't know, Kris. I hope not."

Kris clenched his teeth, gripped the wheel tighter, and sped up. It was only a minute or two before they turned left on Stark Road. Ten miles to the cabin from here, and all of it over a narrow, undulating road badly in need of repair. A challenge to drive quickly on the best day, extra challenging with ice on the road. Kris did well for the first eight miles, but he got caught short coming down a hill with a bend that wound through a small cluster of hunting camps. The truck spun. They came to rest with the back of the truck in the ditch.

"Shit." Kris stepped on the gas but the tires spun. "We might be hung up on something. I'll take a look." He stepped out to survey the damage. Margo came around the front of the truck from her side.

"Don't see it hanging on anything. Just stuck in the mud and the ice."

He opened the driver's door and took the rubber mat from the floor, then ran around to the passenger side for the other mat. "These might get us a little traction." He put one in front of each rear tire, pushing them as far under the tires as he could. He looked up at Margo. "You get in the driver's seat and I'll climb into the bed to add some weight. Go real easy when I tell you."

Margo climbed in. She was a confident, experienced driver. She'd begun driving with her dad long before she had a driver's license, and she'd been in plenty of tough spots. She watched Kris in the rearview. He nodded at her and yelled, "okay." She eased the throttle. The tires spun.

She eased off, rolled down the window, and stuck her head out. "Jump up and down while I give it a little gas." Kris nodded. When she felt the truck begin to bounce, she eased the throttle again. This time it worked. The tires spun, but they caught the mats and gained enough grip to get the truck back on the road. Margo got out and ran around the front and into the passenger seat. Kris threw the mats into the truck bed and got back behind the wheel.

"You're good."

"I've been in plenty of car trouble."

Kris looked in the rear view mirror. "We're in trouble now." He accelerated. "I think that's Dazzle coming up behind us."

Margo turned to look out the rear window. Dazzle's truck was coming around the bend and moving fast. "Oh no."

"Maybe we can get far enough ahead so he won't know where we turn off to the cabin. We have about a mile to Chance Pond Road, then another mile to the cabin. He's in a damn big truck, must be a handful on the ice."

Kris sawed at the wheel and drove on the edge of control for the entire mile to Chance Pond Road. He concentrated on the road, never looking in the mirror. Margo gave him a play-by-play. They opened up some distance from Dazzle, but not as much as Kris had hoped.

As they rounded the last bend before Chance Pond Road, Kris yelled, "Here comes our turn. How are we?"

Margo turned to Kris and said, "He's out of sight right now. He might not see us turn."

The back end of the truck came around hard on the ice as Kris yanked the wheel to the right. He came off the throttle and sawed at the wheel. The truck caught a clear spot on the road and jerked violently when the back end stopped sliding. He hit the gas and they shot up the hill.

Margo was right, Dazzle didn't see them make the turn, but he slowed as he came to Chance Pond Road and caught a glimpse of the back of the truck as it disappeared around the bend up the hill. He followed.

Kris worked it up and over the hill, around the sharp bend at the top, and down the hill toward the camp road. The truck jerked suddenly as it hit small patches of ice. Not enough to lose control, but more than enough to keep Kris nervous. They were close, and he wasn't going to slow down now.

The entrance to the camp road came into view, a row of mailboxes just before it and a tower of name signs on the far side. Kris figured they'd made it, but he didn't think about the changing angle of the road as it neared the mailboxes. He drove too close to the ditch, and the truck found the angle. The truck changed direction without warning and slid off the road without losing any speed. The truck bounced into the edge of the ditch and came to a sudden and violent halt when the front end slammed into the rise where a culvert that ran below the camp road began. The airbags went off with a loud pop, and all went silent as the truck filled with fine dust.

"Margo, you okay?"

Margo was dazed. She nodded and whispered, "Yeah, okay. You?"

"Yeah, I'm good."

They sat in silence for a moment, their minds working through the suddenness of the impact.

"We'd better get out, Margo."

She'd just raised her head toward Kris when the truck suddenly lurched violently again, the sound of crushing, tearing metal filling the cabin. They were both thrown forward into straining seatbelts and bounced back haphazardly. Margo landed on Kris who was lying sideways on the seat.

"What the fuck?" Margo screamed.

They untwisted and sat up. Kris yelled, "We gotta get out!"

He pushed at his door, but it wouldn't budge. "Mine's stuck. How about yours?"

Margo's handle released the latch, but her door was bound too. She threw her shoulder against it. Nothing. She slammed it again. The door opened reluctantly, metal grinding on metal where the truck's cab had been compressed by the impact. Margo jumped out into the wet weeds. Kris shuffled across the seat and did the same.

Kris's truck was bent badly, the front of the bed and the back of the cab pointing toward the sky. Dazzle's flatbed was stuffed into the back of pickup bed. Dazzle was at the wheel of the flatbed, visibly shaken. He saw them standing beside the crumpled pickup and jumped out to the road.

"Margo, you shouldn't have left me!" he grimaced. "I thought you was my friend!" Dazzle was walking on the road along the side of the wrecks in their direction. Dazzle was on one side of the wrecks, Kris and Margo on the other.

Margo hollered, "I am your friend, Dazzle! I am your friend!"

From behind them on the camp road came a high-pitched screeching sound. Kris had heard it before.

"Brendaaa!"

They all turned at the same time and saw an old woman in a nightgown and slippers walking as fast as she could on the slippery road. She was holding a brown lunch bag at shoulder level in front of her.

"Brendaaa!"

"Violet!" Kris called to her, "Shit, Violet!"

She kept coming, ignoring Kris. "Brendaaa!"

Dazzle instinctively retreated, startled by the strange woman. He self-consciously backed away and shuffled around behind the rear edge of the flatbed. He was hiding, shielding himself from her.

"Brendaaa!"

"Violet!" Kris called.

"A school bus, Kris." Margo nudged him and nodded toward the hill.

The school bus was coming down the hill, just like it did every school day morning.

"Brendaaa!" Violet kept on coming, waving the lunch bag in front of her.

"Violet! Violet!" Silas turned the corner of the camp road after her, slipping on the ice and catching himself.

Kris looked at the bus. It was already close enough that he could see the driver frantically trying to gain control. He'd found the angle in the road too. The bus was sliding on the ice.

Kris reacted quickly; he pushed Margo hard, away from the truck. She fell into the wet weeds. Kris fell on top of her.

"Brendaaa!"

"Violet!"

The sound of the impact was like nothing Margo had ever heard. A loud thud, muffled somehow, with more metal-to-metal tearing as the bus pushed Dazzle's flatbed further into Kris's truck and Kris's truck gave way and bent further toward the sky. Then silence.

Margo heard Violet gasp, "Oh my."

Silas stopped in his tracks, his jaw against his chest. More silence.

Kris and Margo lifted themselves from the wet weeds. Kris gave Margo his hand to help her stand.

"You okay?"

Margo nodded.

The bus driver was coming out of the bus with his hands to his head. "Oh my god, oh my god!" He fell to his knees on the road beside the bus and began to cry.

Kris turned and stepped up the ditch toward the truck to get a better view. Violet was standing absolutely still in the road, her hands at her side and the lunch bag on the road beside her where she'd dropped it. Silas was shuffling toward her whispering "Violet" softly, over and over. She didn't acknowledge Silas. Her eyes were fixed on Dazzle's truck.

Kris walked around the wreckage. At first he didn't see Dazzle anywhere, but the scene revealed itself as he passed Violet on the road. Feet and legs hanging from the end of the truck bed came into view. Loose. Ankles bent and the sides of his feet against the ground. Kris slowly moved closer. As he walked past the rear tires, he began to process the scene. He bent down to get a closer look. Blood dripped from the back edge of the flatbed. Confused, not understanding what he saw, he stood. Dazzle's torso lay against the truck bed. His left shoulder was propped against the short bed rail and his head turned toward the road. His eyes were open and vacant. Blood trickled out of the corner of his mouth and from his nostrils. The school bus had forced his torso against the edge of his flatbed. He'd been cut nearly in half.

# CHAPTER FORTY-FIVE

"I'm glad you called me first, Kris." Erik used his handcuff key to unlock the cuff on Margo's right wrist then the cuff on her left wrist. Margo rubbed her wrists. A siren whistled in the distance, coming closer.

"Troopers probably. The ambulance might take a little longer."

Erik turned to Margo. "So you're from Michigan? How'd you end up here?"

"I left my husband. I didn't plan to come here but my son's in school at Paul Smith's so I figured I'd get closer to him."

"Are the troopers going to see anything unusual when they check you out? Previous arrests or anything like that?"

Margo thought for a moment. "I've never been arrested, but the police back in Chelsea know me pretty well."

Erik glanced at Kris and back at Margo. "How's that?"

Margo lowered her eyes toward the ground. Away from Erik. "I've called them for help a few times. My husband beats me up."

Erik and Kris looked at each other.

"Jesus." Silas was standing behind the three. He startled Kris.

"Sorry, Kris, didn't mean to surprise you."

"Didn't know you were back Silas. Violet okay?"

"She's sleeping, Kris. Seeing that bus lose control like that shook her up real bad. And seeing the accident happen. Brings back the memories."

The siren was getting closer.

Erik walked to his car and put the cuffs on the passenger seat. A dark SUV with lights flashing and its siren howling crested the hill.

"Sorry to hear, Silas. Hope she'll be OK." Kris turned toward the oncoming SUV as it pulled to the side of the road across from the wreck. "Troopers are here."

Erik returned to Margo's side. "It's all going to be fine. They'll need to talk with you about the accident. Tell them the truth; you don't have anything to hide."

Margo nodded.

Not too long after the first troopers arrived, an ambulance came along with two tow trucks. And more troopers. They interviewed Margo, Kris, and Silas briefly and talked with Erik. The freezing rain had become heavier, and they decided to let everyone return to their cabins. The interviews would continue inside while the cleanup proceeded. Erik stayed with the troopers. Margo, Kris, and Silas walked down the camp road together.

"Your truck is history, Kris. What are you gonna do for transport?" Silas asked.

Kris stopped walking. Only Silas would call it transport.

Margo and Silas stopped too. Kris glanced back toward the accident. "Shit, Silas. Hadn't even thought about that."

"Why don't you use my truck until you get it figured out."

Kris looked at Silas and nodded silently. The three continued walking. Silas turned at his camp. "See you in a while I guess."

"Right, Silas. Keep an eye on Violet."

Silas raised his hand in acknowledgment and shuffled into his house. Margo and Kris walked up the camp road, over the hill, and down to Kris's place. They didn't talk, the only sound was the crunching of the icy dirt road under their feet.

Inside the cabin, Kris turned on the water kettle and quickly got a fire started. Margo sat in one of the rockers in front of the wood stove. Kris pulled a throw off the back of the couch for her, and she wrapped herself in it. By the time the burning kindling began to set the logs afire, the teapot whistled. Kris poured two mugs of tea, handed one to Margo, and sat in the other rocker. They sipped tea together and rocked.

"I never figured on any of this." Margo stared at the fire.

Kris looked at her. "Not much you can figure about life I guess."

Margo looked at Kris and shook her head. She looked back at the fire.

They sipped tea and rocked. The silence wasn't awkward; it felt alright. Kris let it be. She needed some space. The burning logs crackled and popped.

Margo finished her tea and set the cup on the small table between them. She looked around the cabin. "You've got a nice place here."

"Thanks. Had it for a few years now. Was just a vacation place when I got it."

"Now you're living here, huh?"

"Yeah." Kris sipped his tea.

Margo continued looking around the cabin. "I like it up here. I like it a lot. I'm planning to stay." She looked at Kris. "In this area I mean. It reminds me of where I grew up."

A knock on the door startled them both.

Kris responded, "It's open."

It was the trooper who'd begun their interviews at the crash scene. He opened the door enough to look in and asked, "Okay if we finish up the interviews now?"

Kris motioned with his hand as he got up from the rocker. "C'mon in." He walked toward the door as the trooper entered. At the stove, Kris picked up the teapot to make sure it had enough water, returned it to the stove, and turned on the burner. "Cup of tea or coffee?"

The trooper shook his head, "No thanks." He looked at Margo then back at Kris. "It'll be best if we do the interviews alone."

"Right," Kris said as he turned to Margo. "You want another cup?"

"No thanks, I'm good."

Kris turned the water off. "I'll run up to Silas's place while you two talk. You be okay, Margo?"

Margo nodded. Kris put his coat on and started out the door.

"How long you need?" Kris asked, looking at the trooper.

"About a half hour I'd guess. Based on what I know already, it looks pretty routine. The fatality makes the interviews more important, though."

Kris nodded, stepped out of the cabin and onto the front deck, and closed the door.

# CHAPTER FORTY-SIX

Morning came with a struggle. Rank hadn't slept at all. He heard Sherry moving around and forced himself out of bed. She'd already brewed a pot of coffee. He filled a mug and sat at the kitchen table just like he had the night before, except this morning Sherry was moving at top speed again.

"Here's some cash. Hope it's enough." She took five $100 bills from a plain white envelope and set them down on the table in front of him.

Looking at the bills Rank said, "Shit, should be more than enough." He looked up at Sherry. "I hope they have everything in stock. Little hardware stores like the one in town might not keep something like the tile membrane on the shelf. They might have to order it."

"How about Lowe's? They keep that kind of thing?"

Rank replied, "Yeah, Lowe's would probably have it."

Sherry turned to the coffee pot and filled a mug while she replied. "There's a Lowe's in town. You remember the bar I work at?"

"Yup."

"Okay." Her mug filled, she turned toward him and leaned her back against the counter. "Drive toward that bar, but instead of turning into the parking lot, stay straight. Lowe's is on the left about a mile and a half further down."

"Perfect." Rank nodded and raised his mug as if to toast. Sherry stepped toward him, leaned in, and clinked her mug to his. She took a sip, set the mug on the counter, and hustled back down the hall. Rank watched her walk. Tight jeans and the suede vest. Her bar outfit. Her hair moved lightly on her shoulders as she walked, and her ass moved more than lightly. She looked good to him. She stirred something in him.

She came back out quickly without the envelope.

"I'm busier than fuck-all today, Todd. Working both jobs. I won't be home between. It's too far to drive for a short break. I'll grab a bite in town. I should be back around eight." She downed the last of the coffee and rinsed the mug in the sink. "Be good now. And hey, if you want, stop in on the way to Lowe's and say hi." She winked at him, grabbed her coat, and was out the door before he could reply.

Rank finished his coffee, took a quick shower, and got to work figuring what he needed. He measured the tiled area of the floor to get the square footage, measured the door for the weatherstrip, and left the house. The truck started hard, but it started. He turned right at the intersection and drove away from town, toward the bar.

Driving the truck over the winding roads that lead to the bar was an adventure. The steering was vague, and Rank was having a hard time concentrating. He entered corners with too much speed and often came out of corners on the wrong side of the road. To make things worse, Sherry was screwing with his mind. Too nice. Too sexy. He couldn't stop thinking about her.

His thoughts turned back to Margo when the road straightened. He remembered that it straightened close to the bar, and sure enough, the bar appeared ahead on his right. He slowed as he neared, looking on both sides of the road for a good place to park and watch from. The bar's parking lot was half full. All pickup trucks. He passed it and came to an intersection on his left. The sign read *Chance Pond Road*. A short ways up the road was a pull off with what looked like telephone equipment at the base of a pole. He turned up Chance Pond Road and into the pull off.

There was room behind the pole for his truck. Not screened very well from Chance Pond Road, but not at all visible from the bar, he figured. He got out and looked around. He'd be visible on the road. More than visible. Someone walking in pickup truck country would get noticed fast. He turned to the woods beside the truck. It wasn't too dense. He carefully picked his way into the brush and down a gentle slope in the general direction of the bar. A few minutes of stepping around fallen logs and picking through blackberry bushes landed him in a stand of evergreens near the road. He found a clear spot of ground behind a large tree trunk, and there he sat, watched, and waited.

The spot was good. He could see the entire parking lot and the front entrance of the bar clearly. But he was a little too far away to easily make out faces. He also was worried about getting in and out of the spot in darkness. He decided to buy a pair of binoculars and some brush clippers to clear a trail. And a flashlight. After watching hunters come and go for an hour or so, he decided to get to Lowe's and get his supplies. He couldn't stay here all day; he wanted to get as much of the work done as he could. To keep Sherry happy.

The drive into town from Natty's went quickly; he couldn't stop thinking about Sherry. Being around her was taking the edge off. So was the work. Before he realized it, Sherry's bar was on his left. He turned into the side street and then the parking lot and parked the truck. He sat for a moment and took it in. The same parking lot where he'd parked a couple days before when he'd met her. That day he'd been angry. He wasn't as angry now. He climbed out of the truck.

As he closed the truck door, he suddenly felt exposed. He turned and scanned the surrounding area. No police. None that he could see. He pulled his hat brim down closer to his eyes, stuffed his hands in his coat pockets, and tucked his chin down into his chest as he walked around to the street and into the bar.

It wasn't busy. A couple people at the bar, nobody at any of the tables. Sherry turned as she heard the bar door open.

"Todd! C'mon over here!" She motioned and pointed at a stool near the drink prep station. She was arranging beer glasses on a shelf below the liquor bottles. He pulled the stool out and sat down.

"I can serve beers or liquor, but it's kinda early. I have coffee or soda too. Whatever you want, it's on me." She was smiling and her eyes were sparkling. She looked younger than he remembered.

"Coffee'd be great."

She nodded and turned to fetch a cup. "Cream and sugar?" she asked while she poured, her back to him.

"Black's good."

She set the cup in front of him then rested her elbows on the bar and her chin on her elbows.

"I'm tired as hell."

She didn't look tired to Rank. "Sorry to hear. You look good."

She smiled. "Thanks. Are you on your way to Lowe's or on your way back?"

"On my way there. I guess I might be tired too. Took me a long time to get my ass moving this morning. Sorry about that."

She stood quickly. "Damn, Todd, are you kidding me?" She rested her hand on his forearm. A tingle went through him. "You take all the time you need. Remember what I told you? There ain't no hurry about this. I'm grateful that you're doing it at all." She paused. She let her hand rest on his forearm a little longer, then rubbed it gently, cocking her head just a little to one side and looking straight into his eye. He was starting to get an erection.

She smiled, took her hand off his forearm, and turned back to the sink. She reached in and pulled out another glass. "It's gonna get busy soon. We always get a good crowd for weekday lunch." She placed a glass on the shelf as she spoke.

Rank sipped his coffee. Sherry made small talk while she worked. He didn't have much to say, but it was alright. He was comfortable just being near her. She seemed comfortable too. It felt to him like they'd known each other for a long time.

Rank finished the coffee and stood. "I'd better get going, lots to do on that floor you know." He dug into his pocket for some money.

"Stop that!" Sherry was smiling. "I told you it was on me. No money from you."

"Are you sure, Sherry?"

"Don't be stubborn. Get on out of here. I'll see you tonight." She gave him another wink. She liked to wink.

"Thanks. See you tonight." He stood awkwardly behind the stool, not really wanting to leave. She nodded, smiling, and motioned her head toward the door.

"Right." He walked out to the truck.

He found Lowe's easily. The tile membrane was in stock. 108 square feet. Enough to do the job with some left over if he was careful. It cost a little over $200. He also got tile adhesive and found a weatherstrip for the door that looked like it would work. He was almost at the checkout when he remembered that he needed a few supplies for his stand across from Natty's too. He found the garden department and picked out a large hand pruner.

After he finally checked out, he drove to Walmart, the same Walmart where he'd spent his first night. He bought a small pair of binoculars, an LED flashlight, and batteries. Supplies in hand and his head spinning from being around Sherry, he headed back toward her place.

# CHAPTER FORTY-SEVEN

"C'mon in, Kris. Violet's still sleeping so we need to stay quiet." Silas spoke in a hushed tone as he turned and began walking down the hall. The two walked quietly past the bedroom door and into the living room.

"Tea, Kris?"

"No thanks, Silas. Had plenty already. How's Violet doing?"

Silas shook his head as he sat in his overstuffed recliner. "I'm worried about her, Kris. That was a bad thing to watch. She saw it all."

"Was bad. Really bad. Bad way to go."

Silas stared silently at the floor between them.

"Trooper's talking with Margo right now."

Silas looked at Kris. "He just left here. Wants to talk to Violet when she feels up to it. I told him it might be a couple days. Says he'll come back."

Kris nodded.

"Kris, I have to tell you that I have mixed emotions about what happened to that man."

"You mean Dazzle?"

"I've heard people call him that. I know him by his real name, Dan Zelenco."

They looked at each other silently for a few seconds. Silas wanted to say something but was having a hard time with it.

"What is it, Silas? What's on your mind?"

Silas shifted in his chair. "Me and Violet knew Dan from way back. He was a few years older than our daughter, Brenda." Silas looked back at the floor between them. "I hate to see anyone die before their time, Kris, and the way Dan went just wasn't right. But he wasn't a good man, you know."

"How's that?"

"I don't think he had a lot of friends, Kris. Growing up I mean. There was a while when he came up here to the camp and played with Brenda. She was in grade school I think. He was a couple grades ahead. He rode his bicycle up here."

"Long ways to ride a bike, Silas."

"Yes it is. But he'd do it. Summertime, you know. Up here they could swim or use the boats or the wheelers. Brenda learned how to run the boats and wheelers real young, Kris. She could make some fixes on them too when she had to." Silas's eyes were beginning to fill with tears. He paused and took a breath. "Dan was coming up here near every day for a while. One day Violet needed a little help with something and she called for Brenda, but Brenda wasn't answering. Violet got worried and started out around the property to find her."

Another pause.

"Well, she found her alright. And Dan. Behind the metal shed down near the pond." He looked at Kris.

"That little fucker had her tied up and had a cloth tied over her mouth."

"Holy shit, Silas. Was he hurting her?"

"Not so much in a physical way, but she had some rope burns on her wrists for a couple days after Violet cut her loose."

Silas paused again and took another breath.

"Kris, when Violet came around the corner he was playing with himself."

Kris wasn't sure what he'd just heard.

"You mean he tied her up and he was playing by himself next to her?"

"Jerkin' off, Kris. He was jerkin' off right in front of her. He tied her up to make her watch."

"Holy shit."

"Tell me about it, Kris. Violet came around the corner right when he finished. He was right up close to her. He got some on her when he finished."

Kris didn't know what to say. The two sat in silence again for a few seconds.

Silas continued, "Violet sent him home and told him not to come back. Over the years we heard about him doing it again now and then. In public places. Pulling his thing out of his pants and playing with it in front of women."

"Did he get arrested?"

"Nope, never. There was something about Dan. I don't know if he ever got caught in the act. Almost seems like he got protected. I guess he was connected somehow. I don't know how."

"How'd Brenda take it?"

"I think Brenda took it fine, Kris. I never saw no bad effects I don't think. Violet didn't take it so well. Violet was pretty protective of Brenda anyway, but after that she kept a real short leash. Caused some friction between the two when Brenda got up into high school."

"I can imagine."

"Anyway, it all gave me a bad taste in my mouth about Dan. People say that he was doing even stranger things in his house by himself. I would have thought it was just rumors 'cept for what he did to Brenda."

"What kind of things?"

"Same kind only with sex toys. And pictures of young people."

"Child porn, you mean?"

"That's what the rumors were, Kris. And if it's true, well, maybe we're better off today than we were yesterday, if you know what I mean."

A low moan came from the bedroom, followed by what sounded like Violet calling for Silas.

"Violet's waking up, Kris. I'd better see how she's doing." Silas rose from his chair, and Kris followed suit.

"I should get back to my place, Silas. Trooper might be ready to talk to me now."

Kris followed Silas toward the bedroom. Silas paused at the bedroom door and let Kris pass by. Kris let himself out, shut the door gently, and walked back toward his cabin to talk with the trooper. He wanted to talk to Margo now too. About Dazzle. Silas's saying that it seemed like Dazzle had been protected stuck in his mind. Cindy was protecting him, no question about that, with her plan to rescue Margo when they should have let the police take care of it in the first place. And now he remembered Margo saying something back in the truck. Something like "Dazzle ain't so bad." He hadn't thought much of it then, but now it seemed like Margo was protecting him too, and she didn't even know the guy. What the hell was going on with Dazzle?

# CHAPTER FORTY-EIGHT

Rank drove past Sherry's street and straight to his new stakeout spot across from Natty's. He parked where he'd parked before, the old truck tucked in behind the utility pole in the little pull off on Chance Pond Road. He made his way through the woods carefully and slowly, cutting away blackberry bushes and clearing a rough path as he went. He sat where he'd sat before, but now with binoculars he could see the faces on the people coming in and out of the bar. Not so many this time of day. Customers were mostly hunters, he thought, and those who had come in for lunch were probably already back in the woods.

He sat and watched until he became too anxious to concentrate. He hadn't seen Margo coming or going, and he needed to get some work done before Sherry came home. He worked his way back up his trail to the truck, improving it little by little here and there on the way. It was easier now that he'd cleared a path. He knew it would be easy in the dark also.

The drive back to Sherry's place was uneventful, the monotony broken only once when a group of five turkeys crossed the road in front of him. No other animals. No people. Just woods and a few remote houses. He wasn't really paying attention. He was thinking about Sherry. She was changing him, and he knew it. He also knew that he needed to find a balance between finding Margo to settle the score and keeping Sherry happy. He just didn't know if there was a balance to be found.

Back at Sherry's, he decided to install the weatherstrip first. The slate was going to take some time and there were going to be a few hours when he wouldn't be able to walk on it, so doing the weatherstrip first would mean it wouldn't have to wait until the slate was finished. Plus it was easy. He could get it done before Sherry got home. She was happy when things got done. She was sexy when she was happy. He liked her happy and sexy.

The old weatherstrip came off easily; there wasn't much left of it. It was cheaply made and had been put on in a hurry. A few staples remained, and they were hard to remove. He pried them up with a flat blade screwdriver and pulled them out with a small pair of pliers. The pliers were one of the rusty old tools that he'd cleaned up a couple days ago. They worked like new now. Made him a little proud. Gave him a little satisfaction.

The new weatherstrip was made of white aluminum strips with white rubber tubing. The aluminum strips had pre-drilled slots every few inches. It was installed from the outside with the door closed. Rank had to cut the strips to length with a hacksaw and then screw them to the doorframe while they were pressed against the closed door. The slots gave him a little leeway, a good thing because trying to hold the strip, hold the screws, and screw them in all at the same time was a little tricky. He was finished in about an hour. It looked pretty good from the outside, and the door closed on the rubber tubes nicely. There was a new sound when the door closed that suggested it was tight. He picked up the scraps and returned the tools to the shed.

The slate was next, and it would be a lot more difficult. First he had to remove the slate, not too hard a job since the glue wasn't holding it very well in the first place. He still had to be careful not to break any, though, since he was going to reuse it. He used a hammer and a large putty knife and took his time. Slab by slab. He had to mark them too so that he knew which slab went where. When the slate was up and neatly stacked in the corner, he had to remove the excess glue that remained on the subfloor. That was the hardest part; it took a long time. All he had to scrape with was the same putty knife. Not ideal. He wasn't too far into scraping when his knees began to complain, and he'd already roughed up his knuckles pretty badly a few times, getting a little blood on the subfloor.

He was just about finished scraping when Sherry came through the door.

"Helllooo!"

"I'm in here. Doing the slate floor."

Sherry came in through the dining room after she hung her coat. "Jesus, Todd. How long you been down on the floor like that?"

Rank had shifted from his knees and was sitting on the floor. He smiled. "Kinda have to be down on the floor to do this sort of work."

"You've done enough, Todd. Time to rest a little. Let's have a beer." She turned and walked to the kitchen. Rank struggled to get to his feet and followed her, hobbling a little until he got used to standing and walking again.

Sherry reached into the fridge, grabbed two bottles, opened them, and handed one to Rank. They clinked the bottles and drank.

"I got the weatherstrip up first. Wanted that to be finished before I started the slate. The less cold air on the slate the better. You know, while the glue dries and then the grout." He took another drink.

"Makes sense," Sherry replied. She took another drink and stared at him. Not mad but kind of tired, he thought. She was different. Not so energetic. Not so happy. He took a drink too. Conversation was hard, so they didn't talk too much. She asked to take a look at the weatherstrip and asked if it was okay to walk where the slate had been. She liked it, but she didn't have much to say. She asked what was next on the slate. Rank explained, and she listened, but he could tell that she wasn't really hearing him. She finished her beer, walked into the kitchen, and rinsed the bottle in the sink. She turned and leaned her back against the counter. "I'm sorry, Todd. I ain't much company tonight. Shitty fucking day. And long. Tomorrow won't be so long. Just one job tomorrow. Just the bar." She paused and looked at him.

He didn't know what to say so he just took another drink of beer. She pushed herself from the counter with a resigned shrug. "That's it for me, Todd; I'm beat. See you in the morning." She walked past him and into the hall. Halfway down, she stopped and turned. "Thank you again, Todd. Please don't be angry with me. I really wish I could sit up and talk for a while. I'll just be bad company tonight." She turned, walked into her room, and closed the door behind her.

*Shit*, he thought. He finished the beer and took another from the fridge. He sat at the kitchen table and nursed it.

# CHAPTER FORTY-NINE

Kris met the trooper at the top of the hill between his place and Silas's.

"She's pretty upset."

"Wasn't an easy thing to see," Kris replied.

"Tell me about it." The trooper looked Kris square in the eye. "I've seen a lot of blood, a lot of dead folk killed in nasty ways, but I've never seen anyone cut nearly in half. I watched them EMS folks working with the body. Looked like the only thing holding him together were his clothes. I'm never gonna be able to look at a flatbed tow truck without thinking about that."

Kris nodded in agreement. "You wanna come back to my place and finish up my interview?"

The trooper shook his head. "No, I think I have almost everything I need. Just a couple more questions. We can talk right here if it's okay with you."

Kris nodded. The trooper took notes while Kris answered. The questions were all about the events leading up to the accident. Except one.

"So how long have you known Mrs. Rank?"

"Who's Mrs. Rank?"

The trooper looked up from the clipboard for the first time since he'd started asking questions. "The woman that's sitting in your cabin. She's Mrs. Rank."

"I only know her by Margo. I met her a few days ago when she showed up working at Natty's. Don't really know anything about her I guess, aside from her being held in very high regard by Cindy, the girl that owns the place."

"Based on what you and Mrs. Rank both told me, you put yourself in harm's way to get her out of that motorhome."

Kris nodded. "I tried to get Cindy to call the police. She wouldn't have it. Seemed like she was protecting Dazzle."

"That would have been the smart move. Calling the police I mean. You got lucky."

"Yeah, tell me about it. Was stupid."

The trooper nodded and studied his notes. "I think I've got everything I need. If I have any more questions I have your phone number. I'll call. I don't think I'll need to, though."

"Thanks." Kris extended his hand and they shook. The trooper walked up the camp road and over the hill toward Chance Pond Road. Kris walked down the hill to his cabin.

Margo was still in the rocker in front of the fire.

"Want another tea?" Kris turned the burner under the teapot on.

She looked up and smiled. The first time he'd seen her smile since he'd helped her out of the motorhome. "No thanks. I'll be up all night. Geez, you drink a lot of tea. Can't be good for you."

"Laying on the ground all night at Dazzle's place wasn't good for me. Tea isn't gonna hurt." Kris sat in the rocker next to Margo.

"I guess not. By the way, I never thanked you for pulling me out of there. Thank you."

Kris nodded. They both rocked for a bit without talking. When the teapot started to whistle, Kris got up.

"Jesus, I forgot to call Cindy." He poured water over the tea bag, set the pot down, and turned to Margo. "I'll call her now. You want to talk to her?"

"I'd better. Yes." Margo got up from the chair and walked across the cabin. She stood next to Kris while he dialed the phone. She stood close. Unexpectedly close. Kris didn't move away. It felt good.

Their conversations were short. The window in Margo's room hadn't been fixed yet, so she needed a place to stay for a few days. Kris offered his place. He had plenty of extra beds, and the upstairs loft was divided and private. Margo agreed to that and gave Cindy a short list of the things she needed. Cindy promised to gather them up, but Margo would need to come get them. Natty's was pretty busy.

When Margo and Cindy were done talking, Kris called Silas and arranged to use his vehicle, just to take Margo to get her things. Margo stayed next to Kris and listened. She stayed close. Like a puppy. Almost touching him as he stood against the counter with the phone at his ear. Kris hung up and turned toward Margo. They looked at each other silently for a moment. Kris hadn't really thought much about Margo before, but now, up close, he really saw her for the first time. The entire left side of her face was bruised badly but obviously healing, her bruises green in some places. Her left eye was the worst, open but swollen all around. The eye itself was blood red. A split on her lower lip was scabbed, and her lip and the face around it were swollen. But even as beat up as she was, there was something about her. Something unexpected. It was easy being with her. Easy being close to her. Kris found it easy to understand why Dazzle was attracted to her.

He broke the silence. "We'd better get up to Natty's and get your stuff. Cindy'll be distracted until she's good that you're safe and you have a place."

Margo nodded. She knew Kris was right, but she didn't really want to leave the cabin. She felt safe in the cabin with Kris.

Silas was puttering around the truck when Margo and Kris came over the rise in the camp road. "I've got it all ready for you, Kris. I expect you're gonna use it for a week or two."

"Shit, Silas, I was figuring I'd only use it when I need to. I don't want to put you out."

"I got no plans for it, Kris. Be best if you just keep it at your place so you have it."

Kris wasn't comfortable relying on other people, but he knew better than to argue about it with Silas. "Okay, Silas, if you insist. I'll pay you back. I promise."

"You can pay me back with some of those hot dogs you get down in town." Silas winked. Margo and Kris climbed in and drove out of the camp road.

Natty's was busy but not so busy that Cindy couldn't drop everything when she saw Margo. She ran across the bar and gave her a long, tight hug.

"You okay, baby?"

Margo nodded.

"We'll talk about the whole thing over the next couple days. You need some rest now. How long till you think you might be able to come back and work?"

Margo shook her head and looked around the bar. "I can stay right now, Cindy. The place is busy."

"Not a chance, girl, not a chance. I'm glad you want to come back, but I want you to get a little rest tonight. How about tomorrow?"

"Okay, Cindy. I'll meet you here when you open?" Margo turned to Kris who was standing by the door. "Is that okay, Kris? Can you bring me down here early in the morning?"

Kris nodded.

Cindy gave Margo another hug. "Shit, you've only been gone a couple days and I missed you." She stepped back. "Lemme grab your stuff. I gotta get back to work, and you need to get back to Kris's place." She walked behind the bar and grabbed a duffle bag. "I had this bag, put your stuff in it. Hope you don't mind." She handed the bag to Margo and looked at Kris who was standing by the door.

"Thank you," Margo said softly.

Kris nodded a quick nod.

Margo turned to leave, paused, and looked slowly around the bar. She was glad to be home.

# CHAPTER FIFTY

Myslewiec hadn't slept again. It was getting old. He stumbled into his kitchen, started the coffee pot, and fell into one of the chairs at his kitchen table. The trail wasn't completely cold, but if it didn't go anywhere soon, he knew he'd have to put it on ice and get to work on the other cases that he'd been putting off.

He drank his coffee, put the mug in the sink, and showered. Miller hadn't been able to get a description of any vehicles from the New York hotel. The security camera system had been broken for weeks before the murder, and nobody had taken the time to get it fixed. The hotel's registration forms had entries for vehicle make, model, and license plate, but the desk clerk working the night shift was lazy and didn't insist that those entries be filled in. The victim had no identification, no wallet, no driver's license. Nothing but a few sex toys and pile of dirty clothes.

Miller was already at his desk when Myslewiec got to the office.

"Dido!" Miller was jacked up again. A good sign.

"Dido, we found the wife!"

Myslewiec didn't get it.

"The wife? What do you mean?"

"Remember the guy's wife was missing from Michigan? She turned up in New York. Way up north. Near Canada. Was involved in a fatal accident. That's how she got on the radar. State police investigating the accident. Crazy accident Dido, a pickup truck, a wrecker, and a school bus. The wrecker guy almost got cut in half."

"Cut in half?" Myslewiec stared at Miller.

"Almost. Almost cut in half, Dido. Right above the waist. Brutal. But that's not important right now. What's important is the wife. She's in northern New York. In the boonies, in a town called Cotswald. She's been up there since just around the time the husband killed the kid in Ohio. She told the state police that she got a ride there with some people she met at a rest stop on the New York thruway. They have a camp up near there. The reports say she was beat up recently. Her face is bruised bad."

Myslewiec sat in his chair and thought for a minute. "It ties together. The guy beat her up one time too many. She ran. She made her way up to New York."

"It gets better, Dido. They have a kid and he goes to college up in northern New York."

"So when she ran, she went to the kid?"

"She isn't quite there, Dido. Not with the kid. But close. Close enough. She's in the boonies, like I said. Working at a boondock bar and living in a room there. A place that caters to hunters and guys who drive around in the woods on ATVs."

"She's hiding. Hiding from the husband."

"That's what it looks like, Dido."

"And the husband is moving in the same direction. He's after her."

"It looks that way to me, Dido. We don't have any way to tie the husband to the dead woman at the New York hotel yet, we're still waiting on the prints they pulled from the room, but if he is the hotel killer, he might be working his way toward northern New York too. And he killed the kid in Ohio, so no reason to think he wouldn't kill somebody else."

"How the hell would he know she went that way, though?"

"Maybe he doesn't. Maybe he just guessed that she'd go to the kid."

Myslewiec thought for a minute.

"Let's get some coffee. You might be on to something."

# CHAPTER FIFTY-ONE

"I know it isn't my business, but if you want to talk about how you got beat up, I'd listen." It was an awkward thing for Kris to say, and he felt awkward saying it. He looked awkward too. Margo thought it was kind of cute.

"I guess." She paused and looked at the fire. "I haven't thought much about it since I got here."

Kris didn't know what else to say. He wanted to know more about her, but he was too shy to ask. Felt like he was intruding. They both stared at the fire. Margo started to rock in the chair a little. The chair squeaked. "It isn't something I need to get off my chest, really." She shifted in the chair and rocked a little harder. A few more moments of silence. "I got used to it. He did it a lot more the last couple years." She looked up at Kris. "It's why I came here, right? I mean, I didn't plan to come here, but I finally got away from him and I ended up here."

"Why here?"

Margo shook her head slowly. "It's just the way it happened. When I ran from him, I was only thinking about getting away. I ended up running toward the highway and I hitched a ride."

"You came from Michigan, right?"

Margo nodded and stared into the fire. "Chelsea. West of Detroit. Near Ann Arbor." She went silent.

Again, they both stared at the fire, their shared silence lasting a little longer this time.

Margo broke the silence. "It all happened so fast that I never put any thought to it." She spoke as if in a haze, staring into the fire. "Until now."

"I shouldn't have brought it up. I'm sorry."

Margo looked up at Kris and stopped rocking. "Look, I need to get back into the real world. I need to resolve this stuff. I can't put it in a box and lock it away. I'm glad you brought it up."

Kris got out of his chair, removed the screen from the woodstove, and poked at the burning logs a few times. He put two more logs on the fire.

Margo continued as Kris played with the fire. "The deal is, my son goes to school near here. College."

"One of the schools in Sefton?" Kris asked.

"No. Paul Smith's. A ways from here I guess." Margo shifted in her chair again. "Anyway, the highway isn't far from our house in Michigan, and when I ran from him, I ended up there. I guess I thought about it for a few seconds and decided right then to try and go east. Because Kyle was east. I didn't put much thought into it, I just went with that and made my way to the entrance ramp that went east."

"You hitched a ride at the entrance ramp?"

"Yeah, at the very start of it. Where the cars turn to get on the highway. It seemed like the right place at the time. My first ride got me to a rest stop in New York somewhere. I cleaned up a little there and I slept at a table. No plans. Then this older couple sat down with me. I don't know why. I was a mess. Pretty scary looking, I imagine. I sure as hell wouldn't have come close to anyone looking like I must have." Margo looked at Kris.

Kris nodded and turned to the fire. Uncomfortable. "Hard for me to imagine what you looked like then. I probably would have steered clear."

Margo raised her chin a little, an acknowledgment. "Anyway, these two people wanted to help me, and they were on their way up here. They have a camp on another pond near here."

"French's?"

"Yeah, I'm pretty sure that's it. We stayed at their place a few days before I was ready to go back out into the world. I loved it from the minute I got there. Might be because those people were so nice, but I liked what everything looked like too. I liked what it smelled like. I know it sounds weird, but I felt like I was home again."

"Like where you grew up, you mean?"

"Not like that, not when I was at their camp. And not even the camp really, more like the area. But home like in a place where I was meant to be. I felt a connection somehow."

"You felt like you were meant to be up here in this area?"

"Yeah. I didn't think about it like that, it wasn't that specific, but that's what it felt like. And when we finally went into the town, I really did feel like this area is like where I grew up. When you get away from the woods and closer to the town, there are big fields and little family farms, and that's what it's like where I grew up."

Kris asked, "Where did you grow up?"

Margo realized that she'd been looking at Kris instead of the fire for a while now. He was a nice-looking guy. Not real rugged but no slouch, and not real handsome but not ugly or goofy. Just a nice-looking guy. And real easy to talk to. Almost like she knew that whatever she said to him would stay with him. Wouldn't get spread all around. He could keep private things private. No wonder Cindy liked him so much.

"I grew up in Canada. Ontario, near the border with Detroit."

Kris continued staring at the fire and nodded.

Margo continued without pausing, "Ontario looks a lot like the area near town. Sefton, right?"

Kris nodded. "Sefton. Not much of a town I guess. Without the colleges it wouldn't be anything. Not nowadays."

"It sure is nice around here, though. I like it. I want to stay."

"Divorce the husband?"

Margo paused and considered the question. "I hadn't thought that far ahead. I guess it means that I'll need to contact him sometime."

Kris rocked in the chair. "Yeah. Probably not something you'd want to do for a while. Think he has any idea where you are?"

"I was worried about him chasing me when I was still in Chelsea, but I can't imagine he'd have any idea where I am now."

"Think he'd guess that you'd go to your son?"

Margo looked back at the fire and thought for a moment. "Yes, he probably would." She paused. "But how could he ever find me here? We're way out in the woods, right? This is really remote as far as I can tell. There's got to be miles of woods around us here. And a lot of little towns."

She turned away from the fire and looked at Kris. "It is remote here, right?"

"Yeah. We're pretty far outside of anything up here."

Margo looked back at the fire and shook her head. "I doubt he's coming after me. He's not that ambitious. He'll be sitting on the couch at home watching football or some stupid cop show and drinking. He's only got enough drive to get a new beer now and then. He's not coming after me."

Despite her definitive words, she was unsure about it, that was obvious to Kris.

# CHAPTER FIFTY-TWO

He watched the old clock radio on the nightstand on and off for hours.

2:00, 2:17, 3:04, 3:31, 3:59. *Uncle.*

He got out of bed and put on the clothes he'd worn the day before. In the kitchen he found a pencil and wrote a note on a napkin: *Couldn't sleep. Went for a drive. See you after work. Todd.* He closed the kitchen door gently on his way to the truck, hoping not to wake Sherry.

He drove straight to his stand, parked the truck, and picked his way slowly through the woods to the spot he'd been watching from. The single sodium lamp high above Natty's parking lot lit it well. The lot was empty. Rank adjusted his binoculars for the clearest view, set them on his lap, and waited.

The woods were nearly silent, not a squirrel or chipmunk or bird and no wind to speak of. Occasionally the faintest rustle could be heard in the branches high above him or a tiny cone dropping somewhere nearby. After a few minutes, he heard a vehicle on the road. Distant at first, coming toward him from the same direction he had come minutes earlier. First the sound of the tires crackling across the cold, dry asphalt as it came closer, then the sound of the engine and leaking muffler as it sped past him. A pickup truck. Hunters. The sound faded as it drove into the distance and all was quiet once again.

In the calm and quiet Rank began to think.

*Sherry. Maybe a new shot at life. Up here in the woods.*

*The cops haven't found me. Yet. Maybe they won't.*

*Change my identity. How do you do that? There must be people up here who can do that.*

*Sherry would know someone.*

*Shit. Can't tell Sherry. Has to be a secret.*

He repositioned himself. His ass was cold.

Another vehicle came and went. The parking lot remained still. He heard rustling in the woods behind him. A squirrel maybe, or a bird. Not a big animal.

He couldn't get Sherry out of his mind. He pictured her walking away from him down her hall toward her bedroom. Pictured her tight jeans and the way she swayed. Confident. Sexy. He imagined the smell of her perfume. Her eyes.

He shifted again. The ground was cold. The sound of another vehicle rose from the distance, but it was different this time. Slowing. A small pickup with a cap pulled into the far side of the lot and parked. Rank trained the binoculars on the truck. The driver opened the door but didn't get out right away. He could see the back of the driver's head looking down at the seat and gathering up something. The driver got out of the truck, closed the door, and walked around the front end toward the bar door. It was a woman. Short brown hair. A little stocky. The owner, he remembered her. She's the one who'd spoken with him and Sherry the night they ate there. She's the one who'd told Sherry that the woman from Michigan was working at the bar.

The owner stood at the door to the place and found the key, unlocked the door, and went inside. Quiet again. Lights came on inside, visible in the small high windows on either side of the door. A neon sign came on in the window to the left. Budweiser. Rank became anxious. His thoughts of Sherry disappeared. He waited.

Another vehicle came and passed the parking lot without stopping. He noticed that the sky was just beginning to lighten. Dawn was closer. He trained the binoculars on the window to the right of the door. No movement. He put the binoculars down and thought, trying to remember the inside of the place. He hadn't been paying close attention when he and Sherry had eaten there, and he hadn't thought about anything but Margo once he'd discovered she was there, but he did remember that the kitchen was in the back. The owner must have gone straight to the kitchen to start cooking.

Another vehicle, this time from behind him and to his left. Coming past the spot where he'd parked the truck. He turned to watch. A pickup truck with no cap and an open bed. A rolling stop at the intersection. Two people inside. The truck turned to its right and moved toward him, then turned immediately into the parking lot and parked directly to the left of the door.

Rank trained his binoculars on the cab of the truck. The driver and passenger were looking at each other. Talking. Rank could see that the driver was a man, but the passenger was partly hidden by four or five stickers on the cab rear window. Dump stickers maybe. The passenger's head turned quickly to the door, opened it, climbed out of the truck, and closed the door. It was a woman. It was Margo.

She gave a quick wave to the driver and was inside the bar before Rank could think. The truck pulled out of the lot and drove back up the road to Rank's left. Rank watched the driver through the binoculars until the truck disappeared up the hill.

A guy. Margo was with a guy. Rank's anger grew. He looked back at the bar. Still again. Quiet. Margo inside. Rank's heart was racing. Margo was inside the bar.

No longer caring about secrecy, Rank jumped up and hurried back to the truck, branches on the ground cracking under his feet. He threw the binoculars onto the passenger side of the bench seat, and they bounced and fell off the far side between the seat and door. He slammed the door shut, started the truck, jerked the shift lever into reverse, and stomped the gas pedal. The rear tires spun wildly on the dirt, and the truck jerked out from behind the pole. He turned the wheel sharply, and the truck lurched as the tires caught pavement. Barely in control, Rank stomped the brake pedal and slammed the shift lever hard. It passed the drive position and settled into the position numbered two. Rank didn't notice. He stomped the gas pedal. Tires chirped as the truck lurched forward.

He let off the pedal and drove slowly past the bar, staring at the door. All was quiet.

Margo was inside.

Once past the bar, he stomped the pedal again and sped away toward Sherry's place.

# CHAPTER FIFTY-THREE

Rank pulled into Sherry's driveway just as Sherry was closing the side door. *Shit*, he thought. He hadn't counted on her still being home. He got out of the truck.

"You okay, Todd?" Sherry asked.

He put on his best smile. "Yeah, couldn't sleep."

She walked close. Stood directly in front of him. Looked him straight in the eye. "I saw your note. It was really nice of you to leave it for me." She reached out and took his hand. "Thank you." She smiled and tipped her head a little to the side.

"You're welcome." He was uncomfortable. Sherry was confusing him.

She raised herself on her toes, leaned forward, and kissed him lightly on the cheek. She settled back onto her feet. "Hey, I don't work tonight. What do you say we go have a few beers and a burger somewhere?"

Rank nodded. "That sounds great."

She raised his hand a tiny bit and let go. "Awesome!" She turned and walked to her car, bouncing like a little girl. As she opened the car door, she turned back toward Rank. "Take a nap if you can, Todd; get some rest. Never know, might be a long night!" She winked and smiled as she lowered herself into the driver's seat. Rank didn't move. He couldn't. His head was spinning. Sherry turned him on. He waved as she drove away. He stood in the driveway for a few seconds after she left. Motionless. So many thoughts racing through his mind that he couldn't think at all.

He went into the house and made a cup of coffee, then took it to the front entryway and stood in front of the stripped floor. He sipped the coffee and stared at the floor. He needed to lay the slate, needed to finish the job. For Sherry.

It was a little slow, cutting and fitting the uncoupling membrane and then fitting the slate tiles back into the same positions where they'd been laid originally. He'd drawn a little map before removing them, and he'd marked them all on the back. He had them all in place by ten and made himself another cup of coffee. He'd used a fast drying mortar, and the package said he could grout in two hours. He sat at the kitchen table and sipped the coffee.

His thoughts turned back to Margo. What was he going to do about Margo? He couldn't let her run away like she'd done. He touched the eye patch with his fingers, ran them across it from left to right. He put the coffee cup into the sink and walked down the hall. Sherry's door was open a crack. He'd never seen inside her room. He opened the door and stepped in, immediately greeted by the smell of Sherry. He closed his eyes and breathed through his nose. Her smell calmed him. Opening his eyes and looking around, he saw that her room was messy. The bed wasn't made. Her sheets were cream-colored and flowery, and she had a pink blanket and a quilt. Her pillows were stacked, one tossed on top of the other. A glass half full of water was on the floor beside the bed.

Looking around a little more, he noticed that she had an old wooden dresser. Maple, he thought. Tall and narrow, not low and wide. A jewelry box sat on top with the lid open, and a mirror was attached to the dresser behind the jewelry box. Makeup bottles, lipsticks, and creams were scattered around the jewelry box. A guitar leaned against the dresser on the far side, and a full-length mirror stood on the floor beside the guitar. Clothes were strewn on the floor. Dirty, he guessed. He spotted a thong on top of a pair of jeans. Black. He turned and walked back toward the kitchen, checking to make sure he really was alone in the house. He peered out the side door. No vehicles in the driveway except his truck.

He tiptoed back into Sherry's room and went straight for the thong. He held it against his nose and breathed through it. It was musky. Strong. He imagined her at work. Moving fast behind the bar. Hot. Sweaty. He breathed in again. He was getting hard. He rubbed the thong across his cheek and looked at it. Smaller than he'd expected. He imagined her in it, her ass round and white. He held it against his nose one more time, took one last smell, and tossed it back on top of the jeans.

He closed the door gently, as if he was trying not to wake her. He went into his room, grabbed his duffle bag, and sat on the edge of the bed. Digging around, he found his Ruger and its box of shells. He set the box on the bed and checked the magazine before setting the Ruger beside the shells. He dug back into the bag and found the fat chick's pistol. He looked it over closely.

Small with a black plastic handle and a silver steel barrel and trigger. Shaped kind of like the guns he'd seen in World War II movies, except smaller. He removed the clip. It held eight rounds. He put the clip back in and set the pistol on the bed beside his Ruger. He dug back into the duffle bag and found the box of shells for the pistol.

Rank began to think as he set the duffle bag back on the floor. He didn't know what he was going to do, but he knew that he needed the guns to do it. Maybe not both guns. Not yet. Some kind of plan was starting to form, and he decided to let it take its time.

He walked back out to the entryway and looked at the slate, then back into the kitchen and looked at the clock. He still had over an hour before he could grout. He walked out the side door and across the yard to the shed. Inside, he started looking for something he might carry the guns in. He saw nothing on the bench or on the shelf below. Nothing on the floor, nothing hanging on the walls. He went through one of the toolboxes, a simple open box, and found a half-used roll of duct tape. Thinking it might be handy, he set it aside and put away the first box. The other toolbox had a removable tray on top. In the box below the tray, he discovered an old leather tool belt under a speed square and a keyhole saw.

He took the tool belt out of the box and shook the sawdust off of it. The tool belt had five pockets: two large pockets on each side and a small pocket in the middle. The two large side pockets each had a smaller pocket sewn to their fronts. "Perfect," he spoke softly to himself.

He put the tray back and closed the toolbox, then closed the shed back up and walked back into the house.

In his room, he set the duct tape on the bed and began trying out the belt. Neither of the pistols fit well in any of the belt's pockets. He stood and put the belt around his waist, adjusting it for fit. He tried again to put the pistols into each of the larger side pockets and then the shell boxes. Wasn't going to work. He laid the pistols and shell boxes back on the bed.

The belt was awkward. He walked into Sherry's room, picked his way around the clothes on the floor, and stood in front of the mirror. The belt made him look like one of those home improvement guys on TV. Stupid, he thought. He turned to leave but stopped and picked up the black thong. He smelled it again as he walked back into his room. He put the thong in his duffle bag, then removed the belt. He walked back to the kitchen and made another cup of coffee to sip while he waited to do the grout.

# CHAPTER FIFTY-FOUR

Kris returned to his cabin after dropping Margo off at Natty's. It was early, a lot earlier than he usually started his day. He thought about building a fire but decided to start working instead. With an early start he might get most of the day's work finished by early afternoon, and he could go back to Natty's for a late lunch. Or maybe an early dinner. He made a cup of tea and walked out to his office in the outbuilding.

He'd been at work for a few hours when Silas knocked on the door.

"It's open, Silas." Kris leaned back in his chair and motioned Silas to come in.

The door creaked a little as it opened.

"Kris, how you doing today?" Silas was wearing a white wifebeater and a pair of blue work pants. Kris couldn't remember the last time he saw Silas dressed flamboyantly, like he used to. "Same old shit, Silas. Same old shit."

Silas grinned and sat in the chair next to Kris's desk.

"How's Violet doing, Silas?"

Silas shook his head. "She ain't the same, Kris. Not that she's been too good for a few years now, but seeing that accident really changed her."

"How so?"

Silas leaned forward. "Kinda weird, Kris. She's got more energy, ain't laying around all day now. Up and about. But distant, like nobody else is in the house with her. Doesn't even talk to me. Looks right through me like I'm not there." Silas sat back in the chair.

"Jesus, Silas, that's strange. Did you talk to her doctor about it?"

Silas shook his head again. "No, but I have to take her for a checkup in a couple weeks. If she's still the same I'll ask about it." Silas stared at Kris and a grin came to his face.

"What are you grinning at, Silas?"

"Well, Kris, one good thing came out of it. She ain't making Brenda's lunch anymore."

"Crap, Silas, I was enjoying those lunches, you know."

"You didn't enjoy peanut butter and mayonnaise!" Silas laughed a little and then became serious again. He leaned forward. "Reason I came to talk to you, Kris, is that my wood pile's been hit pretty damn hard in the past couple days."

"How hard?"

"I'll bet there's a half a cord missing since last week, Kris. Every time I go into town or away from the cabin for an hour or two, some more wood goes missing. I can't figure on it. Worst part is that Violet's in the cabin while it's happening. The way her head's working now, I ain't surprised that she doesn't realize it." Silas paused and stared at Kris for a moment, then continued, "Shit, even if she stood on the front stoop and watched them take the wood she probably wouldn't think twice about it. But it worries me, because if they've got the balls to take my wood right from the woodshed, they might get brave enough to go inside one day and see what else they can steal." Silas leaned back in the chair again. "Gets worse, Kris. I can't find my axe now."

Kris leaned forward in his chair. "Your axe, Silas?"

"The axe I use to split wood." Silas paused for a moment. "Well, the one I used to use when I could still split wood. I still use it once in a while. When I looked for it this morning, I couldn't find it. I always keep it in the same place, Kris. Now I'm afraid that whoever's been stealing my wood took my axe too. Either that or I'm starting to lose my mind." Silas looked to the floor and shook his head. "Either way it don't matter. Violet might be in some danger, Kris. I'd never forgive myself if Violet got hurt."

The two sat silently for a few minutes. Kris thought.

"Silas, I haven't been a very good friend I'm afraid. I knew this was going on, but didn't know it was this serious. I think I know how I can help you out."

"How's that, Kris?"

"Just tell me when you're gonna be gone, and I'll watch your place from the top of the rise there." Kris pointed to the top of the small hill that separated his cabin and Silas's.

"You'd do that for me, Kris?"

"Of course I would, Silas. We can catch the bastards red-handed and get that wood back for you."

Silas agreed that it would be a good idea and told Kris when he planned to be away over the next few days. They talked a little more small talk and Silas left Kris alone to continue working. Kris got up from his chair and walked out with Silas to grab another cup of tea. He hadn't had breakfast and he was getting hungry, but he didn't want to eat until he got to Natty's later on.

On the short walk between the outbuilding and his cabin, he began to think about Margo. She'd only stayed at his place one night, but it was a comfortable setup. He felt like he'd known her longer. Easy to get along with her. While he waited for the water to boil, he imagined what she might be doing right now. Wondered how many hunters were in Natty's. Wondered how many of them were hitting on her.

The teapot whistled him back to reality. He poured the tea and walked back to the outbuilding. He'd had a decent morning, got a lot done. If he got back into his work now, he thought he could finish by three. He was looking forward to one of Cindy's burgers. And to seeing Margo.

# CHAPTER FIFTY-FIVE

Myslewiec tipped the mug and drank the last gulp of cold coffee. The bag of Krazy Kurls was empty. He crumpled it and tossed it into the trash can beneath his desk.

"The prints are positive, Dido." Miller rushed into the office. Myslewiec turned and looked at him without saying anything.

"They matched the prints they found in the hotel room with our man. They had him on file in Michigan. He'd beat the wife enough to get tossed in the local holding cell a few times."

Myslewiec remained silent. He was tired and a little surprised by this new development.

"He killed two, Dido. Two. We'd better get in touch with that town in New York and tell them what we have."

Myslewiec nodded.

# CHAPTER FIFTY-SIX

Natty's, it turned out, wasn't too busy at all. It was almost empty. For the first day in a few weeks, the steady stream of hunters had become a trickle. Cindy didn't mind; she'd made good money over the past few weeks, even though it had been a lot of work. Taking it a little slower for a day suited her fine. Plus, Margo was back and she was happy to have a little time to talk.

"It's gonna take another day or two to get your apartment back in shape. The window couldn't be fixed; it was beat up too bad. So we had to order a new one 'cause they didn't have the right size in stock. Just a piece of plywood nailed up there, not fit for living in yet." They were sitting at the end of the bar having a coffee. The place was now empty. A couple hunters had left a few minutes earlier and nobody else had come in yet.

"I'd be surprised if Kris wouldn't let me stay a while longer, Cindy."

"Me too. I'll fill him in on it, though, and make sure he's okay with it. If he isn't, we can find you a place for a couple days."

Margo sipped her coffee. "He's a real nice guy, Cindy; he'll be okay with it. He set me up real good upstairs at his place. It's got a part-wall that splits the upstairs into two rooms. I'm in one room, and he's in the other. It's pretty private, and Kris makes sure he keeps to himself. Real polite and gentlemanly."

"That's Kris for you. You know, I've never been upstairs at his place, and fuck knows that I've hit on him a few times!" Cindy laughed. "Hey, I forgot to tell you that while you were going through that shitstorm with Dazzle, Walter and Nancy stopped in to say goodbye. They headed back to Rochester."

# CHAPTER FIFTY-SEVEN

Rank finished wiping the grout haze from the slate tiles and stood to admire his work. *Sherry's gonna be happy.* He picked up after himself, dumped the dirty water from the bucket, and cleaned it, rinsed and wrung out the rags he'd used, and returned it all to the shed. Back in the house, he went straight to his room and pulled Sherry's thong from the duffle bag. He held it to his face and breathed through her sweat. He put it in his shirt pocket. For good luck.

He looked at the pistols and shells and thought about what he might do. *No way to carry both pistols. What do I need them for anyway?* He returned them to the duffle bag and took the tool belt back to the shed. Frustrated and confused, he walked back into the house and pulled his Ruger from the bag, put it into the front of his pants, and covered it with his untucked shirt. He left the house and got into his truck. No plan. He left Sherry's place and turned right at the intersection. Toward Natty's.

## CHAPTER FIFTY-EIGHT

A single hunter came through the door and sat at the bar. Both Cindy and Margo said hello as they got off their stools and went back to work. Margo walked around behind the bar and Cindy went into the kitchen to check on things.

"What can I get you?" Margo laid a bar napkin in front of him.

"I'll have a beer from your tap. Bud I guess. You still serving food?"

"Sure we are." Margo put a glass below the spigot and pulled on the tap handle. "I don't think Cindy's started making dinner yet, but I'll check with her. Even if she hasn't, we can do up burgers and sandwiches." She set the full glass on the napkin in front of him.

"No need to check on dinner, a hamburger would be just fine."

"Sounds good. Tomato, lettuce, onion? Fries or chips?"

"Tomato, lettuce, onion on the side if that's okay, and chips are fine. Ketchup and mayo too please."

Margo nodded. "You've got it." She turned and walked to the kitchen door, stuck her head in, and relayed the order to Cindy. She came back out, grabbed a bottle of ketchup and a place setting from below the bar, and put them in place in front of him. "Any luck out there?"

He took a drink of the beer and set the glass back on the napkin. "Nothing. I've seen three does since I started a few days back, one today. I ain't got a doe permit, though, and I can't afford the fine, so I'm letting them go. Nothing with points yet."

"That's too bad. How much longer are you going to hunt?"

"Another day or two, then I need to get back to work."

Margo leaned on the bar. "Where's work?"

He took another long drink from the glass. "Down near Syracuse. I work for the power company. Line work. Sucks now, gets cold and snow starts. Lines ice up." He finished the glass and set it down.

"Refill?"

"Yeah, please."

Margo set the glass below the spigot and pulled the tap handle again. "I imagine winter is a tough time for you guys."

"When the lines ice up and we have to be out all night it kinda sucks. But the worst is when people lose control of their cars on the ice and take out a pole."

Margo set the glass in front of him.

He picked up the glass. "They almost never do that in the daylight, always in the middle of the night after they've been out drinking." He took a drink. "Nothing like dragging yourself out of bed in the middle of the night to go work in freezing cold weather."

Cindy came from the kitchen with a large plate: the burger, tomato, lettuce, and onion on the side like he'd asked, a big pile of ripple chips, and two little white paper cups of mayo. His eyes got wide as she set it down in front of him. She turned and walked back into the kitchen.

"That's a lot of food there. Thank you!" He opened the ketchup bottle and poured some on top of the burger.

# CHAPTER FIFTY-NINE

Rank drove slowly past Natty's, peering at the door. One truck in the lot, plus the owner's truck. Not busy. He turned right at the intersection of Chance Pond Road and drove up the hill past the spot he'd been parking his truck while he watched the bar from the woods. He drove on. Aimlessly. Trying to figure out what to do.

Chance Pond Road crested a hill and then wound down through a stand of mixed forest. A small green cabin, neat and tidy, stood beside a stream to the right as the grade of the road transitioned from down to up. He drove up over the next hill and down the other side. The roadside at the bottom of the hill was torn up; the vegetation was flattened and tire tracks made deep grooves in the mud and grass. *An accident maybe*, Rank thought. Just beyond the mess a camp road cut off to the right. A post littered with homemade nameplates stood at the road's entrance. On the far side of the camp road, the trees thinned and a pond opened up on his right. It was small and still, and Rank could see cabins scattered along the shore. He noticed smoke rising from the chimneys of a couple cabins.

A decrepit house, its yard littered with abandoned cars, trucks, gas grills, and old furniture stood on his left, and then a trailer home, its blue paint faded from years of neglect. Beyond the pond, the road climbed again and turned to dirt as it entered a dense stand of evergreens. A narrow dirt road cut to his left, a large stone painted with red letters marking the entrance to a hunting camp. Further on, someone had cleared trees and left the remnants scattered, maybe in preparation to build. The road began to descend again, steeply this time, and became rough. The truck bounced and slid, its worn suspension unsteady on the washboard surface. Near the bottom, the road smoothed, turned sharply to the right, and eased toward level.

He drove past an intersection with another dirt road to his left, this one with a large steel gate. Another hunting club, he guessed. A little further on, the road split a marsh and then began another uphill climb that terminated at a paved road.

Rank sat at the intersection for a few moments wondering which way to turn and thinking.

*Margo's why I came here.*

*Why I've been so angry.*

*But that was then.*

*Not so angry now.*

*Not angry anymore…Sherry.*

*But Margo's at the bar.*

*I came for Margo.* He touched the eye patch. His little excursion had wasted some time, and he needed to get to Margo while he could. *The bar's probably to the right.*

He turned right.

Back on asphalt, Rank drove slowly. The road split another marsh, then climbed into a dense patch of mixed forest. A few small camps began to appear, some rough and a few a little more elaborate, then suddenly Rank was passing through a small village of hunting camps. Nearly all were occupied. Pickup trucks and SUVs littered the road, and the smell of wood smoke filled the air. A deer hung from a tree branch next to one cabin. Rank thought that hunting season must be nearly over.

The hunters village disappeared as quickly as it had appeared, the road winding down a long hill and then up again. The forest changed too, from mixed to coniferous and back. Rank didn't notice. His mind wandered, unable to grasp a single thought. Unable to focus. He saw the trees. He saw the road. He heard the sound of the tires on asphalt, the creaking and groaning of the truck. Thoughts of Sherry flashed in and out of his mind, warm and welcoming, interrupted by Margo, cold and distant. Natty's lot suddenly appeared on his left. Abrupt. Unexpected. Jarring. Two trucks. Same as before. He slowed. Watched the door. Unable to think. He drove past, stomped on the gas pedal, and swore at himself.

# CHAPTER SIXTY

Kris made a few last corrections to the file he was working on and saved it. Not a bad day, and still early. Earlier than he'd expected. A good thing, he was hungry. He closed up the outbuilding and walked across the yard to the cabin to wash up and brush his teeth. When he finished, he walked out and climbed into Silas's truck. It felt strange to him, he was uncomfortable using someone else's vehicle.

He drove slowly past Silas's place, then turned left on Chance Pond Road. He passed the mess that remained from the accident and thought that he should try to clean it up a little someday soon. That mess might be a reminder that Violet and Silas didn't need.

At the intersection in front of Natty's, Kris had to wait for a pickup truck to pass. As Kris pulled out behind the truck it suddenly slowed, the driver leaning close to the truck's window and looking toward Natty's for a few long moments. Then, just as suddenly as it had slowed, the truck accelerated and sped away. *Strange*, Kris thought. *Must have changed his mind*. He shook his head as he turned into Natty's lot. He shut the truck down and went into the bar.

Natty's was nearly empty. Kris paused at the door and looked for Margo. There was one guy sitting at the bar, nobody else in sight. As Kris walked toward the bar, Margo came out from the kitchen. She smiled broadly when she saw Kris.

"Hey!"

Kris replied with the same. "Hey!" He pulled up a stool and sat.

"Might be too early for a whiskey, eh?" Margo leaned on her elbows in front of Kris.

Kris rested on his elbows, his face close to hers. "Probably. I figured I'd come get a burger. Haven't eaten today."

"We might be able to fix something up for you." Margo smiled. She remained on her elbows looking into Kris's eyes. The low light in the bar softened her face. The bruises didn't look as bad as they had in Kris's cabin. Kris thought for a moment that he could see what she looked like without them. He liked what he saw.

"Kris, what are you doing down here so early? You ain't gonna start drinking whiskey this early, are you?" Cindy was drying a small pot as she walked out from the kitchen.

Kris sat up straight and Margo stood.

Cindy paused for a second. "Shit, you two look like your parents just caught you making out!" She laughed.

Margo and Kris looked at each other. Kris blushed. "I just came in for a burger, Cin. I haven't had anything to eat all day and I didn't feel much like making something at home."

"Well why didn't you say so? Medium rare, right?"

"Close as you can get to that would work just fine."

"Kris," Cindy lowered her chin and looked through the tops of her eyes like a schoolteacher correcting a fifth-grade student, "you know better than that. You want medium rare, you are gonna get medium rare, baby." She turned and walked toward the kitchen, still talking as she went. "What'll you have on it?"

"Lettuce and tomatoes, Cin. And American cheese please." Kris looked at Margo. "I'd try a Bud too, if you don't mind."

Margo grinned at Kris. "So long as you don't get too drunk. Cindy says I can't stay in my room still. I'm going to need to lean on you for another night or two, and I don't want to be cleaning up after you." She winked.

"I promise. Not too many beers. And you can stay at my place as long as you want."

"Damn good burgers." The guy down the bar had just finished his and was licking ketchup and grease off his fingers. "Damn good." Kris and Margo looked at him. He looked at Kris. "First time I've ever been in here. Won't be the last, I can tell you that."

Margo asked if he was finished, and he nodded. "What else can I get you?" She picked up his plate.

"How about one more beer?"

"You've got it." Margo turned and took the plate back to the kitchen.

"They talk to you like you've been here a few times." He put his hand on his knee and turned toward Kris.

"I come in now and then. I live right up the road."

"There's houses out here? I thought it was only hunting camps."

"Well, it isn't really much more than a hunting camp."

"How'd you come about living out here full time? Seems like it might be some work."

"You're right about that, harder than living in town."

Margo set the beer in front of Kris and started pouring one more for the hunter.

"I didn't plan to live up here full time. I used the place for a bunch of years, fishing mostly. Didn't come up till April and closed it up in October."

"So your place is on a lake?"

"Chance Pond. Pretty small but decent fishing. Bass, perch, some small pike."

Margo set the beer down in front of the hunter. "I'd like to hear more about this too, Kris. How you came to be here I mean. Not about fishing." She leaned her elbows on the bar again.

Kris drank from the glass and set it down, making sure to set it on the napkin that Margo had laid out for it.

"Well, I worked down near Boston for a long time, small company. Figured I'd work there forever. But that wasn't part of the plan I guess." He took another drink. The napkin stuck to the bottom of the glass.

Margo and the hunter were silent. Waiting for him to go on. Kris looked at them both for a few seconds and took another drink. Uncomfortable being the center of attention. "Shit, you don't want to hear a big long story about me. Enough to say that I got laid off and couldn't find another job, so I sold my place down there and moved up here. Didn't really think much more about it than that." Kris took another drink. "Margo, you make me tell you much more about me and I'm gonna need to drink a lot of beer."

Margo shook her head and smiled. "I'm not going to make you do anything you don't want to, Kris."

The hunter leaned forward. "Did you winterize the place? I mean, you said you used to close it in October."

Kris looked at him and nodded. "Best I could."

"Well tell me about that, will you? I've been looking at a hunting camp down the road that's for sale. I always wanted a place outside of things." He took a swig from his fresh beer. "By the way, the name's Gerry." He extended his hand.

# CHAPTER SIXTY-ONE

Rank drove fast along the winding forest road. Too fast. The truck wasn't up to the task and bounced wildly through the turns, wheels in the weeds now and then. Rank didn't care. He kept his foot on the throttle and worked the steering wheel to keep the truck on the road. He was mad at himself for passing the bar.

Before he knew it he was turning into Sherry's driveway. He jammed the shift lever into park before the truck had fully stopped, the truck jerking and Rank sliding forward in the seat. He sat. Numb. His mind racing, no clear thoughts. Margo and Sherry battled for attention, the past he wanted to bury and the new chance he might have.

He stepped out of the truck and into Sherry's house. It was warm, the heat was always turned to seventy-two. He turned on the coffee pot, put a filter in the basket, and filled the filter with coffee and the reservoir with water. He gave the carafe a quick rinse, returned it to the coffee maker, and pushed the start button. In the cupboard, the mugs were neatly lined up, each handle facing in the same direction and at the same angle. He grabbed one and set it next to the coffee maker.

As he waited for the coffee, he walked to the slate tiles and had a look. The slate looked like new. He was good at the handyman stuff. Margo had always criticized his work, always wanted more. Sherry wasn't like that. Sherry was happy to have the help. Sherry made it easy. He walked back to the coffee maker, leaned on the counter, and looked out the kitchen window. He realized that he hadn't really paid any attention to Sherry's property. He didn't know how much she had. Where the property lines were.

Out the window he could see her lawn, a meadow really, stretching about fifty yards. At the far edge were woods. Mixed, mostly hardwood trees with a few evergreens. With the leaves fallen, he could see a ways into the woods. A few large stones, a few fallen trees. No animals. No movement. The coffee pot sputtered, signaling the end of the drip. He filled his mug and went outside.

He walked across the meadow slowly toward the back woods. It was quiet. Still. The air was cold and fresh. He paused halfway and sipped his coffee. He turned and looked at the back of the house. The vinyl siding was old, and it had faded where the sun could reach it. Small, high windows marked the kitchen and bath. The larger window on the right was Sherry's room. He remembered what Sherry's room looked like inside. How it smelled. He unzipped his coat a little and felt for Sherry's thong in his chest pocket. Still there. He'd better put that back before Sherry got home. A little panicked, he walked quickly back to the house and returned the thong to the pile where he'd found it. He walked back through the kitchen and topped off the mug before going back outside.

Not quite as slowly this time, he walked back toward the woods and into it. Leaves crunched below his feet as he stepped over fallen logs and picked his way past pricker bushes. Not too far in, he came to one of the rocks he'd seen from the window. It was bigger than he'd thought. He brushed some twigs and leaves off it and sat facing Sherry's house. He sipped the coffee. The fresh air felt good, but as he sat, he realized that it wasn't really all that quiet. A few different kinds of birds were chirping in the distance all around him, and a small animal was moving behind him to his left. He sat motionless and listened. He didn't move a muscle. He forgot about his coffee.

He didn't know how long he'd been sitting when the sound of a car pulled him back to reality. Sherry pulled into the driveway, the car's tires crunching on the gravel. She got out of the car and walked directly into the house without realizing that he was sitting in the woods behind it. He felt a little guilty. He got up from the rock, dumped the cold coffee from the mug, and hurried toward the house.

Sherry was admiring the slate tiles when he walked into the kitchen from outside.

"Hi," he hollered as he closed the door.

Sherry burst into the kitchen. "It's fucking beautiful, Todd!" She ran to him, threw her arms around him, and squeezed. He felt awkward. She sensed it and pulled away, but she couldn't contain her enthusiasm. "It looks so much better than I'd imagined! How did you learn to do such beautiful work?"

Rank was embarrassed. He looked down at the floor. "I dunno how. I guess I just did it."

"You're being modest, Todd. She touched his chin with the tips of her fingers and gave a gentle nudge, a signal that he should lift his head. He looked at her, she at him. She leaned toward him, rose up on her toes, and kissed him on the mouth. A small kiss, light and soft. He was startled. She lowered herself and tipped her head to the side. "I promised you dinner tonight. I need a shower." She turned and walked down the hall, talking as she went. "Maybe Natty's again, Todd?" Her bedroom door closed.

Rank sat at the kitchen table. If his head had been spinning earlier, it was spinning faster now. Her kiss had surprised him. It was perfect. Soft and sweet and warm. He'd forgotten about Margo, at least for the time being. The bathroom door closed and the shower began running. Rank sat still at the table. Thinking about the kiss.

The water ran for what seemed like a long time, then stopped as quickly as it had started. He heard some shuffling in the bathroom: Sherry moving things, opening and closing doors and drawers, the water in the sink running. He couldn't imagine what she was doing, but he tried. A tap-tap-tap sounded like her toothbrush hitting the edge of the sink.

The bathroom door opened. Rank looked toward the hall. Sherry walked toward him, her hair wet from the shower and a towel wrapped around her. She didn't speak as she came closer. She stopped directly in front of him, close. She looked him in the eyes and smiled. "We have some time before dinner and I'm nice and clean." She pulled off the towel, brought it to her head with both hands and began drying her hair. Freckles covered the top of her breasts. Her pubic hair was light brown. She continued looking straight into Rank's eyes. "What do you think, Todd?"

He stammered, "You're, you're beautiful," uncomfortable looking at her naked body but unable to resist.

She grinned and continued drying her hair, her breasts swaying as her arms moved. "Thank you, Todd, you're sweet to say so, but I meant what do you think we should do until dinner time?" She stopped drying her hair and lowered the towel to her side. She didn't cover herself back up. She stood naked in front of him.

Rank looked up into her eyes. He knew the answer, but he couldn't speak. She reached her hand toward him. "C'mon, Todd." He took her hand and stood. She walked him down the hall.

# CHAPTER SIXTY-TWO

The phone call over, Myslewiec set the handset into the cradle and swung around in his chair. "Sefton police are happy to know about the situation."

"Happy?" Miller was confused. "They're happy? The guy's a fucking killer, Dido."

"Look, what can I tell you. I explained it all to them. They even looked him up in NCIC."

"Dido, the bastard killed two people. C'mon." Miller leaned back in his chair.

"I know, I know." Myslewiec leaned forward and put on his best motivational attitude. "We gave them everything we have. They know he's likely to be up there near them somewhere, and they'll keep an eye out. Now we can turn back to our other cases and get some shit done, right?"

Miller nodded reluctantly. "Our other cases suck, Dido; there's nothing else that's this good."

# CHAPTER SIXTY-THREE

Two beers later, Kris had said about all he could say about winterizing the cabin.

"I'd love to see the place, Kris." Gerry took the last swig from his bottle.

"Right up the road, Gerry. I have to go back anyway. Follow me up there, and I'll give you the nickel tour."

"What would you think about looking at the place I'm thinking about buying? Would be great to get another opinion."

"Where'd you say it is?" Kris took the last drink from his bottle and set it on the bar.

"About a mile down the road here. It's near a bunch of other hunting camps."

Kris turned and looked out the window. "Has it got electricity? Getting dark out there now."

"Shit. It's got electricity, but it isn't turned on. I'm around another day or two, and the hunting hasn't been great for me. Maybe you'd be willing to look at it tomorrow in the daylight?"

Kris nodded. "Sure." He turned to Margo who was drying the last glass from the bunch she'd been washing. "I'd better pay up."

Margo nodded, put away the glass, set the towel down, and turned to the register.

Kris turned back to Gerry. "What do you say I follow you to your place first? That way I'll know where it is and I can meet you over there tomorrow. Then we can turn around and you can follow me to my place."

"Works fine." Gerry climbed off his stool.

Margo set the checks down in front of the men.

"Any idea what time you'll be done tonight, Margo?" Kris took a twenty from his wallet and handed it to her with the check. "Keep the change."

"Cindy tells me we're closing at eleven."

"I'll come back in a little early and have a whiskey. You might need to drive us back to the cabin."

Margo smiled and winked. "What if I want a whiskey too?"

Kris cocked his head to the side and blushed. Gerry handed Margo a twenty as well.

"See you later, Cin," Kris hollered as he and Gerry walked out of the bar. Cindy came out of the kitchen just as the bar door closed behind them. The place was empty. Margo was looking at the door. "Slowed down a lot, Cindy."

"Hunting season's almost over. It'll stay steady now until spring, slow on weekdays and busier on weekends."

Margo was quiet. Cindy could see that she was worried. "Shit, girl, it's okay. We'll make enough to keep it going and we'll get a little rest. You don't need to worry about the job, or the place to stay. We'll keep the same arrangement until springtime and see what it looks like then. How's that sound?"

"Cindy, you're a sweetheart. I love this place, and I love working with you." She gave Cindy a hug.

"One thing, though, Margo," Cindy smiled, "I'd like a crack at Kris too, you know."

"What do you mean?"

"Well, it don't take a rocket scientist to see that he's taking a likin' to you, girl. And seems like you kinda like him back."

Margo grinned a little bit. "You're not far off about me liking him, Cindy. I mean, who wouldn't, right?" Cindy nodded. Margo shifted on her feet. "I just ran away from the bastard that beat the crap out of me for years. It's going to be a while before I'm ready to deal with another guy and all his baggage."

"I'm part kidding, Margo. I've been tossing hints to Kris for a long time now and he's never bit. I don't expect he's gonna change his mind about me. I've come to terms with just being friends." She paused, then spoke in a lowered voice as she leaned a little closer to Margo. "But if you and him start getting into it, you gotta promise to give me all the details."

Gerry's place was about a mile down the road, just like he'd said. Simple and plain, a small single-story cabin with a door in the center and two small windows, one on each side. The siding was the same as most local camps, plywood with vertical grooves, and the roof was tin. The weeds around it hadn't been cut for quite a while, but the lot was wide and open on either side of the cabin. Gerry stepped out of his truck, motioned to Kris with a flashlight, and started walking around to the side. Kris got out and followed.

The camp was located well apart from the other hunting camps; only a small corner of one other camp was visible from the yard. It felt isolated, remote. It sat back from the road a little too, with enough room in front for a few vehicles. "Got a propane tank back here, and there's a gas stove inside. No heater, though." Gerry spoke without missing a stride. The two walked around toward the back, walking in a wide arc at the side of the cabin to avoid a pile of cement blocks and old bricks that lay next to it.

"Be easy to put one in," Kris added.

Gerry nodded. "Water tank over there." He pointed the light on a white plastic tank, about four feet square and in a metal frame.

"Those are expensive. Good you have it."

"I wish it was light enough to see."

"We'll walk through it tomorrow. Let's get up to my place and I'll show you around." They walked around the water tank and the far side of the little cabin. Gerry shone the light on the cabin in different spots, and Kris looked at it the best he could in the darkness. Not much to see.

It took them ten minutes to get back to Kris's place. He'd turned the front spotlight on when he'd left, figuring it would be dark by the time he got back. The spotlight was high on the cabin. It lit the entire front and parts of the side.

"How about a whiskey while we look around?" Kris turned the key in the lock and opened the door.

"Sure." Gerry climbed up the two steps in front and followed Kris inside.

# CHAPTER SIXTY-FOUR

Sherry blowing softly on Rank's cheek woke him.

"You were out for a while. Little Death I think I've heard it called."

Rank looked around the room for a moment, trying to get his bearings. "What?"

"Little Death. It's when you fall into a deep sleep after good sex. And, Todd, the sex was really good!"

"Oh. Little Death. I get it. That's what it's like." Rank looked into Sherry's eyes and whispered, "Yeah, the sex was good."

"How about another go?" Sherry fondled Ranks balls.

"That why you woke me up?"

Sherry nodded.

"We already went three times, baby. I dunno if I can get it up for another right now. I'm an old man, you know."

Sherry laughed. "You're *not* old." She paused and gave his balls a quick squeeze. "No worries, Todd. Three massive orgasms in one afternoon is a record for me anyway. I'm just getting greedy." She kissed him on the cheek, threw the covers off, and jumped out of bed. "I'm gonna take a quick shower."

Rank watched her ass and breasts jiggle as she walked around the foot of the bed. She paused and turned to him, cocked her head a little and grinned. "Wanna wash my back?"

Rank tossed the covers back to the other side and climbed out.

The hot water in the shower and Sherry's skilled hands relaxed Rank, and before he knew it, he was entering her from behind. He fondled her breasts and squeezed her nipples as she rocked back into him and moaned, the hot water streaming across his back. He hadn't had this much sex with Margo in months, let alone in one afternoon. An orgasm later they were dressing together in Sherry's room, and within a few minutes, they were in Sherry's car, sitting at the intersection. Rank was spent. Sherry had more energy than she'd had before all the sex.

"What do you think, Todd? Natty's, right?"

Rank didn't want to run into Margo. "Uh, Sherry, I like Natty's a lot, but there's all sorts of places in Sefton that look kinda good too."

Sherry thought for a moment. "You like Thai food?"

"Sure do."

Sherry turned to the left toward Sefton. "There's a weird little Thai place in town. Used to be a donut shop," she looked at Rank as if to emphasize, "a really good donut shop." She looked back at the road. "They turned it into a Thai place and the food is great. Yellow Curry Vegetables is to die for!"

"Sounds fantastic, baby." Rank put his hand on her thigh and squeezed it. "You mind if I call you that?"

She put her hand on his and shook her head no. "You keep fucking me like you did today and you can call me anything you want." She moved her hand from his and rubbed his crotch.

The flashing lights jarred them both from their dreamy post-sex haze.

"Shit. What did I do?" Sherry pulled to the side of the road and stopped. The police car pulled in behind them and the spotlight came on lighting the inside of the car. Sherry sat still and rolled down the window.

"License and registration please." The cop shone a flashlight onto Sherry's face. "Oh, hi, Sherry."

Sherry looked into the flashlight. "Erik? Sounds like you but I can't see past the light."

"Sorry." He pointed the light toward the ground. "Yeah, it's me."

"Wow. It's been a while. You haven't been in Magee's."

"Busy as hell. Chief has us all working overtime on the football coach case and a few of the guys decided to get the flu. It's why I'm doing a double and out cruising around tonight."

"You're right, I didn't think you did traffic anymore."

Erik shone the flashlight at Rank. "Not technically traffic, Sherry. I had a call up in Cotswald. Jake Cameron beating up his wife again. I don't much like driving around, and this friggin' car's a rat. Radio's not working right, on and off all the time. Sometimes if it isn't working I can give it a whack on the side and it'll come to life. Most times it just doesn't work. I'm kinda sick of hearing all the chatter from the station anyway. Same old shit. Nothing new. So not having a working radio isn't so bad I guess." Erik pointed the flashlight toward the back of the car. "I was behind you on my way back to Sefton, and I noticed that you have a taillight out."

"I do? A taillight?"

"Passenger side. Hey, I don't need your license or registration; you're good. Just see about getting it fixed, okay?" He motioned his head toward Rank. "Who's your friend?"

Sherry looked at Rank and back to Erik. "This is Todd. Todd Rank. He's staying with me for a while, doing a bunch of the handyman work I need done in trade for room and board."

"Where do you come from, Todd?" Erik kept the light on his face, studying the patch on his eye.

"Michigan."

"Can I ask what brought you up to the North Country?"

"Passing through is all. My kid goes to school up at Paul Smith's, and I always liked it up here, so I figured I'd make an extended stay and check it out. I'm out of work back in Michigan like everyone else, so I have some time I guess."

Sherry spoke up. "He's done a great job for me so far, Erik. Sealed up my windows, fixed all the leaky shit in the bathroom, and you should see the job he did on the slate in the front entry."

Erik pointed the flashlight toward the ground. "If you're happy, I'm happy, Sherry. You all have a good night now." He walked back to his car.

Sherry put it in gear and pulled away, Erik in the cruiser following her. Rank was silent.

"You okay, Todd? You acted kinda scared."

"I don't like cops much I guess, and I sure don't like them putting a light in my face."

"Me neither, Todd. Erik, he's okay, though. We went to school together. I've known him since I was five or six. Funny he turned out to be a cop. He was kind of a mama's boy when he was a kid."

Rank stared straight ahead. He'd been seen by a cop. Studied by a cop. He knew he needed to resolve the Margo problem quickly. He was kicking himself for not doing it today.

"What are you thinking about, Todd?"

He looked at Sherry, still silent. She looked good in the soft moonlight that was seeping into the car in waves as it passed through the trees beside the road. He thought about their sex. "Nothing really I guess. Remembering this afternoon."

She put her hand on his thigh and gave it a squeeze. "I'm gonna remember this afternoon for a long time, Todd. Unless you give me a few more of those rockin' orgasms and make me lose my mind again." She moved her hand from his thigh to his crotch and rubbed it. "And by the way, I hope that you're not just passing through anymore. Like you told Erik."

Rank smiled and shook his head as if to say no. He was far away again. Margo had taken over.

# CHAPTER SIXTY-FIVE

"So really, the generator is the key." Gerry was asking even though it sounded like he was telling.

Kris sipped his whiskey and stared at the generator. His flashlight lit the interior of the little building that housed the generator and gas caddy pretty well. "Pretty much. Electric service up here is sketchy, goes out all the time. Insulate the best you can, wrap the pipes with heat tape, and be ready to run the generator a lot." Kris looked up at Gerry. "But if you're just gonna be up here for hunting season, you could carry water in. No real need to have water in the pipes. Only need a lot of water to fill the toilet tank."

"Shit, and since it'll just be me I expect, I don't really need to flush the thing too much."

"Nope. Keep it simple. Save your money."

"Kris!" The voice came at almost the same time as the pounding on the door around the side of the camp. Kris hollered "out here" in the direction of the front door. He looked at Gerry, and they both walked quickly around the corner.

"What's up, Silas?" Kris asked when he realized who was at the door. Silas looked ragged in the glare of the spotlight that lit the front of the cabin.

"Violet's gone Kris"

"She's gone, Silas? Where the hell would she go?"

"I took a nap, Kris. I shouldn't have had that nap. But she was asleep. I've always been able to take a nap when she's asleep, Kris."

Silas wasn't ragged after all; he was frantic.

"Calm down a little bit, Silas. We'll find her."

"I already walked up to the road. I yelled for her. She ain't out there, Kris."

"Let's look again, Silas." Kris set his whiskey glass on the step and walked quickly past Silas and Gerry. Gerry and Silas followed, but Kris was moving fast.

"Violet!" Kris called as he walked up the camp road, "Violet!" He shone the light around the woods to his left, then up the road, then off to the right. He paused occasionally to get a closer look at something that didn't look normal.

"Violet!" Kris crested the hill and started down. Silas's cabin was in sight now. As he got closer, he could see a shadowy figure sitting on the front step.

"Silas? That you, Silas?" Violet called toward Kris.

"No, Violet, it's Kris. Silas is coming right behind me."

Violet was in her dressing gown with her bare legs stuffed into a pair of green gumboots.

"Violet! Where the hell did you go?" Silas was huffing from the walk. He sat beside Violet, put his arm around her, and softly said, "You scared the piss out of me."

Violet looked at Silas and replied, "I just went for a walk, Silas, that's all. You were sleeping, and I figured to be back before you woke up. I'm sorry."

Kris hadn't ever seen Violet acting sane. She seemed to have her mind intact for a change.

"Let's get in the house, Violet; it's cold and you hardly have any clothes on." Violet stood, Silas followed. "Thank you, guys." They walked into the house and closed the door.

Kris and Gerry walked back up the road.

"That was something." Gerry shook his head.

"What do you mean?" Kris asked.

"Well," Gerry stopped in the middle of the road and turned toward Kris, "I never thought about what it might be like to live in a place like this being that old I guess."

"What do you mean a place like this?"

"Just that it's pretty far from everything. She could have wandered for a long time and there'd be no other people around that might see her."

Kris thought about it. "You're right. If they were in town she'd have been walking on the sidewalks I guess, and there'd be a few other people around that might see her. Police especially, they're around town quite a bit I suppose."

"Right. And what happens if they need to get to the hospital?"

Kris was silent. Not something he wanted to think about too much. The two resumed the walk back to the cabin, silent the rest of the way. When they got to the trucks, Gerry turned to Kris and extended a hand. "Thanks for showing me the place. I'd still like to have you take a look at mine if you think you'll have some time."

"I expect I'll be able to. How about we plan to meet at your place first thing in the morning, once it's light out?"

"Sounds good." Gerry climbed into his truck and shut the door. Kris stepped back to give him some room as he backed the truck onto the camp road.

With Gerry gone, Kris walked to the generator shed and closed it up. He retrieved the two whiskey glasses from the step on his way into the cabin. Back inside, he lit a fire and walked around the cabin, straightening things and picking up what needed to be picked up. He noticed that some ash had settled on the wood stove. He dug out the hand broom and swept it off. One thing led to another, and before he knew it he'd been all around the cabin sweeping and dusting.

*Margo's coming back*, he thought to himself, *women like things clean.*

Pleased with the cleanup, he washed the two whiskey glasses and put one away, then poured fresh whiskey in the other and sat down in front of the fire.

# CHAPTER SIXTY-SIX

"What's wrong, Todd?"

Rank didn't look up from his plate. "I dunno." He was worried, but he knew he had to fake it, pretend everything was alright. His cover depended on it. He looked at her. "I think I'm just blown away. I never expected to fall for you."

Sherry reached across the table. Rank took her hand. "Todd."

He tickled her palm with the tips of his fingers. She yanked her hand away. "Todd!" She leaned forward and whispered, "You be careful, Todd, you might get me horny again!"

Rank smiled. "Maybe that's what I'm trying to do!" He knew he could pull this off. He also knew that his time was limited. The cop didn't recognize him in the car, but he had a good look. It was only a matter of time now.

Sherry paid for dinner and kept her hand on Rank's thigh the entire ride back to her house, rubbing gently. She laid a long, deep kiss on him the instant they stepped inside the house, even before she closed the kitchen door. She led him straight to the bedroom, stripped his clothes off, and went down on him. She was good; she knew just when to stop to keep him going. She stripped, pushed him down on the bed, and climbed on top.

A few minutes later, she lay in his arms, near sleep and wet with sweat. When she began to snore, he gently rearranged himself so that she was no longer resting on him. She rolled over. He lay still. Waiting.

When he sensed that she was asleep for good, he slowly rolled himself off the bed. He picked up his clothes and walked on tiptoe into the next room. He dressed, picked up his duffle bag, and made his way quietly to the kitchen door. He opened it slowly, carefully stepped onto the porch, and shut it as quietly as he could. He hustled down the steps and into the truck, fired it up, and drove away.

He drove slowly past Natty's parking lot. Empty. Made sense; it was late. Or early. He hadn't checked the time. He drove to the spot where he'd parked before. He did his best to get the truck in behind the pole as deeply as possible to try and conceal it. He picked his way to the spot he'd been watching Natty's from. He sat and waited.

# CHAPTER SIXTY-SEVEN

Kris put a couple fresh logs on the fire and closed the doors to the wood stove. He always closed the doors when he wasn't going to be tending the fire. He opened the vents at the door bottoms, and he could hear the fire burn faster. The vents directed a flow of air at the base of the fire and fanned the flames. Kris figured that the logs would be consumed by the time he and Margo returned, but the coals should still be red-hot, and he'd be able to get another good fire going easily.

He walked around the cabin with his empty whiskey glass and checked to make sure everything was neat. He ran up the stairs, switched on the lamp on the nightstand beside Margo's bed, and brushed the quilt to make sure it was straight. He stepped back and looked at the room. The light was soft and warm on the sloped wooden ceiling above the bed, and the reds and greens in the quilt looked deep and rich in the warm glow. Pleased with his work and comfortable that the place was ready for her, Kris rinsed his glass in the sink and went out to the truck to drive to Natty's.

There were a few trucks in Natty's lot. Not as many as on a weekend night, but as many as he'd ever seen on a weeknight. Hunting season was nearly over, and the guys must be living it up a last time or two until the next year.

Kris found a stool near the kitchen end of the bar. Margo set a glass of whiskey down in front of him.

"Now how'd you know I was gonna have whiskey?" He grinned at her.

"C'mon, Kris, I'm not a complete dumbass. I've known you for what, a few days now?"

Kris didn't know if he saw a sparkle in her eye or if it was just the light in the bar. He sipped the whiskey and told himself it was just the light. She leaned on the bar in front of him and got close enough to whisper. "Cindy's gonna close up in a few minutes. She's tired as hell, she's been here almost nonstop for the last few weeks, right? I don't know how these guys are gonna take it."

"They'll be fine about it." Kris raised his glass as if to toast her. "Thank you very much for the whiskey."

Margo stood back and smiled. "You are very much welcome, Kris."

Cindy came out from the kitchen. "Kris, you sexy bastard." She put her hand on his and winked at him. "How about you take me home with you and Margo and we do a three-way?"

Margo shook her head. Kris blushed. Cindy leaned closer and whispered, "You know you'd like it." She stood and walked to the center of the bar. "Last call, gents. I have to close up so I can go home and get laid." Laughs erupted and one hunter called to her, "Take me home, Cindy!"

"Your wife wouldn't think too highly of me, Jeff." More laughs. "Tell you guys what, seins' how it's near the end of the season, this last round tonight is on the house." The laughs turned into whoops and then applause. Margo started pouring beers.

After the last customer left, Cindy shut the lights off in the kitchen. Kris finished his whiskey. Margo washed and dried the glass and put it away.

"Can you get here early tomorrow morning, Margo? I'm thinking we ought to be ready for a bigger crowd now with the hunting season almost over. They'll be losing their ambition, starting out a little later and enjoying the last day or two a little more. The ones that are still around are getting tired now."

Margo looked at Kris.

"I'm here to help. I can get you here whenever you want me to."

"What time, Cin?"

"I'm thinking around four-thirty or five. That be okay?" She looked at Margo and then Kris.

"Like I said, whenever you want." Kris stood and pushed the stool closer to the bar.

Margo nodded. "Okay then, between four-thirty and five. Honestly, Cin, might be closer to five." She nodded a little toward Kris, letting Cindy know that she was depending on Kris for a ride and didn't want to put him out too much.

"That's fine, baby. If anybody comes in I'll hold 'em off till you get here."

Margo was animated on the ride back to Kris's place. She talked nonstop, telling him all the details of the evening. It was obvious that she liked working at Natty's. Inside the cabin, she took her coat off, hung it behind the woodstove, and sat in the rocker.

"You got the energy to have a little bit of a fire, Kris?" The chair squeaked as she rocked.

Kris nodded and opened the doors to the stove. "Sure do." He put a couple new logs on the coals. They ignited quickly. He sat.

"Hey, before you get comfortable, do you think I might be able to try some of your whiskey?"

Kris was a little surprised. "Sure you can! Shit, I needed an excuse to have another sip myself." He rose from the chair and started into the kitchen, only to pause and turn just after he passed her. "You want it neat like I have it, or with some ice?"

Margo rocked a little faster as she thought. "I probably should have a little ice. Not too much, though; I want to taste it like it's supposed to taste."

"Three cubes. I like odd numbers." Kris pulled two glasses from the cupboard, put some ice in one and fetched the Wild Turkey from on top of the refrigerator. He filled the glasses, and with the drinks in hand, he walked back to Margo. He handed her the glass with ice and whiskey, and they clinked before he sat down. He watched her sip it. She stopped rocking and sat forward in the chair. Slow and deliberate. A small sip. She licked her lips. She turned her head toward Kris and smiled. "That's really good!"

"Shit." Kris began to rock.

"What do you mean 'shit'?"

"Gonna have to buy Turkey a lot more often now that I don't have it all to myself."

Margo laughed and sipped again. "Well, now that I'm making a little money I can chip in."

# CHAPTER SIXTY-EIGHT

It was still dark and very cold, but Margo was awake and ready to go. Kris, not so much. Margo was almost bouncing out to the truck. Kris was shuffling. They didn't really talk much on the way; Kris was too tired.

In Natty's parking lot, Kris mustered enough energy to tell Margo his morning plans. "I'm coming back for breakfast. Going back to the cabin for a while now, then meeting that guy from yesterday to go look at his camp."

"Okay, see you then!" Margo shut the door and bounced into Natty's. Kris backed out of the lot and drove back toward the cabin.

Upon seeing Margo, Rank ran back to his truck and crouched down to hide until the pickup that had brought her passed by. He jumped into the truck and sped to Natty's. He pulled up sideways in front of the door, leaned across the seat, and swung the passenger door open. He dug the roll of duct tape from his duffle bag, made sure the pistol was in the waist of his pants, and got out of the truck. He left the driver's door open and the truck running. He stood for a moment between the truck and Natty's front door and looked up and down the road. No vehicles in sight. He went inside the bar.

Margo was getting some coffee mugs from under the register, her back to the door. She stood and turned when she heard the door open. She froze when she saw Rank.

Rank ran around the bar. Margo was too stunned to react. He grabbed her by the arm and spun her around, holding her wrist behind her back tightly. She screamed. Cindy rushed from the kitchen.

"What the hell—"

Rank pulled the pistol from his belt with his free hand and pointed it at the back of Margo's head. He turned to look at Cindy over his shoulder. "Stay there and stay quiet!" he hollered. "You move and you'll both die right the fuck now!"

Cindy stood motionless.

Rank put the gun on the bar and took the duct tape from his coat pocket. Margo saw the gun in the corner of her eye. She wasn't taking his shit anymore. She jerked and twisted, and he lost his grip. She grabbed the gun from the counter, turned it toward him, and pulled the trigger. The bullet grazed his shoulder and ripped through a framed picture on the far wall. Rank screamed and grabbed her hand in time to force it toward the ceiling. Her second shot brought a little plaster down over their heads. He forced her hand down on the bar hard. She let go of the gun. It bounced once on the counter and rattled to the floor on the far side between two stools.

"Fuck!" Rank yelled.

Adrenaline masked the pain in Margo's wrist as it hit the bar. She fought for a little balance and jammed her knee into Rank as hard as she could. He buckled and lost his grip. Margo stepped back.

Cindy raced around the bar and found the pistol. She straightened up and aimed it at Rank.

"Your turn to stay quiet, motherfucker!" Cindy was scared and angry. She was shaking, and Rank could see it. Rank stood still for a moment and then dove beneath the bar. Cindy froze. He grabbed a glass, stood back up, and hurled it at Cindy. The glass hit her hard on the forehead. A lucky throw. She went down. She dropped the gun.

Rank turned back to Margo and grabbed her hand again. She fought, but Rank easily overcame her struggle. He slammed her face down on the bar, forced his knee into her back, and found the duct tape. He pulled some away from the roll with his teeth, pulled her hands together, and spun it around her wrists once. It was enough to disable her. He paused and rested, his weight hard against her.

He wrapped more tape around her wrists, tighter this time. Margo winced. Rank pulled her off the bar and shoved her toward the kitchen door. He turned her and pushed her around toward the entrance. Cindy was on the floor unconscious, her head bleeding badly. Rank scanned for the pistol, spotting it on the floor near the pool table. He pulled Margo toward it.

As he bent down to pick it up, Margo kicked him in the shoulder. He spun and lost his balance, hitting the back of his head on the pool table as he fell. He landed hard on his ass. Margo ran toward the door, awkward with her hands bound behind her. As she turned backward to pull it open, she saw the flash from the pistol, heard the fast whistle of the bullet, and the crack of the wood as it split beside her head. She froze.

Rank rose from the floor, the pistol trained at Margo and his free hand on the edge of the pool table to help keep him steady. He shook his head as if to clear it and walked toward Margo grinning. He grabbed her by the arm, pulled her away from the door, and opened it. He shoved her outside and into the open door of the pickup truck. She fell face first on the seat. She kicked as hard as she could as he tried to force her legs into the truck. He cursed and slammed her back with his fist. She screamed in pain. He pushed her legs into the truck and closed the door.

He ran to the driver's side, reached in, shoved her into an upright position, and climbed in. He slammed the gear lever hard, missing drive and ending up in second gear again. He stomped on the gas pedal. Dirt and stones flew as the rear tires struggled to find grip on the gravel parking lot. The back end of the truck swerved toward Natty's, and the rear fender slammed against the doorframe as Rank fought the steering wheel for control. The truck bounced and swerved, and Rank struggled to straighten it out. He kept his foot hard on the pedal, kept fighting the steering wheel. Margo bounced against the door. Her head slammed against the window. The front tires hit the pavement, and the back end made one last short slide before the rear tires caught and the truck jerked violently. Rank drove away from the bar as fast as he could.

# CHAPTER SIXTY-NINE

The knocking on the door washed across Sherry's mind a time or two before she realized she wasn't dreaming. She rolled over and whispered, "Todd?"

Morning light was beginning to stream through the window. The bed was empty beside her. More knocking. Louder maybe, she didn't know. She sat up and looked at the empty side where Rank had slept. She threw the covers off and grabbed her robe, putting it on while she walked down the hall.

"Todd? Todd? That you out there?" As she came to the end of the hall, she could see the figures at the door well enough to see that they wore uniforms. "Whoa." She opened the door. It was Erik and another cop. "What's up, boys?"

Erik's voice was low, almost a whisper. "Sherry, is the man that was in your car last night here in your house?"

"I dunno, Erik. You want to come in?"

Erik nodded and put his finger to his lips. Sherry nodded, stepped aside, and shut the door behind them.

"Where would he be, Sherry?" Still whispering.

She pointed down the hall. "Maybe in the room on the left. What's going on?"

Erik put his finger to his lips, again telling her silently to be quiet, and then whispered, "Stay right here." He pulled his gun, and the two cops carefully walked around the table. He pointed the gun into the dining room and looked around. He backed out, motioned into the dining room with his head, and walked down the hall while the other cop walked into the dining room. At the room Sherry had pointed out, Erik stood against the wall beside the door with his gun ready in his right hand. He turned the doorknob with his left hand, swung the door open, and spun into the room. Sherry heard him move around in the room and come out. He went into her room and did the same and then into the bathroom on his way back to the kitchen.

"He isn't here, Sherry." No longer whispering.

"What the fuck is going on, Erik? You're scaring me."

The other cop came back through the dining room. "Nothing."

"Erik?" Sherry implored.

"Lemme check outside quick, Sherry, then I'll fill you in. Stay here."

The two cops went outside and looked all around the house, into the woods out back, and in the shed. They holstered their guns and stood beside the squad cars talking for a few minutes. Erik came back into the house while the other cop sat in his car and talked on the radio.

"What the fuck is going on, Erik?"

"Sit down, Sherry," Erik said softly, motioning to a chair at the table as he pulled another chair out for himself and sat. "We have reason to believe that the guy who was in your car last night is a wanted murderer."

"You're shitting me."

"I wish I was kidding, Sherry. When's the last time you saw him?"

The past few days raced across Sherry's mind. She saw flashes of Todd: at the bar when she first met him, proudly showing her his work on the windows, on his knees on the floor scraping the glue where the tiles had been, grimacing above her during an orgasm.

She shook her head and muttered, "Shit. Shit. Shit."

"When was the last time you saw him, Sherry? This is important."

She looked up at Erik. "Last night, after we got home from town. Must have been around eleven."

"Any idea where he might be now, Sherry?"

"Jesus, Erik, I've got no idea." Truth was, Sherry's mind had gone blank. The shock of realization had set her back. She'd fallen for this guy.

"Anything could help, Sherry. Anything."

"Tell me something about him, Erik. Maybe that'll help me think."

"Okay." Erik sat back in the chair and thought. "He came from Michigan, beat up his wife back there, and she ran away from him. They have a son going to school up at Paul Smith's. We think she came up here to be closer to the kid, and that he chased her up here."

Sherry sat still. Something was coming but she wasn't shaking it loose yet. Erik waited for a minute then continued.

"The wife turned up near Chance Pond. She was involved in an accident up there that we had to investigate. She's been working at Natty's for a week or so."

The realization went through Sherry like a bolt of lightning.

"Natty's!"

"What about Natty's, Sherry?"

"I took him to Natty's for dinner a couple days ago. Cindy was talking about the new girl. Must be his wife!"

"He might know she works at Natty's?" Erik asked.

"He knows. He knows. He sat and listened. Cindy went on and on about her. He asked a couple questions. Like what did she look like and things like that. Didn't seem like anything to me at the time."

"He's driving his own car, Sherry?"

She thought for a minute and muttered again, "Shit."

"Sherry. His car."

She came out of her stupor. "Right, his car."

"His car." Erik leaned a little closer.

"It's a truck. A pickup truck. Pretty beat up. Green with dirty white cap."

"Do you remember the plates, Sherry?"

Sherry sat silently staring at nothing in the distance.

"Sherry?"

She turned abruptly toward him. "What?"

"The license plates. Do remember the license plates? Were they from Michigan?"

"Shit, I don't know. I didn't pay any attention." She laid her head on the table and began to cry.

# CHAPTER SEVENTY

"Where are you taking me?"

Rank kept his eyes on the twisting road and kept his mouth shut. He was pushing the truck hard, using every inch of road and a few inches of the gravel shoulder where there was some.

"Where are we going?" Margo's head ached, her wrists and shoulders were on fire, and her thighs were cramping from trying to hold herself on the slippery vinyl bench seat. She looked at Rank and realized that more questions were pointless.

A sudden metallic scraping sound accompanied by the loud, raw sound of the engine startled Rank. "What the—" He slowed. "Fucking truck."

They rattled and scraped down the road for another half mile. Rank was obviously confused, thinking about his situation and wondering what to do next. They came around a bend and a cabin appeared ahead on their right. Rank slowed to a crawl as they came to the cabin. As they passed the front door, he jerked the wheel hard and accelerated onto the yard, the truck bouncing and jerking on the uneven ground. He drove around the back and turned the truck past a propane tank. He stopped and jammed the gear lever into park.

"What's this place?" Margo asked.

Rank didn't answer. He jumped out of the truck and tried the back door to the cabin. Locked. He opened the truck's rear gate and dug a flat pry bar out of the toolbox. He jammed the bar into the doorframe and put all his weight on it. The frame gave a little. He adjusted the bar and pried again. The frame gave and the door swung open. He went inside.

Margo struggled to try to free her wrists enough to open the truck door. The tape was tight and strong; she had no chance. She sat back on the seat, leaned her head back on the headrest, and started to cry.

Rank came back out. He dropped to the ground and inspected the truck. He stood. "Muffler broke, tailpipe's dragging," he told Margo, as if she cared. He stood beside her door and looked the place over.

"This place'll do." Then looking back at Margo, he added, "Quit crying."

He opened her door and grabbed her hard by the arm. He pulled her from the truck. She hadn't expected it. She stumbled and fell, the back of her head slamming against the ground. Rank pulled her up enough to drag her into the camp.

It was dark and musty inside the cabin, dust and cobwebs covered everything. Rank pushed her to the floor, kicked her legs out of the doorway, and closed the door. He dragged a wooden chair from a table on one side of the room and propped it against the door. Then he took his pistol from the waist of his pants, set it on the table, and sat down.

"You hurt me, Margo."

Margo, lying on her side on the wood floor, stared at him.

"I haven't really thought this out. Dunno what I'm gonna do here." Margo was silent. The still air inside the cabin seemed colder than the air outside. It smelled stale. The floor was dirty. She felt the grit on her cheek.

Rank stared at Margo and thought. He could have killed her at the bar and been done with it. Now what. Restless, he began rummaging around the cabin. He didn't know what he was looking for, but he knew that something would strike him. Out the back door he found a small pile of rebar. That gave him an idea. He pulled a three-foot piece from the pile and went inside. He set the rebar down on top of the gas stove that stood among a few plain cabinets on the back end of the camp, opposite the table. He opened two drawers and found a box of matches in the second. He turned on one of the stove's burners, lit a match, and tried to light it. Nothing. He went back outside to the propane tank, pulled up the cover, and twisted the valve to the left. Back inside he lit another match. This time a blue flame burst from the burner.

*Perfect.*

He turned the burner off and pulled a chair to the center of the room, turning it to face the stove. He looked around the camp again, then went back outside. Behind the water tank was a small pile of boards. He found one that wasn't completely rotted, checked his coat pocket for the duct tape, and returned to the cabin. He gave Margo a kick in the back. "You still with me?" She groaned.

He propped the board up against the center of the chair's back and secured it tightly with duct tape. He gave the board a firm pull to make sure it was solid.

Satisfied, he returned to Margo, grabbed her by the armpits, and pulled her up. She didn't help him. "Christ, you put some weight on, didn't you?" He dragged her to the chair and forced her down into it. Before she realized what he was doing, he wrapped the duct tape around her face and pulled her tightly to the board. She tried to scream, but the tape covered her mouth. He wrapped the tape three more times around her face and the board he'd taped to the chair, then tore it off the roll. Next, he taped her feet and legs, and then when she was bound and unable to move, he tore the tape from her wrists, pulled her arms around either side of the chair, and taped them back together behind the chair. She struggled, but Margo couldn't move.

"We don't have a lot of time." Rank lit the stove, laid the end of the rebar in the flame, turned toward Margo smiling, and waited.

# CHAPTER SEVENTY-ONE

The door opened and the other cop leaned into the house. Sherry raised her head from the table, her eyes red from crying.

"Erik, we just got a call. Something happened up at that bar near Chance Pond. Some hunters went in and found a woman unconscious. Signs of a struggle."

"Natty's!" Erik looked at Sherry and back at the other cop. "Call for backup. I don't want to leave Sherry alone. You stay here with her. Have the backup meet me at Natty's"

"You got it." The cop backed away from the door and closed it.

"I'll have him stay in his car and watch the place, Sherry. You gonna be okay?"

Sherry nodded.

# CHAPTER SEVENTY-TWO

Kris finished cleaning the ashes from the woodstove and looked at the clock. "Close enough. Time to meet Gerry," he said aloud, talking to himself. He washed his hands, put on his coat, and headed for the truck. Outside, Kris could see that there was enough light now to see without electric lights. He got in the truck and started out the camp road. As he crested the hill and Silas's place came into view, it occurred to him that Silas might like to take a look at this cabin too.

He pulled the truck to the side of the road in front of Silas's cabin. He climbed out of the truck, made his way up the ramp that Silas built for Violet, and knocked on the front door. His knocking set the dog off, and it ran to the door barking. Silas followed, trying to quiet the dog.

Silas opened the door. "Hello Kris." He was still in his pajamas.

"Silas, I'm going down to look at a hunting camp with the guy that was at my place last night. I figured you might like to see it too."

"I'd like to Kris, but Violet's finally asleep, and I need to try and get some shuteye myself while I can. We had a rough night."

"Sorry to hear Silas. Is Violet okay?"

"I think so Kris. She was up and moving around most of the night. Hard to get her to calm down and sleep. It's happened before. Tell me about that cabin next time I see you."

"Alright Silas, you get some rest then."

Kris climbed back into the truck and drove down Chance Pond Road. At the intersection in front of Natty's he turned left, toward the cabin. The drive was quiet, and he took his time. He didn't want to get there too much before Gerry. He pulled up in front of the cabin and sat staring. Something didn't feel right.

Inside the cabin Margo was trying to scream, jerking in the chair, its legs scraping and bumping on the wood floor. Rank was enjoying the show; she was terrified, and he was in complete control. He looked at the rebar, not glowing yet. He wondered if the flame would be hot enough to make it glow orange. He decided to wait and see, he wanted to watch Margo react to the red-hot poker. The bar was getting hot in his hand. He set the end on the counter, found an old towel in a drawer, and wrapped the end of the rebar.

Kris got out of the truck quietly and left the door ajar so he wouldn't make any noise. He crouched down below the window lines and carefully snuck around the camp. A green pickup with a cap was parked out back. It hadn't been there the night before. It wasn't Gerry's; his was red, was newer, and didn't have a cap. Kris snuck back to the front of the cabin and made his way below the window. He carefully raised his head to see inside. The window was dusty, and it wasn't fully daylight yet, but he could make out a man standing at the stove heating something and somebody in a chair. Struggling.

He tried to focus on the person in the chair, make out who it was. He listened.

Rank watched the rebar, now ignoring Margo and her pointless struggle. The end of the poker was beginning to turn a little orange. "Looking ready, Margo." He had to raise his voice to make sure she could hear him over the noise she was making. He took the rebar from the stove and turned toward Margo. "Let's see if it's hot enough." He laid the hot end of the rebar on her neck. Her skin sizzled and smoked, and the volume and pitch of her muffled screams rose dramatically. Rank held it tightly to her neck and watched her struggle.

Kris, still watching through the window, heard the guy say "Margo" and realized what he was seeing. He ran to the pile on the side cabin and picked up a cement block. Too heavy. He dropped it and picked up a brick, then another. He ran back to the front of the cabin. He threw the first brick through the window and then quickly threw the second.

Rank jerked the rebar from Margo's neck and straightened as the glass in front of him shattered and flew into the room. Something hit the table hard. A brick. The brick slid across the table and struck Rank's pistol. The pistol spun off the table to the floor, ricocheted off the wall beside Margo, skittered past Rank's feet, and disappeared under the stove. A second brick hurtled through the upper part of the window and came down on the table. Rank stood and watched. Stunned.

Outside, Kris took a few steps back and made a running leap headfirst through the broken window. The window was fairly close to the ground, and he managed to get himself a little more than halfway through, landing on his stomach on the table. The glass shards that remained in the window frame tore at his thighs. He ignored the pain and awkwardly pulled himself through.

The shattering glass and bricks had surprised Rank, but this man suddenly diving into the room enraged him. He stepped around Margo toward the table and swung the rebar down hard as Kris rolled off the table to the floor. The rebar missed Kris's shoulder and struck the table. Kris hit the floor chin first and pushed himself to his hands and knees trying to stand as quickly as possible. Rank stepped toward him and swung again. This one connected; the rebar hit Kris square on the shoulder. Kris buckled but managed to stay on his hands and knees. Rank raised the rebar again to strike another blow, but Kris lunged at Rank's legs, striking him at knee-level and pushing him back against Margo. Rank's weight tipped the chair into the wall, Margo's head striking it hard and stopping the chair's movement. Rank fell backward into her and the leaning chair, stumbling and trying to maintain balance.

Kris reared back and punched Rank in the face. Rank's head jerked and his feet lost what grip they had. As he fell, he hit Margo and the chair, causing the chair legs to lose their grip on the gritty floor. Margo's head slid hard down the wall as the chair fell onto its side along with Rank. Kris leaned in and grabbed Rank by the shirt. Unbalanced, Rank swung the rebar with one hand and struck Kris in the face. Kris lost his grip and stumbled back, then lunged again as Rank twisted and struggled to rise to his feet.

Kris managed to grab Rank's head, but not before Rank had begun to uncoil. The rebar hit Kris hard across the temple, and he collapsed. The fury of the past few moments had ended as suddenly as it began. Rank took a few breaths, wiped his sleeve across his bloody mouth, and surveyed the scene. Margo lay still on her side, bound to the chair, moaning softly. Kris lay unconscious on the floor next to them. Rank spun toward the stove and thrust his hand under it, desperately feeling for the pistol. Nothing. He stood, frustrated and shaken. Margo moaned a little louder.

"Damn!" Rank raised the rebar and brought it down hard on Margo's leg. A muffled scream and then silence. He dropped the rebar, stepped around Kris, turned back to him, and kicked him hard on the side of the head. He pushed the chair from the back door and ran to his truck.

Rank flung open the passenger side door of the truck and reached into the duffle bag for the other pistol, but the sound of a truck door closing in front of the camp stopped him. He put the pistol in his belt, closed the door, ran to the other side of the truck, got in, started it, and drove around the side of the camp toward the road. Looking in the rearview mirror as he began to turn around the side of the camp, he saw a hunter running around the other side toward him. His truck bounced and lurched on the uneven ground. He kept his foot in the throttle as he cleared the camp and passed the two trucks parked in front. The tires squealed when they found purchase on the pavement, and the truck lurched down the road. Rank didn't know where he was going. He just knew he had to go.

Kris was coming to when Gerry burst into the cabin. "Holy shit!" Gerry bent down to Kris as Kris wiped at the blood on the side of his head.

"You okay, Kris? What the hell went on in here?" Gerry looked over at Margo, on her side and taped to the chair. He pulled his hunting knife from its sheath as he stood. The tape around her wrists was first. He cut both sides of the wrapped tape, carefully so as not to cut her wrists too. She brought one hand around, the tape still attached to her wrist. Gerry moved toward her head. "Okay if I sit you up? It'll be easier to cut you free." Margo grunted. Gerry took that as a yes. He set the knife on the table and wrestled her carefully to the upright sitting position.

Kris was standing now, dazed but coming around. Gerry carefully cut the tape from behind Margo's head. Instead of trying to pull the tape from her mouth, he bent down and cut the tape around her feet. She stood and began to slowly pull the tape from her mouth. She winced and stopped. Gerry stepped back and stared, dumbfounded and unsure about what to do next.

# CHAPTER SEVENTY-THREE

"Yeah, he had an eye patch." Cindy held a damp towel on her forehead where the glass had struck. Erik was taking notes. A few hunters were hanging around, including the two who had found Cindy lying on the bar floor. "And like I told you, I dunno what he was driving. Me and Margo were inside the bar trying to get ready for the breakfast crowd when he came in."

Erik stared at the notebook. Cindy pulled the towel from her head.

"Shit, Ricky, I'm fine. Go find that son of a bitch and Margo!" Cindy was impatient.

"Got backup coming, Cindy. I can't leave you here alone right now."

"I'm fine, Ricky, I'm fine." Cindy threw the towel down and got up from the stool. Turning to the hunters, she shouted, "Whadda you say, boys? How about some friggin' breakfast?" A few grunts and nods came from the spectators, and Cindy headed into the kitchen. Erik shook his head and put the notebook in his pocket. He'd already done his due diligence; photographing the scene and bagging the evidence. He sat and waited.

Rank had only been on the road for a few moments when two police cars came from the opposite direction and sped past him, lights ablaze. Surprised and rattled, he watched them disappear around the bend in his rearview mirror, sure that they would turn around and return for him. He drove another quarter mile wondering what to do when he came to an intersection with a dirt road. He made a last minute decision and turned hard to the left. The front end of the truck pushed a bit on the loose gravel, and the back end swung wide. Rank struggled with the steering wheel and maintained control, speeding into the woods. In the rearview mirror, he saw the cloud of dust he'd created hanging behind him. *Fuck, they'll see me.* The dirt road was straight as far ahead as he could see. He pushed the pedal to the floor.

At Natty's, the two police cars pulled into the parking lot. "Did you see any vehicles on your way here?" Erik asked as the cops climbed out of their cars.

"We just passed a green pickup with a white cap. He was going the other way."

"Where did you pass him?"

"He was between here and where the Chance Pond loop meets up with this road."

"So he could have turned up Chance Pond Road?"

"Yeah, that's possible."

"Did he have a passenger?"

The cop thought for a moment. "I don't think so. He was going like hell, though. In a big hurry."

"Call it in, that's the guy we want. Let's get a car at the intersection with Route 56 fast. Better have an eye on Tupper too, and South Colton, in case he uses the Five Dam Road." Erik turned to one of the cops. "You watch this place." He turned to the other. "You backtrack toward French's Pond. I'll take the Chance Pond loop in case he turned up there." Erik climbed into his car.

Rank was driving desperately, faster on the gravel than he was comfortable with. The dirt road twisted hard to the left and up a steep incline. The old truck bounced hard on the washboard surface and loose stones beat the undercarriage. Rank wasn't in a careful mood; he kept his foot in it hard. At the top of the incline, the road remained straight. The truck bounced and bucked. The front end wobbled. Rank could feel something loose through the steering wheel. Something he hadn't felt before. He kept his foot in it hard.

# CHAPTER SEVENTY-FOUR

Kris thought for a second. "I used some duct tape to hold some gauze on a big cut once. I was hiking and had to get back off the mountain. Hurt like a bitch getting it off. I used cooking oil when I got home. Took some time, but it worked."

"Ain't got cooking oil, Kris." Gerry looked at the floor and thought. Margo slumped back into the chair, frustrated at being unable to get the tape off. Gerry looked up suddenly and exclaimed, "WD!" He ran out the door. Kris and Margo looked at each other, neither knowing what he meant and both surprised by the sudden outburst.

He returned as suddenly as he left, holding a blue can up for both of them to see. "WD-40! I always keep a can in my truck. Works for a lot of things." He gave the can a shake and spoke to Margo, "Okay, close your eyes. I'm gonna spray some around the tape on your face here and we'll give it a few minutes to soak in."

Kris got up and went to the back door. "What if that fucker comes back?" He turned and spotted the rebar. He bent down and grabbed it. "Shit!" he recoiled, dropping it back to the floor. "It's hot as hell." He shook his hand in the air and walked out the back door.

Moments later, he returned with a chunk of rebar that he'd found lying in a pile behind the cabin.

Gerry looked back at Margo. "How about trying to peel that tape off now? Just try a little corner, and go real slow. Then if you can peel a little away, we'll put some more WD on it." Margo nodded and began to peel. It still hurt but not as much. She could bear it. She peeled the tape slowly away from her mouth first, so she could talk.

# CHAPTER SEVENTY-FIVE

The dirt road spilled out onto pavement at the bottom of a long, shallow downgrade. The loose feeling in the steering seemed worse to Rank with the truck on pavement, and the truck wandered from side to side. Rank had to make exaggerated turns with the steering wheel to keep it on the road. Didn't matter; he kept his foot hard on the throttle. The pond he'd passed before appeared on his left now. Still tranquil. As he passed the camp road, the truck wandered quickly to the left across the road. Rank couldn't steer fast enough, the tire fell from the road to the dirt shoulder, and there was a loud snap. The steering wheel became light and the truck veered hard to the left into the ditch. The stop was sudden and violent when the front end met the bank on the far side. The impact sent Rank's head into the steering wheel.

Dazed by the impact, Rank shook his head and looked over the steering wheel. Woods. Mixed hardwood and evergreen. A hill. He couldn't see much of the hill past the top of the windshield. He remembered the pond and the camps. Most would be empty this time of year. A chance to rest and think. He got out of the truck, checked for the pistol in his waistband, and started climbing into the woods.

The hill was steeper than he thought. He scrambled over fallen logs and through blackberry bushes and dodged around small evergreen trees. The hill crested and a downslope began. More thickly wooded than the upslope. Slower going. He pushed away low branches and tripped on unexpected stones and stumps. At the bottom, he came to a level area that was predominantly hardwood. For the first time he could see for a distance. An old stone wall cut across about fifty yards ahead, and beyond it was what looked like a small woodpile. A neatly stacked woodpile. He figured some cabins must be close.

He began to catch his breath; walking through the hardwood was easy. Nobody behind him. Yet. He stepped over the stone wall. Not so much a formal wall; it was simply stones piled together, and as such, it was low and wide. The woodpile was much closer to the wall than he'd thought, just on the far side of the stones. He stepped over, his legs wide, and he planted one foot on the far side of the wall. Picking up the other foot, he stumbled and caught himself with his hand. He steadied himself and swung his leg across. The momentum caused him to take a few steps in a trot, a little out of balance. With the last step came a loud metallic snap and an unimaginable searing pain at his ankle. He fell to the ground.

# CHAPTER SEVENTY-SIX

The WD-40 had worked, at least it had worked well enough that Margo had been able to get the tape off her face without too much damage.

"It was my husband, Kris. He found me."

"I figured as much. You Okay?"

"Yeah. My wrists are sore and my neck's stiff, but I'm good all in all."

"Your neck has a big burn or something." Kris moved a little closer.

"He burned me with that metal bar."

"I'm hoping he isn't coming back, Margo."

Gerry interrupted, "That said, maybe we ought to get out of here while we can."

Kris stood and extended a hand to Margo. "Good call."

Margo took his hand and stood. The tape still clung to her wrists and her pant legs. Kris was looking past the tape. They held hands for a moment and looked at each other silently. Gerry, seeing Margo and Kris holding hands, muttered, "Alrighty," and walked out the door. Margo and Kris released hands and followed him. They walked around to the front of the cabin.

As Margo climbed into Kris's truck she said, "We should get back to Natty's. Cindy got hurt too."

Kris nodded and turned to Gerry. "Gerry, I broke this window, and I'll fix it."

Gerry nodded as he climbed into his truck. "I'll follow you back to the bar in case there's ways I can help." The truck doors closed, and they pulled onto the road, Kris and Margo leading and Gerry following.

In Natty's parking lot were three police cars and a couple pickup trucks. Kris didn't remember ever seeing police cars at Natty's. Cindy ran to Margo when she came through the door and threw her arms around her. "You alright, girl?"

Margo nodded."

Cindy tipped her head to the side and scowled. "Wha'd that fucker do to your neck?"

"He burned me." Margo was stoic. Cindy's eyes welled up.

"Miss, were you involved in this incident?" It was one of the cops.

Margo turned her head toward the cop and nodded.

He continued, "I'll need a statement from you." He looked at the burn on her neck. "Maybe the best thing will be to take you to Sefton Hospital and get that neck taken care of. I can talk to you after that. You can ride with me."

Margo looked at Kris, silently seeking his opinion.

Kris responded without hesitation, "Makes sense, Margo; your neck looks pretty bad. If that gets infected it'll be a bigger problem than you need right now. Plus he's still on the loose. You'll be safe with the police while you get to the hospital."

Margo turned to the cop and asked, "Do you think that Kris here could drive me to the hospital? That way

I'll have a way to get back. We can follow you or you can follow us. How about that?"

The cop started for the door. "Works for me. Let's go."

# CHAPTER SEVENTY-SEVEN

Rank writhed on the ground. The pain was agonizing. He had no clue what had happened.

"Gotcha, you no good wood thief!" Violet stood over him. He had no idea where she'd come from. Rank writhed and moaned.

"How's that bear trap feel, thief?"

"Bear trap?" Rank could barely speak, he was near blacking out from the pain.

"Thes right. A bear trap. I knew I'd get you. You'll think twice about stealing our wood again."

"I didn't steal no wood, lady. Please get me outta this thing!"

Violet looked at him with a squint. "If you didn't steal our wood, then how come you ran right up to my woodpile here?"

"Fuck, lady, I'm not stealing anybody's wood. Get me outta this thing. will you?"

Violet squinted at him for a few moments, her head tipping from one side to the other as she thought. After a few moments, she said, "Well, even if you are the one stealing our wood, I'm gonna have to let you out sometime I s'pose." She bent down and grabbed at the bear trap. His leg twisted and the trap pulled tightly against the chain that held it to a nearby tree. The trap's teeth tore further into Rank's ankle. He screamed and jerked violently. Violet let go and stood. Surprised. She blinked and tipped her head as she caught her breath.

"Well, if you're jess gonna scream every time I try to help we ain't gonna get nowhere fast."

"Lady, just pull the trap apart so I can get my leg out. Don't twist it, just open it!"

Violet squinted at him for a moment before she bent down to try again. The trap spring was heavy. It was hard for her to pull it open. She gave it a yank, but it twisted again. Rank screamed. His body twisted toward his leg. Violet let go and stood again. She was visibly shaken and out of breath.

"I ain't trying to hurt you. Thet thing's hard to open."

"You should have thought of that before!" He moaned and writhed.

Violet was starting to get anxious. "I don't think I can open it without twisting it some."

"Well just do it as fast as you can. Tell me when you're gonna start." Rank was sweating even though it was cold. His head was spinning and his stomach was starting to turn from the pain.

Violet squinted at the trap for a few moments. She stepped to the side and straddled Rank's leg, then bent down and grasped the jaws gently. She took a deep breath and shouted, "Now!" She pulled as hard and fast as she could. Rank screamed and twisted further, kicking his leg and pulling the trap from Violet's hands.

Violet stood panting, her words separated by gasps for air. "Mister, I ain't gonna be able to open that trap for you."

"What? Christ, lady, get somebody who can!" Rank turned his head toward the ground and threw up.

Violet squinted at the trap for a few moments. Rank writhed and moaned, the side of his face deep in his own vomit. Suddenly, Violet gave a quick nod of her head and muttered, "I know." She turned and walked toward the woodpile. Rank watched as she stepped around to the far side and bent a little, as if to retrieve something. She came back around carrying an axe.

"What are you gonna do with that?" His eyes widened.

Violet rested the axe on the ground and leaned it against her leg. She spit into her hands. "I saw a TV show where a fox got caught in a trap." She rubbed her hands together. "He chewed his leg off and he got out."

Rank screamed, "Holy shit, lady," Violet picked up the axe, raised it as high as her tired arms would let her. "—you ain't gonna—" She swung it down on Rank's ankle. The axe missed the target and bit deep into his calf. Rank screamed and twisted. The trap tugged against its chain. He vomited again.

Violet pulled the axe from his calf. She was gasping for air from the effort. "Shit." She raised the axe again, not as high this time; she was weak. Rank screamed as the axe came down. This time she hit bone just above his ankle. His scream changed pitch, and his body jerked uncontrollably. The axe came out of Violet's hands and fell to the ground.

Violet straightened up and staggered backward as she looked at his bloody leg. She was completely out of breath. Dizzy.

"I'll get it this time," she gasped, struggling to speak. She picked up the axe. The unbearable pain had put

Rank into a stupor. He moaned but didn't protest as she struggled to raise the axe again. She got it as high as her knees when her arms gave out. The axe fell by its own weight, bringing Violet's arms with it as she lost her grip. Violet's eyes rolled back in their sockets, her chin raised, and her head tipped back. The heel of the axe head dug into Rank's calf and bounced off the bone. Violet collapsed to the ground. Rank screamed and twisted. The axe fell to the ground between them.

Rank barely had enough sense to see that the lady had collapsed. It was a small relief that, for the time being, the axe wouldn't fall again. He vomited again, now only bile. He closed his eyes.

He opened them when he heard leaves rustling. Heavy steps. A large animal. Rank couldn't get out of the trap, and even if he did, he wouldn't be able to walk on the mangled leg. He reached for the pistol in his belt, held his hand and the pistol close to the ground just under his side so it couldn't be seen, and waited.

Erik peered at Rank from a distance.

"Hands up."

Rank didn't move.

"Police. Hands up."

Rank picked his head up, looked at Erik, moaned, twisted to find a spot without vomit and laid his head back down. For just an instant, he could smell the musty soil under the birch and maple leaves that pressed to his cheek.

Erik walked around in front of Rank with his pistol drawn and bent down to check Violet's pulse. Nothing. Her lips were blue, and she was already cold. His pistol aimed at Rank, he shifted and looked at Rank's leg. A ragged, bloody mess. The guy wasn't going anywhere. He knew he had to get help here quickly if he didn't want Rank to bleed to death. He stood slowly, pistol trained on Rank, and surveyed the surrounding area. He could see for some distance through the hardwood. It appeared that there was no one else nearby. The woods were still and quiet.

The pistol shot cracked through the cold air and echoed across the hardwoods. Erik jerked down into a defensive position and swung his head and eyes toward Rank, expecting another shot and preparing to fire. There was no need. Rank lay motionless. Limp. The pistol resting in his lifeless hand next to his forehead and blood pouring onto the birch and maple leaves from the bullet's entry hole.

# CHAPTER SEVENTY-EIGHT

"You gotta tell me that one again, Dido. I can't believe it!"

Myslewiec paused and tipped the bag of Krazy Kurls toward the ceiling, emptying the last few crumbs into his mouth.

"A bear trap? Holy crap, Dido. A bear trap? Who'd believe that one?"

Myslewiec nodded and grinned as he chewed and swallowed the crumbs, then spun his chair back toward his desk and opened the folder that contained their newest case. Miller spun back toward his desk too, shaking his head and mumbling, "A fucking bear trap. I can't believe it."

# CHAPTER SEVENTY-NINE

Burials wouldn't happen until spring at St. Mary's Cemetery. The bodies of those who passed when the ground was frozen were stored in a receiving vault until the thaw. Still, Silas had a graveside service for Violet. A dozen people and a priest gathered at Violet's future grave under the gray skies that often foretold a storm. Standing near the top of the hill with Margo on one side and Cindy on the other, Kris wondered if the skies were just as sad as Silas. He wondered, as he always did at funerals and wakes and now at this graveside service, when it would be his turn.

Silas didn't speak at the service, he wept silently, and he barely spoke at all in the weeks following Violet's death. Kris visited him often, played some cards now and then, and always brought Silas hot dogs when he went to the store. Kris helped Silas bring back the wood from the pile that Violet had made, the wood she took and stacked whenever Silas wasn't looking. Why she had done it would probably puzzle Kris for the rest of his life. Turns out that Silas hadn't even realized that his bear trap was missing, he was so worried about his wood. One day while they were playing cards, he told Kris that every time he went to the shed he looked at the spot where the bear trap hung and thought about Violet.

He also told Kris that he went to the shed a lot, sometimes just to look at that empty spot. Kris tried his best to help Silas take his mind off of Violet. He failed miserably.

It finally did snow, later in the evening after Violet's service. It snowed a lot of snow, and it snowed all night and right up until dark the next day. Kris kept the fire going and took care of Margo. He agreed to take her to Paul Smith's College to see her son as soon as the roads were clear. Margo passed the time rocking in the rocker, sipping whiskey, and reading old books. She even enjoyed some of the books. Mostly, though, she watched the fire.

Natty's was closed because of the storm. The hunters were all gone for the season anyway. Margo's room at Natty's still wasn't ready. Cindy told her that unreliable contractors were about the only kind she could afford. She'd expected them to finally get to it that day, but with the storm, it was going to have to wait a little longer. Contractors in the North Country made their living however they could, and most of them plowed driveways, parking lots, and roads when it snowed. "Shit, you can't be putting in a window during a snowstorm anyway," Kris had said, "and you're always welcome to stay with me." Margo liked staying with Kris.

It took Kris a couple hours to clear the way out the day after the snow stopped falling. He realized that he liked it at the cabin when it snowed. Everything still. Everything quiet. No jet skis or motorboats rumbling around the pond. No cars driving back and forth along the camp road. No kids running between the camps. Surprisingly, Fisco had moved back to town, either unable or unwilling to deal with the extra effort that came with the snow and the cold. Nope, the camps were empty. Except for Silas just up over the hill, Margo in a rocking chair reading old books, and Kris. And a fire to tend, and a little whiskey to drink. Peaceful. Kris didn't mind the first storm of his first winter on Chance Pond at all.